Praise for *The Wish List*

"An incredible story filled with romance, suspense, and some utterly delightful magical beings."
—*Huntress Reviews*

"*The Wish List* is an entertaining read that drew me in and had me rooting for the characters. I'll be looking forward to the next book in the series."
—*Once Upon a Romance*

BOOKS BY GABI STEVENS

The Wish List
As You Wish

As You Wish

GABI STEVENS

TOR®

paranormal romance

A TOM DOHERTY ASSOCIATES BOOK

NEW YORK

This is a work of fiction. All of the characters, organizations, and events portrayed in this novel are either products of the author's imagination or are used fictitiously.

AS YOU WISH

A Tor Book
Published by Tom Doherty Associates, LLC
175 Fifth Avenue
New York, NY 10010

www.tor-forge.com

Tor® is a registered trademark of Tom Doherty Associates, LLC.

ISBN 978-0-7653-6504-0

First Edition: May 2011

Printed in the United States of America

0 9 8 7 6 5 4 3 2 1

To two special authors who have given me encouragement, strength, and understanding when I most needed it:

Lori Wilde, who got to know me at my lowest point in my writing life and still offered me her friendship, advice, and kindness.

And especially Jodi Thomas, who has offered guidance and wisdom and love, and has always believed that I'd make it. Jodi, your words sustained me when I didn't believe in myself.

Ladies, I don't think you know how much you mean to me. Maybe now you do, a little.

ACKNOWLEDGMENTS

Once again, I am grateful to many people without whom I couldn't do this terrible and wonderful job.

Marlene Stringer, who, I'm convinced, wears a large "S" on her chest for when she changes into her role as Super-agent. (I would have said a large "A" on her chest, but that would give entirely the wrong impression.) She takes care of the little headaches so I can concentrate on the big one, namely writing.

Heather Osborn, a wonderful editor who doesn't let me fall on my face with egregious errors in my story, and often shows me ways to make my fables even better.

Melissa Frain, who also helped me through the rough spots.

Darynda Jones, who read this book as a manuscript to see if it stood on its own. I have saved the two e-mails you sent while reading it, and I look at them whenever I start doubting myself. I'd quote them here, but no one would believe I didn't write them myself. Thank you.

Stefanie, who gave me the inspiration for two of my characters. Baby girl, you may never read one of Mom's books, but someday I hope you find your own happy ending.

Bob, as always, for making tacos.

And to all my readers who loved *The Wish List*. You don't know how much your response has meant to me. May you always find magic in your lives.

As
You Wish

1

∽◦◦◦∾

CORDELIA'S RULES FOR HER
DAUGHTERS

•

*Choose Your Associates Carefully. Your Friends
Are a Reflection of You.*

Fairy godmother deemed unstable

The huge, bold headline demanded Reggie's attention.
She bent closer to the *Quid Novi* to read the subtitle:

*Eminent wizard sought for questioning. Caution urged
in dealing with the pair.*

Reggie lifted one eyebrow. Really? The Arcani newspapers had reported little else for the past week and a half.
The fairy godmother candidate and her arbiter had evaded
the Council and their Guards, and disappeared without a
leaving a trace. Ten days later, the best trackers had found
no hint of them. Reggie could understand why the Council
was growing panicky, but she wasn't nervous. Why would
two fugitives come to her bakery?

Regina Scott straightened up. She didn't have time to read the *Quid Novi*. She didn't even have time to read the *San Diego Union*. Besides, the news of the Arcani world didn't concern her. She wasn't Arcani. She was a Groundling.

It happened on occasion: two Arcani gave birth to someone without magic. Like her. It was rare, but it happened. Her parents had despaired over it, but she had come to terms with her lack of power many years ago.

To a Groundling, the *Quid Novi* would look like a cheesy free rag. Only an Arcani could read the magical newspaper. Reggie herself could read both only because her parents had long ago cast a spell allowing her to see the magical words.

She tidied the two separate stacks. The headline of the *Union* dealt with the latest stock market upset. The Groundlings would never hear of the two renegade Arcani.

For a moment she envied the pair. If she were on the run, then she wouldn't have to attend her sister's engagement party this evening. It promised to be a nightmare. She would be the object of pitying glances, and she'd have to endure people talking to her as if she were stupid instead of just non-Arcani. Not to mention the pity they'd feel because her *younger* sister was engaged, whereas she had no prospects.

With a sigh she tucked a strand of her unruly dark hair behind her ear and returned to the task of wiping down the tables in preparation for the day's customers. With magic these mundane jobs might take less time, but there was no point in wishing for something she didn't have.

Heavenly smells wafted from the kitchen where Tommy and Joy were creating their special treats. She inhaled deeply. As soon as she finished cleaning the tables, she'd go check on them, pour herself a cup of coffee, and then open the bakery promptly at seven.

Four sharp raps at the front door jerked her attention from her thoughts. She glanced at her watch. Six fifteen A.M. That was early even for Nate. She peered through the glass of the front window and saw three figures standing on the stoop. Leaving the cleaning rag on the table, she reached to unlock the door. It swung open before she touched it.

"Good morning, Reggie," said an elderly woman with iron-gray hair. She was tall despite her age, and she embraced Reggie without waiting for Reggie's response.

"Aunt Lily," Reggie said in surprise. She looked at the other two women. Why were the godmothers here? She hugged the second one, then the third. "Good morning, Aunt Rose, Aunt Hyacinth. Isn't it a little early to come visiting?"

"Not at all," Rose said with her customary smile. "You keep baker's hours. We knew you'd be up. If you don't mind, I'll go say hello to Tommy and Joy before we start." Her white hair swishing in its stylish bob, Rose strode to the kitchen.

"Good morning, Reggie," Hyacinth said. Of the three women, she looked the least happy with the hour. Her short-cropped silver hair stuck up in many directions. "You wouldn't have a cup of coffee to spare, would you?"

As Reggie grabbed a mug and turned to the coffee-maker, she heard Aunt Lily say, "We are not here to socialize, Hyacinth. This is not a coffee klatch."

"Who said I wanted to socialize? If you want me to function at such ungodly hours, I need coffee." Hyacinth grimaced and sat at one of the tables that occupied the room.

Reggie gave the filled mug to Hyacinth. "Cream and sugar?"

"No, thank you. I need the jolt from the undiluted brew." Hyacinth lifted the mug and sipped.

"Coffee, Aunt Lily?" Reggie asked.

"No, thank you, dear. Some of us enjoy these early hours." Lily gave a pointed look to Hyacinth, who merely growled in return.

Rose reappeared from the kitchen followed by two plump bakers dressed in jeans and T-shirts with long white aprons over their clothes. A smile split Tommy's wide, flat face, but Joy's face crinkled in concentration. She carried a plate covered in turnovers. Reggie felt a rush of pride as she looked at them. Too many people wouldn't see past the slightly off features to the talent that lay beneath. The two bakers weren't related, but they were best of friends. Tommy had Down syndrome and Joy had . . . well, Joy was just Joy.

"Good morning, Aunt Lily," Tommy said and threw his arms around the taller woman.

"You're looking wonderful, Tommy," Lily said with pleasure sparkling in her voice.

"I am. I have a good job. But Aunt Hyacinth doesn't look happy." Tommy leaned into Hyacinth's face. "Try one of Joy's turnovers. They're apple. You will smile."

Tommy's words coaxed a curve to Hyacinth's lips. "Then give me one of those magic turnovers. I could use some help to smile this morning."

Tommy became earnest. He wagged his finger at Hyacinth. "You can't say that. Reggie told us we can't use the word 'magic' in the bakery. The Groundlings can't know."

"It's okay, Tommy. Aunt Hyacinth didn't mean it that way," Reggie said quickly. "Besides no Groundlings are here now."

"Except you," said Joy, as she placed her plate on the table.

Except me, she thought. A brief twinge of self-pity struck her, but she dismissed it as easily as it arrived. She had long since ceased to worry about the unfairness of life. Joy and Tommy were Arcani, but had special needs. She was, well, normal, but she wasn't Arcani.

"These look delicious." Rose took a chair at the table, lifted a turnover, and sniffed it. "And smell even better."

"I'm baking more for breakfast." Joy turned to Reggie. "Don't worry. I checked the oven. It's at three-seven-five degrees and the timer still has six-one-three on it. I won't burn them."

"You never do. You're very careful." Reggie wished Joy wouldn't worry so much about every detail, but she also knew that the strict adherence to routine allowed Joy to bake her amazing creations.

Rose bit into a turnover. "This is terrific."

"Yes, it is. I have to make more now, so I'm going back to the kitchen now." With a little wave, Joy returned to the back room of the bakery.

Tommy sighed. "I suppose I should go too. Joy needs my help. We work together. We are a good team." He followed Joy.

Hyacinth wiped a little apple filling from her lips, popped it back into her mouth, and closed her eyes in enjoyment. "No wonder everyone raves about this place. Do you think Tommy and Joy know they're using magic to bake these?"

"No," Reggie said. "It's just automatic with them. I watch them carefully so they don't drain themselves."

"You've done a fine thing here, Reggie," Lily said and took a seat at the table.

"I haven't done much really. Tommy and Joy have a real gift for baking. I'm just helping them make a success of it."

"It will be hard to give it up, won't it?" Rose said.

"Give it up?" Reggie drew her brows together. "I'm not giving it up."

"You need to hire someone to help with Tommy and Joy," Lily said.

"Well, yes. The bakery is doing really well, and I was considering expanding, but I can't hire just anyone." They had made a success of the bakery, and the logical step was growing the business, but how had the godmothers known that?

"Of course not," Hyacinth said. "You need someone you can tell everything to."

"Everything? That Tommy and Joy are Arcani and use magic to bake? That some of our customers are Arcani as well?" Reggie shook her head. "I don't think so."

Lily waved her wand and a slim box appeared on the table. "You need to hire someone because you have a new job." Lily opened the box.

Two wands, one of yellow wood and one of black, lay in the case. Gold encased the handle of the yellow wood. Cabochon rubies, emeralds, and sapphires dotted the filigree work. Silver entwined the ebony wand. Stark geometric designs complemented the glittering, round diamonds in the handle.

Reggie stared at the two wands. "I can't use a wand. I don't have magic."

Lily smiled patiently. "Who opened the door this morning?"

"I assumed you did. I didn't have the chance to turn the key."

"That's because you had already unlocked it," Lily said.

"No, I didn't. I hadn't even pulled the key out yet. Or I forgot to lock it again. I've been forgetting all week."

"No, Reggie, you haven't forgotten. You unlocked it with magic." Aunt Rose's eyes glittered in excitement.

"I couldn't have." Reggie gazed at them in confusion.

"Fairy godmothers don't receive their powers until they

turn twenty-seven. Merlin wanted us to understand how Groundlings live," Rose said.

Reggie's heart started to pound and a flow of excitement washed through her. Was it possible? Could she have magic? After all this time?

In a gentle tone, Lily said, "Three times three times three. It's a magical number, dear."

"Your birthday was last week," Hyacinth added. She sipped her coffee.

"Yes, but—"

"And you turned twenty-seven. Come on, girl. Put it together." Hyacinth eyed her.

Lily sent Hyacinth a chiding look.

"What? It's still early," Hyacinth muttered.

"Are you saying I'm getting magic?" Reggie whispered.

"No, we're saying you have magic," Lily said.

Reggie's heartbeat kicked a notch higher. "It's not possible."

"Of course it's possible." Rose giggled. "You're the next fairy godmother."

As her knees grew weak, Reggie plopped into a chair. "You're joking, right?"

"No, dear. You're one of the new three," Rose said.

"For this region," Hyacinth said.

They sounded serious.

"So you must choose." Lily pushed the case with the two wands toward her.

The aunts couldn't be serious. Was this their birthday present? Couldn't they have just given her a rabbit or something? She stared at the three godmothers. Anticipation and eagerness glowed on each face.

She glanced at the case. The two wands lay as if waiting for her. She reached out and paused. Her hand hovered above the box. A definite warmth emanated from one of the slender rods. Hesitant, almost shyly, she picked up the golden wand. Her fingers closed around the handle, and she could imagine it snuggling into her palm. It rested within her grip securely and comfortably.

"I knew it," Rose said. "I just knew you would pick that one."

Then Reggie noticed the empty spot in the case meant for a third wand. "Where is the third one?"

"With its owner," Lily said. A hint of misgiving appeared in her expression.

The rogue godmother. Reggie remembered the headline from this morning.

Even Rose lost her smile. "We can't tell you everything right now. We just don't have the time."

A sense of unease skittered through Reggie. Something was wrong. They were hiding something.

"Speaking of time, we should get going," Hyacinth said. She stood. "We've been here too long. They're bound to have heard by now."

"Who's bound to have heard? And heard what?" Reggie asked, still gripping the wand.

"The Council. Your name should have appeared on the wall right after you picked your wand," Lily said. "They'll be sending your arbiter shortly."

Hyacinth frowned. "And probably a contingent of Guards to see if they can catch us."

As if proving Hyacinth's words true, the bell on the door jangled as the door swung open. All four women gasped and whirled to face the intruder.

A man stopped in the doorway, and Reggie breathed a sigh of relief. "Good morning, Nate. You're not the first one here today."

Nate still hadn't stepped in. He filled the doorway and had to stoop slightly. Despite the promise of a warm summer's day, he wore his customary attire. Today a long black leather duster, clearly expensive, reached his calves. Black leather gloves encased his hands. A gray knit hat covered his head and forehead down to his brows. A white muffler, silk if she guessed right, wrapped the lower half of his face so that only his eyes were visible. And what eyes. Ice blue and intense, those eyes were more expressive than many people's entire faces.

Despite six months of daily visits, Reggie didn't know much about Nate. They had only exchanged a few words in these past months. He was a fiercely private person, and she respected that desire. Through observation, she had learned he was uncomfortable around people, so she opened the bakery early for him. She glanced at her watch. Six thirty, his usual time. He generally ordered coffee and an egg croissant. Sometimes he took a few of Tommy and Joy's special creations home with him, but he never stayed longer than half an hour and was always gone before the breakfast rush started. She knew that he was Arcani because he read the *Quid Novi*.

Nate's gaze darted from one woman to another. "You're the fairy godmothers." His voice was gravelly and rough, as if he wasn't used to talking.

"Guilty," Rose said. Her smile had returned.

Nate glanced at Reggie and noticed the wand in her hand. "I thought you couldn't do magic."

"Surprise," she said. "Looks like I'm a fairy godmother. I guess."

"No guessing needed. You are, dear." Lily stood. "We have to go."

Hyacinth downed her coffee and grabbed another turnover. When Lily gave her yet another chiding look, she shrugged. "Hey, if you're going to wake me, I need sustenance."

Rose crossed to Reggie and kissed her cheek. "Take care, dear."

"We know you have questions, but we can't stay," Hyacinth added, standing beside Rose. "Leave us a message."

"You won't be able to call us directly. We don't carry our cell phones around anymore. Did you know they can track you with one of those?" Rose clicked her tongue.

"We'll be able to tell you more the next time we see you," Lily said, giving her a hug. "I promise. Try not to worry."

About what? Reggie wondered.

"Good-bye, dear." Lily joined her companions. "Are we ready, ladies?"

"Ready."

The three women shimmered briefly, and then they vanished.

Reggie stared at the spot for a moment.

"So you're the new fairy godmother, huh?" Nate said.

She shook herself and examined the wand she still clutched in her hand. "That's what they said."

Nate moved to his regular table. "Have you tried any magic yet?"

"No. I've only had this thing for three minutes." She tucked the wand into the pocket of her apron. "Coffee?"

His eyes crinkled. "Yes, but it can wait until you test your skills."

Reggie opened her mouth to protest, then changed her mind. She retrieved the wand and felt the warmth in her palm again. She looked at the now empty plate on the table the godmothers had occupied. She focused. "*Vení.*"

The advantage was that she had been raised in an Arcani household. She knew the words and what to expect. The reality was that she had never done magic before. Except for unlocking the door apparently, but she hadn't been aware of that. Her nose wrinkled, and she gritted her teeth as she concentrated.

The plate rattled on the tabletop. She held her breath. The plate levitated a fraction of an inch above the wood, hovered, then edged off the table. It floated toward her.

She expelled her breath, and with the rush of air, the plate wobbled and crashed to the floor.

Tommy burst from the back room. "I heard something break. Oh, hi, Mr. Nate. Did you break something?"

"No, Tommy. *I* dropped a plate." Reggie quickly stowed her wand in the pocket again, and then grabbed a dustpan and brush from a closet in the corner.

"Well, don't worry. I drop things all the time."

"Thanks, Tommy." Reggie swept up the shards from the ground.

"I've got to go back to the kitchen now."

"Everything good back there?" Reggie asked.

"Under control, boss." Tommy made the okay sign with his thumb and forefinger and left.

Reggie dropped the broken plate pieces in a wastebasket and returned the brush, dustpan, and the abandoned cleaning rag to the closet. She washed her hands at the sink behind the counter, then grabbed a mug and poured a coffee for her customer.

"A little bit underwhelming, wouldn't you say?" she said as she placed the coffee in front of Nate.

"Nah, not for a first try." Nate hesitated. "You don't seem excited."

She looked at him. "I suppose the idea will really hit me later, and then I can freak out."

He shook his head. "You did read the paper this morning."

"No, just the headline." She glanced at the stack of *Quid Novi*. That headline blared at her again. Oh. She was the second of the new fairy godmothers, wasn't she? The first one was making headlines. "Right. The other one is missing."

"It's more than that." Nate pointed at the papers. "The Council wants to question the fairy godmothers. The ones who just left."

"They do?"

"Apparently they've been avoiding the Council's questions." His gravelly voice held no comfort. "They'll probably want to talk to you too."

"Well, I can't tell them much." Her family wouldn't like it if she upset the Council. Maybe she didn't have to tell her family right away.

Crap. The party. She had forgotten about it. If the Council made her late for the party, her mother would never forgive her. Reggie shut her eyes. Today was not the best day for becoming a new godmother.

"Are you okay?" Nate's voice broke through her thoughts.

"I may not be later." She opened her eyes and smiled. "I'm fine. Can I get you an egg croissant today?"

He nodded, then grabbed a *Quid Novi* and buried himself behind the paper.

Retreating behind the counter, she selected a fresh croissant and carried it into the kitchen. Tommy stood by the stove where he was already scrambling two eggs. A wave of guilt struck her. How could she leave Tommy and Joy to become a fairy godmother? They needed her. She knew how capable they were. They had been her classmates. They were her friends.

Her mother had insisted she attend an Arcani school. No Groundling school was good enough for her daughter, and despite the advice from the teachers and counselors, despite her lack of magic, despite her own pleading, Reggie remained at an Arcani school. In special education. The teachers

taught her everything they could, but she couldn't participate in most of the regular classes without magic. Only when
she was old enough did she drop out and enroll in a local
community college and get her first real education. Her
parents had not been happy. They had been even less happy
when she started the bakery.

Reggie sliced the fresh croissant in half, and Tommy laid
a neat crescent of scrambled eggs with melted cheese on the
bread. Reggie placed the sandwich on a plate. Tommy had
already moved to help Joy dust her latest pastries with powdered sugar. They were a team here.

"Those look beautiful, Joy." Reggie placed her arm
around Joy. Joy giggled and continued to work. Reggie took
Nate's breakfast out to him.

"Do you want anything with that?" She asked the question every morning and then waited for the same answer.

"No, this is good." Nate pulled the croissant behind the
paper and disappeared from view again.

So she was a fairy godmother, huh? Too bad she had other
duties this morning. Reggie glanced around the bakery. The
display cases were filled and ready for the day, several pots
of freshly brewed coffee awaited the first customers, and the
eating area was tidy. She glanced at her watch again. Nearly
seven. Time to open.

Before she could flip the sign, the door opened again. Reggie had to consciously tell herself not to let her jaw drop.
Sophronia Petros swept into the bakery trailed by a muscular
man who looked like he belonged on a battlefield, not in a
bakery. Sophronia wore a flowing cream dress with a large
pashmina thrown with artistic casualness around her shoulders. Every hair on her expensive blond head fell neatly into
place in an elegant coiffure. What was her mother's greatest
rival doing here?

Sophronia took in the atmosphere of the room and

wrinkled her nose delicately as if she didn't like the smell. Reggie's dander rose.

"How . . . quaint." Sophronia said the word as if it were an insult.

Reggie pasted a fake smile on her face. "Good morning, Mrs. Petros. What can I do for you?"

"Oh, you must call me Sophie. We're going to spend so much time together." Sophronia rearranged her shawl. "I'm your arbiter."

2

❧

CORDELIA'S RULES FOR HER
DAUGHTERS

•

*Learn to Appreciate and Recognize Good
Wine. It's a Useful Skill.*

REGGIE'S INSIDES CONSTRICTED. She had forgotten that Sophronia was on the Council. Crap. This day, which already had the potential to be a nightmare, had just turned worse.

"As soon as I saw your name appear on the tablet, I knew I had to volunteer to be your arbiter." Sophronia smiled like a snake at a mouse.

Reggie nearly squeaked. "Lucky me."

As the Guard took a position at the door, his eyes alert for any threat, Sophronia ambled around the bakery. She ran her finger over a tabletop and then brushed it off as if she had picked up crumbs. Reggie bristled. She had just cleaned that table. It was spotless.

"Only one customer?" Sophronia waved toward Nate.

Nate lifted his head from the paper. The muffler still covered his face, but the croissant was half-gone.

"We're not open yet," Reggie said. "And I won't be able to, if your goo— Guard doesn't unblock the door." She had almost called the Guard a goon. That would have gone over really well.

"You'll just have to be a little late today. With the recent events, I can't risk an attack. The last godmother candidate seems to have an agenda against the Council." Sophronia pointed at the headline on the newspaper. "They sent Keith here to protect me."

Reggie examined the Guard. Nate was taller, but this guy was huge. Flabbergasted, she scrutinized Sophronia. Did she really expect someone here to cause trouble? The Guard stood on alert as if he did.

Sophronia peered into the display case, then straightened. "I didn't realize you were so talented."

"I'm not. That's all Tommy and Joy's work."

The woman affected a guileless expression. "Surely not."

"I just supervise." Reggie knew Sophronia wouldn't understand the fierce pride she felt for her two colleagues.

"Very smart of you. They do all the work and you reap the benefits." Sophronia's smirk held a challenge.

"They earn more than I do," Reggie said between clenched teeth.

"Well, really, dear, that's rather silly. They wouldn't function without you, and from what I've heard, your little . . . business is taking off. You'd be much better off if you took a bigger percentage. And they'd never know."

Reggie opened and shut her mouth a few times before shaking off her indignation. "I would never do that."

"Hmmm." The smug sound gave ample evidence of Sophronia's opinion.

Reggie bit back the caustic remarks she wanted to loose. She crossed her arms over her chest instead. "Listen, Sophronia, I appreciate your coming by and letting me know you're my arbiter. Is there some sort of schedule you need to tell me about? Tests I need to prepare for? I've got a busy day ahead of me. . . ."

"Of course. Your sister's party is today. Ian is such a lucky young man. Are you baking for it?"

As a matter of fact they were, but she didn't need to tell Sophronia about it. Reggie tilted her head back to look up at the woman. Wait a minute. A quick glance affirmed her guess. Sophronia wore heels. At five feet two inches, Reggie knew she wasn't tall, but neither was Sophronia. The heels were just a tactic to try to intimidate her. "Mother expects me to arrive early."

"Well then, I shall see you tonight at the celebration." Sophronia smiled down at Reggie.

Naturally her mother would have invited Sophronia. How better to rub the engagement in Sophronia's face? Her two daughters were already married, but neither had snagged someone like Ian.

"As for the rest, there is no set schedule. I shall drop by unannounced to see how your powers are progressing, what magic you can perform. I shall be asking you questions and note your responses." Sophronia tried to peer into the kitchen. "So what did you think of the fairy godmothers?"

Reggie looked at her, perplexed. "I've known them for years."

"Are they still here?"

"No."

"What they did they tell you?" Sophronia's tone hadn't changed, but her expression took on an edge.

"That I'm the new godmother."

"And?"

"Nothing. They gave me a wand and left." Reggie held up the wand.

Before Reggie could react, Sophronia reached out and grabbed the wand, but instead of snatching it out of her hand, a bright spark flashed from the tip accompanied by a loud bang.

"Ow!" Sophronia cried out and snatched her hand back. She shook it as if she had been burned. Keith leapt forward from his place at the door with his wand at the ready, but Sophronia waved him away. "What did you do to me?"

"I didn't do anything." Reggie gazed at the wand, which lay peacefully in her hand. She hadn't felt more than a slight jerk in her palm.

"You'd best watch yourself, young lady." All pretense of friendliness disappeared from Sophronia's face. "Attacking a Council member is a serious offense."

"I didn't attack you." Reggie stepped away from Sophronia.

"Then you'd better tell me where those three women are."

"The godmothers? I told you they left."

"Really?" Doubt laced Sophronia's voice. "You know they are wanted for questioning."

"I've heard." She glanced at Nate, who was following the exchange with watchful eyes. "Why?"

"Don't you read the papers? Haven't you paid attention to the news lately?"

"Not really. I've been working. We've been busy."

"Their first choice for godmother has made threats against us, and we need to know if the godmothers are behind it. If you don't want to end up like the other one, a fugitive, you should cooperate with us. Tell me where the godmothers went."

That wasn't right. Everyone knew the godmothers didn't choose their replacements. The Magic did that. Reggie shook her head. "I don't know."

Sophronia's voice dropped in tone. "Yes, you do. They told you something. It's your duty to tell me."

Reggie took another step back. "No, they didn't. They said they'd come back, but I don't know where they went."

"I think you do. I think you're hiding something." Sophronia took a step closer. Her wand was now in her hand.

"She isn't." In a fluid, graceful movement, Nate stood from his table. His newspaper fluttered to the floor. His blue eyes narrowed slightly. "They didn't say anything."

"Who are you?" Sophronia asked, recoiling slightly.

"It doesn't matter," Nate said. "The point is Reggie isn't lying, and you seem to be threatening her."

"Threatening? I?" Sophronia raised a hand to her chest. "Do you know to whom you are speaking?"

"Yes. Sophronia Petros. Member of the Council, and from today's actions, I'd say first-class bitch."

Reggie bit her lips to prevent a bark of laughter. The shock on Sophronia's face made her wish she had a camera.

"How dare you?" spluttered Sophronia.

"No, how dare you? This should be an exciting and happy day for Reggie. Instead you come in here, throwing around your prejudices and insulting her and her colleagues. Have you no shame?"

"Shame? You're hiding behind a scarf and hat. You won't even show your face and you're accusing me of having no shame?" Sophronia's gaze narrowed. "What are you hiding?" She lifted her wand and aimed it toward Nate.

A deep growl rose from Nate's throat. Sophronia's eyes widened, and her wand trembled. Even the Guard seemed to be taken aback.

"Don't even think of using that on me, lady." Nate's voice was low and even. "You don't want to see me angry."

Before the situation could escalate further, Reggie moved between Nate and Sophronia. For whatever reason, she didn't fear him. She placed her hand on the arm of his leather duster. "I'm sorry, Nate. You didn't come here for trouble. I'm sorry I couldn't provide you with the privacy you wanted this morning."

The squint of Nate's gaze softened as he looked down at her. He didn't say anything for a moment, then nodded. "You've a good heart, Regina Scott. You'll make a great fairy godmother." Nate turned toward the door.

"You sound like you're never coming back," Reggie said, not knowing why that made her suddenly sad. His morning appearance had become a constant in her life.

"Oh, I'll be back." Nate's eyes crinkled as if he was smiling under the scarf. "It'll take more than a Council . . . dog to keep me away. But if she's smart, she won't come when I'm here." He strode to the door and glared at the Guard, who tried to stand his ground only to wither under Nate's fierce gaze. He stepped aside to let Nate through. The door jingled as it closed behind him.

"Well, what an unpleasant man," Sophronia said. She brushed imaginary dirt from her shawl. "I would pick different friends if you wish to pass my standards and make it as a fairy godmother."

Somehow Reggie knew that no matter how she behaved, she had little chance of meeting Sophronia's standards.

"But apparently he is adamant that you know nothing."

Because you'd take his word over mine. Thanks for your vote of confidence. Reggie drew a deep breath. "Nate was here when the godmothers were. He witnessed everything."

"Then maybe the Council should speak to him as well. Nate is his name? What's his last name? His address?"

"I don't know. I don't require customers to fill out an application to eat here."

Sophronia's lips thinned. "Sarcasm won't help your case with the Council or me."

Despite the irritation she felt, Reggie kept her expression calm. "I told you everything I know. If the godmothers return . . ."

"They will. And when they do, you must contact us. It's your duty."

Reggie opened her mouth to promise, then hesitated. "I'll do the right thing."

"Good." Sophronia took one last glance around the bakery, then marched into the kitchen anyway. Before the Guard could follow her, she returned. "You weren't lying. No one was there."

"What about my bakers?"

"Well, yes, they were there, but really, they hardly count."

Anger flooded Reggie's cheeks with heat. "Was there anything else?"

Sophronia bestowed her smile again. "You should practice your magic. You've years of work to catch up on."

"Thanks. I'll do that." Maybe she'd practice by turning Sophronia into a toad.

"Good. I'm so glad we came to this understanding. We'll get along just famously. Well, dear, I must be off. I'll see you tonight at the party. Ta-ta." Sophronia kissed the air above Reggie's cheek, then swept through the door as breezily as she had entered, as if nothing unpleasant had happened. The Guard lumbered out behind her.

Reggie collapsed into a chair. The bakery wasn't even open yet, and she was exhausted. She turned her wand over in her hand.

A wand.

She smiled, focused on the OPEN sign, and said, "*Verte*."

In her palm, the wand's handle warmed. A moment later the posterboard flipped to reveal the CLOSED side.

"Yes." Exhilaration sparkled in her, even as her hand trembled. This was going to be easier than she thought.

And then the sign flipped again. And again and again and again, until it whirred like helicopter blades. The lanyard it hung on became hopelessly twisted. Reggie dropped the wand on the table, and the sign settled against the window.

With a chuckle, Reggie crossed to the sign, unraveled the cord, and laid the OPEN side next to the glass.

She had magic.

But as much as she might like to try out her new powers, she still had a bakery to run. She picked up her wand, and concentrated. "Sanctum."

The wand vanished, but she could still feel its tug from the other plane where it now waited for her next summons. She had seen her parents stow their wands before, but had never believed she would do so with her own one day.

The joy of it seized her and she spun, wrapping her arms around herself. Until she stumbled a little. With a laugh at herself and her clumsiness, she caught her breath. The magic had left her a little drained, but happy. She had magic. Not under her control yet, but she had magic.

This might not be such a bad day after all.

NATE REACHED HIS home after a short hike. His house sat behind his neighbors' with only a long, narrow drive to connect it to the street. No one could bother him here, which was as he liked it. He locked the door behind him and threw his duster onto the coat tree in the entry. Wide windows in his living room offered a spectacular view of the ocean, but he paid it no heed. With a singular purpose, he strode to a large mirror in the hallway.

Flicking on the light switch beside the mirror, he peeled the hat from his head and raked his gloved fingers through his flattened hair. Spotlights lit the large oval mirror. For a moment he peered at his refection, then grabbed the end of the scarf. Once, twice, he unwound the white silk from around his face, then let the material drop to the floor. His eyes narrowed as he took in his image.

A roar of anguish ripped through him. His head tilted back with the sound, and the howl filled the room behind him with near deafening volume. He tore the gloves from his hands and stared at them. Claws came to sharp points at his fingertips; the fingers themselves were covered in fur that disappeared into the sleeves at his wrists. The urge to gouge at his face overcame him, but instead he dug the sharp nails into the drywall beside the mirror. The weak Sheetrock powdered beneath his touch.

His fingers embedded in the wall, Nate forced himself to look in the mirror. Except for his eyes, a beast stared back at him. His ears were pointed and tufted, his hair unruly and coarse. His nose wasn't a nose at all, but a snout, and from beneath that snout at the corners of his mouth where uneven teeth lined his gums, two tusks curled upward to lethal points. The ruddy orange hair that covered most of his head extended to his face as well. Only his eyes remained human at all, and at times he doubted that much as well.

Disgust filled his eyes. His lip curled into a sneer that would have expressed his repugnance except his mouth didn't curve that way, and so his expression took on the look of a beast about to feed.

Nate released his grip from the wall. He pulled his wand from his pocket. Despite his appearance he was as much a wizard as any in the Arcani world. He pointed the tip at his face. "*Restitue.*"

He felt the familiar wave of power drain from him into his wand. He felt the magic flow over him, touching him, tingling. And then he felt the familiar disappointment when once again the magic failed to restore his appearance.

Seven years. Seven years of hiding, of rumors about his reclusion. Seven years of searching for some sort of counter spell.

But this time despair didn't wash over him. He turned from the mirror and retreated to his living room. Daylight brightened the space. Normally he avoided the room until dusk, but today he pressed his face against the glass of the windows and looked out over Del Mar and the ocean. The coolness of the glass didn't penetrate the hair on his cheek, but he knew it was there nonetheless. He had to plan.

Who would have thought when he stumbled upon the Star Bright Bakery that it would hold the hope for his release from the curse that bound him? Until today, he thought he had just found a place where he could, for a few minutes a day, enjoy stepping into the world. Regina Scott never questioned him, and Tommy and Joy were sweet and simply accepting. The bakery was a haven, a sanctuary outside of his house. A place he was drawn to day after day. He couldn't have predicted that Reggie was the next fairy godmother.

A smile, or at least the attempt of a smile twisted his muzzle. He didn't know much about fairy godmothers except that they had special magic endowed upon them by Merlin himself. He probably would have met the outgoing ones at some time if he hadn't withdrawn from society, but now it didn't matter. Reggie had fallen onto his path without any effort on his part. And he wasn't about to muck up this chance to undo the curse. He knew when to be ruthless, how to achieve his goals, and this situation was one of those occasions.

When that self-important arbiter had shown up and bullied Reggie, he had seized the chance to stand up for her. He had seen the gratitude in her eyes. Now he just had to build upon that beginning and strengthen their bond. And he knew just how to do it.

A twinge of guilt twitched inside his gut for an instant, but he brushed it aside. He had helped Reggie and would help her again. And if in return she could remove the curse from him, well, that was just fair.

The sun rose higher in the sky. He glanced at the clock. Seven thirty A.M. He had many hours before his next move. He had ample time to prepare.

3

CORDELIA'S RULES FOR HER DAUGHTERS

•

It's Just as Easy to Marry an Important Man as a Nobody.

REGGIE APPEARED ON the terrace of her parents' extensive grounds. Above the faux marble stones, strings of lights floated in the shape of hearts, and fairies and sprites twinkled in the trees and bushes. Reggie wasn't surprised to see them. Even if only to decorate, no one refused an invitation from Cordelia Scott.

Dusk settled over the land, and stars arrived in the night sky. The sunset had been breathtaking—nature herself seemed eager to acquiesce to Cordelia's demands.

After delivering the pastries and cakes to the kitchen, Reggie had made her way to her old room and changed out of her blue jeans and T-shirt into the clingy little red dress she now wore. She would have felt more comfortable if Tommy and Joy had stayed, but Tommy decided his Xbox held more appeal, and Joy wanted to watch Indiana Jones again. In truth, Reggie'd rather be at home in her apartment over the bakery too, except she'd received a command from her mother and she had no good reason to miss her sister's engagement party.

With a sigh, Reggie turned to the bar. Maybe a drink would help.

"There you are, Regina." Her mother's voice called her away from the wine she craved.

"Hi, Mother." Reggie kissed Cordelia's cheek. Her mother wore a trim beige suit with enough cleavage to show off the ruby necklace Dad had bought her. Matching earrings dangled from her earlobes. "You look great."

"Thank you. Didn't you wear that dress last year to the yachting party?" Cordelia asked.

"Probably." Reggie tried to suppress the automatic defensiveness her mother brought out in her.

"I would have bought you a new one," Cordelia said.

"A new dress isn't the point. Tonight is Del's night. No one should be focusing on me." Reggie gazed over the expanse of lawn. Guests sat at tables scattered over the grass. In addition to the sprites and fairies, luminous glass balls in various colors lit the grounds. "Where's Del?"

"Adelaide will be making a grand entrance in about an hour. By the way, I expect you to be up here when she does."

Fun. "Okay, Mom." Reggie saw Ian Talbott standing at a table talking to some wizard with gray hair. "Isn't Ian making the grand entrance?"

"Don't be silly. We're presenting your sister. Ian'll be here to take her hand from your father." Cordelia smiled and waved to her future son-in-law.

Ian waved back, then headed for them.

"And really, Regina. Couldn't you have done something with your hair?" Cordelia lifted a curly strand that had escaped Reggie's hastily pinned twist. "If you'd just let Rudolfo—"

"Sorry, Mother." Her dark, curly hair had always been a source of contention for Cordelia.

Ian sauntered up to them, his face wearing a smile a politician would be proud of. "Reggie. So good to see you again. How's my favorite soon-to-be sister-in-law?"

Cordelia giggled, giving the expected response to his humor, but Reggie merely stared at him. "Hi, Ian. 'Soon-to-be.' Does that mean you've set a date?"

"Not yet, but I'm sure Cordelia has it all under control." Ian beamed at the woman.

"I do indeed. I have several dates and venues selected. We just have to sit down and make the decisions."

Mother was in her element, Reggie noted. A party tonight, wedding details to settle—Cordelia had to be ecstatic. Reggie cringed inwardly. What was Mother going to do when she found out Reggie was the new fairy godmother? No party. She would be adamant. Or maybe she wouldn't have to tell her. . . . No, that wouldn't work. Tomorrow. She would tell Mother tomorrow. Even then, Mother would never forgive her for not telling her first.

"Something wrong, Reggie?" Ian asked. "You look as if you've detected some awful smell."

"What?" Cordelia whirled in alarm, sniffing at the air.

"Just thinking of an appointment I have tomorrow. Nothing you have to worry about, Mother. The party's perfect." Reggie patted her mother's arm.

"It had better be," Cordelia said. "Your father spent enough money on it."

"Where is Daddy?" Reggie asked.

"He's talking to a Council elder," Cordelia said with a vague wave.

"Which gives me a wonderful opportunity to make a

contact. It always helps to know another elder. I might be able to influence his thinking on some important matters." Ian's gaze already searched the guests for his quarry.

"Just don't forget the presentation in an hour."

"I won't." Ian descended the stairs to the lawn.

"He is so dedicated," Cordelia said.

"And ambitious." Reggie watched her sister's fiancé walk away from them in search of more important conversation.

"Nothing wrong with that. You could use a little more ambition yourself," Cordelia said in that tone only a mother could achieve.

"The bakery is doing fine, Mother." Maybe when Cordelia found out about the whole godmother thing, she'd finally be satisfied. Guilt pinged at Reggie's conscience. Tomorrow. Definitely. She would tell her mother first thing in the morning.

A distinguished looking gentleman approached them. His hair was thick and dark with just a hint of gray at the temples. His suit seemed an elegant extension of his presence— rich, suave, and impressive. He stopped in front of Cordelia and lifted her hand to his lips.

"Mrs. Scott, thank you so much for the invitation to your charming soiree." His French accent only added to his polished air. "You make a foreigner feel most welcome."

"My pleasure," Cordelia said. "May I introduce my daughter, Regina Scott? Regina, this is Luc LeRoy. He's new in town, so I thought he should meet some of us."

"How do you do?" Mr. LeRoy said.

"Please call me Reggie," she said at the same time.

"Then I must be Luc. I love how informal you are here in America. Someone should write an article on how our place of residence influences the behavior of the Arcani." He smiled at her, and Reggie felt the pull of his personality. If he wasn't important yet, he soon would be.

"How are you finding our part of the world, Luc?" Cordelia asked.

"If only everyone were as friendly as you are, dear lady." He gave a slight bow. "San Diego is lovely, although I ran into a little difficulty finding the perfect lodging. I'm afraid I am imposing on some friends for the time being. They have loaned me their house while they are away."

His voice was almost mesmerizing. That accent, his poise, his attractiveness—they all worked together to envelop the listener. Reggie shook herself as she realized that a dopey smile curved her lips. "How did you meet my mother?"

"We have some mutual friends. They offered to introduce me to important Arcani here in San Diego. Your charming mother was among them."

"You remember that wine tasting you father and I went to last week." Cordelia preened under Luc's attention. "Since Luc was new in town, I thought I'd invite him to the party."

"What brought you to San Diego?" Reggie asked.

"I had some business I needed to take care of here, and since this is the Time of Transition, I thought I would stay for a while. I like being near a Council city."

Time of Transition. The time when new fairy godmothers were chosen. That ping of guilt returned, and she averted her gaze from her mother. "So your business is with the Council?" Reggie asked.

"Only peripherally." Luc smiled. "But I don't wish to bore you with the details. This evening is for the celebration of your engagement." He bowed to her. "May I offer my congratulations?"

"Oh, not me," Reggie said quickly.

"My younger daughter, Adelaide." Cordelia lowered her tone. "Reggie is unattached at the moment."

You don't need to sound embarrassed, Mother. Reggie gave Cordelia a hard look.

"An oversight of the greatest measure, I am sure." Luc's gaze took her in.

This guy *dripped* with charm. Reggie needed to change the subject. "What part of San Diego does your friend live in?"

"I'm not sure precisely what it's called, but I believe—"

He didn't have a chance to finish. Sophronia waltzed up to them. She wore a bright turquoise-blue suit with an outrageous collar that threatened to poke an eye out if someone walked by unaware.

"Cordelia, dear, how are you?" Sophronia and Cordelia exchanged air kisses. Sophronia shook her hair in an artful manner. "Doesn't that suit speak your name? And it's your color. Beige."

Cordelia didn't blink. "La, Sophronia. Don't you look divine as well? That extravagant cut, the flamboyant color—it hides your age quite well."

Reggie didn't blink at the exchange. She was too used to the way these two women acted around each other. Luc, however, watched with an expression that mixed amusement and shock.

"Don't mind them. This is the way they behave with each other," Reggie whispered.

"I'm glad you told me," Luc whispered back. "I was worried I might get injured if I stood too close."

Reggie chuckled. "You get used to it."

Sophronia turned from Cordelia. "Reggie, dear, so good to see you again. Not dressed for the bakery tonight I see."

"No, Sophronia. Thanks for noticing." Reggie eyed the woman's smile. It didn't bode well.

"Now, now. I told you this morning to call me Sophie."
Sophronia tsked.

Reggie realized she had made a grave error in keeping
her new status a secret.

"Sophie? Since when are you two so friendly?" Cordelia
asked.

"Didn't you tell your mother?" Sophronia's eyes widened in mock surprise. "Reggie, you should be ashamed of
yourself."

"No, I thought I'd wait until tomorrow." Reggie prayed
Sophronia would hear the plea in her voice. "Tonight is for
Del."

"Don't be silly," Sophronia said. "You can't keep such
news to yourself."

"News?" Cordelia looked at Reggie. Uncertainty marred
her hostess expression.

"Tomorrow, Mom, I promise—" Reggie feared what was
about to happen.

"Darling," Sophronia cried. "Reggie has been chosen as
one of the new godmothers."

Cordelia froze. Sophronia's look of triumph wasn't a celebration of Reggie's new position, but a coup over her rival.
Reggie glanced at her mother's face and cringed at the hurt
evident in her features. Even Luc looked taken aback.

"Mother, I swear I meant to tell you. Tomorrow." Reggie
grabbed her mother's arm.

"It's true?" Cordelia's voice was barely above a whisper.
Reggie nodded.

For a moment Cordelia said nothing. Then she threw her
arms wide and embraced Reggie. "My baby girl."

Surprise stunned her, and then Reggie squirmed in her
mother's embrace. This display wasn't real. Her mother was
acting.

Cordelia held her out at arms' length. "Why did you think you had to keep this secret?"

"I didn't, Mother." Reggie tried to put the right emphasis in her tone. "It's not the right time. Del—"

"But this is the perfect time. I'm already throwing a party." Cordelia turned from her and waved her hand. A waiter appeared at her elbow. "Go find your boss and send him to me." Cordelia's eyes glistened with new energy.

Reggie recognized that expression. Sophronia had severely underestimated Cordelia. Mother wasn't about to allow Sophronia a victory. Not only was Mother about to steal Sophronia's thunder by making a huge deal out of the information, she was going to prove how important her family was. And with aplomb.

Horror and dismay filled her. "Mother, no. Not tonight. The party is for Del . . ." One look at her mother's face stopped her. A wave of futility washed over her. Her mother wasn't about to listen to her.

"Nonsense, Reggie. You're too self-sacrificing." Cordelia patted Reggie's shoulder. "That's why you were chosen. You're always thinking of others. I should have known you were headed for greatness."

Reggie couldn't hold back the resentment that shot through her. Her mother had harangued her, judged her, and voiced disappointment in her for years. A wind gusted around her. More of her unruly hair slipped from the knot at her nape. Her breath came in uneven bursts as she struggled to contain her anger.

The first bulb in the string above her popped, followed by a second, the third, then the rest in rapid succession until they sounded like popcorn. The now defunct light strand fell to the ground tangling in their legs.

"Honestly. You can't depend on quality these days."

Cordelia pulled her wand from the inner pocket of her suit jacket. "*Repará.*"

The light rope rose from the ground, reshaped itself into a heart, and started twinkling again.

"I'm deducting that from their bill," said Cordelia.

A whisper tickled her ear. "That was you, wasn't it?"

Reggie jumped at the voice. She turned her head to see Luc watching her with a crooked smile on his face. She had forgotten he was still there. "I don't know."

"You were feeling something particularly strong, and your emotions caused that little accident." Luc nodded. "I've seen it before."

He had? Reggie sighed. He probably had more knowledge about the Time of Transition than she did. "I guess I should get used to little power surges, huh?"

"Didn't the godmothers tell you . . . anything?" Luc asked in surprise.

"They didn't have time. They told me I was a godmother, gave me a wand, and disappeared. Apparently there's been some sort of trouble, and they couldn't stay." Reggie shook her head. "I would have liked a little more preparation."

"What of your arbiter?"

"Sophronia's my arbiter, and I have the feeling she won't be forthcoming with much information either." Reggie glanced at the woman. Although Sophronia still smiled, a hardness had settled over her expression.

Luc raised an eyebrow. "I imagine not. *Pauvre petit,* this is what I believe you call a pickle."

She chuckled ruefully. "I can think of stronger terms than that."

"Then let me offer you assistance. I would be more than pleased if you would call on me for help should you need it." He gave her a little bow.

"Thank you, Luc." His offer sounded sincere. His charisma definitely held appeal. He would do well in this crowd.

The catering boss appeared before Cordelia. "Mrs. Scott, I understand you wanted to speak to me."

"Yes, I need to know if the guests have all arrived?"

The caterer snapped his fingers and his clipboard appeared. He consulted a list. "All but a few, madam."

"I guess we can safely say if they haven't shown up yet, they aren't coming." Cordelia nodded. "Change in plans. I need to make an early toast. Can you supply more champagne for the later one?"

He looked at his list again. "We ordered plenty. It shouldn't be a problem."

"Excellent. I need you to start pouring now and passing among the guests to gather them for an announcement."

"Very good, madam." The caterer took out his wand and touched the embroidered insignia on his jacket. Almost at once the waitstaff looked up at him. The caterer waved his hand and headed into the house. The waiters finished their immediate business and followed him.

"Efficient," Luc said as he watched the process. He seemed to be lost in thought for a moment.

Reggie tried to formulate a plan to stop her mother, but before she could say anything, her mother spoke again.

"What happened to your hair?" Cordelia let out an annoyed sigh.

Reggie touched the twist. It was a mess. That unintended display of power had ruined what little semblance of elegance she had achieved.

"You have just about enough time to run upstairs and fix it before the toast. Hurry up."

"Yes, Mother." Reggie darted into the house and up the stairs to her old room. In truth she was grateful for the respite from the party and her mother. And Sophronia. And the one-upmanship. She needed a break. In fact, she was tempted to lock the door of the bathroom and not come out again.

Just as she pulled the clip from her hair, she heard the door to her room open.

"Reggie?"

"In here, Del." Reggie pulled the brush though her hair and tried not to wince as the bristles encountered a tangle.

Adelaide walked into the bathroom. Reggie looked at their reflections in the mirror. Del was tall enough not to be petite, lithe, with flowing blond hair, green eyes, and a cute, pouty mouth. Reggie's hair threatened to frizz if she brushed it any more, and her muddy brown eyes were insignificant, even if the eye shadow she wore made them look larger. Her sister looked like their father, while she was some weird mixture of their parents. She could only be sure that somehow she was the product of a genetic mutation.

Del stood beside her and peered into the mirror. "Did you come to get me? Is it time yet?" Del pressed her lips together as if she were coaxing her perfect lipstick to look even more perfect.

"Not yet." Reggie grabbed her hair, twisted it, and reapplied the clip. As if mocking her, a strand of hair escaped at once and dangled on her cheek. The rest looked okay. She wasn't going to achieve any better, so she left it.

"Isn't this exciting?" Del hadn't moved her gaze from her reflection. She adjusted a perfectly placed tress. "I can't wait to make my entrance."

Reggie swallowed hard. "Look, Del, I have to tell you something."

"Can't it wait? I don't want to think about anything to-night." Del tossed her head artfully and smiled at herself.

"No, it can't wait." Reggie left the bathroom and sat on the edge of her bed.

Del followed her. "All right. If you have to tell me now."

"I do." Reggie drew in a deep breath. "Today I found out that I'm a fairy godmother."

Del's eyes widened. "You? But you don't have magic."

"Apparently I do." Reggie wasn't surprised at her sister's reaction.

"But you? Why?"

Her expression must have revealed her thoughts because Del hurried on. She gave a flip of her hand in a gesture that was reminiscent of their mother. "You know I didn't mean it that way. This is great news. So why are you acting as if something's wrong? Ian will be thrilled he has a connection to you. And Mother must be ecstatic. What did she say?"

"That's the problem. I wasn't going to tell her until after the party."

"Oh Reggie, you're so nice. Thanks for thinking of me." Del beamed at her sister.

"Yes, but she found out, and now she's waiting for me downstairs so she can make an announcement to everyone." Reggie winced as she waited for her sister's reaction.

Del's eyes grew wide and her mouth dropped open. Her brow furrowed. "But this is *my* party."

"I know. But you know Mother."

"I can't believe this. Tonight is supposed to be about my engagement." Her agitation palpable, Del paced by the bed.

"It still is. I promise after this toast I'll sink into the background."

"How could you do this to me?" Agitation filled every one of Del's steps.

"I didn't do anything to you. It's not like I planned it." The old familiar impatience surfaced in Reggie as she dealt with her self-centered sister. "I didn't start out the day by saying, 'Hmm, I wonder how I can ruin Del's big day.'"

"Well you have, haven't you?" Del's cheeks held more color than could be explained by her makeup.

"Don't worry. I can always fail to actually pass the test. Sophronia's my arbiter. Then this will be just another way I've embarrassed the family." Reggie stood. "I have to go. I just thought I'd warn you."

She left the room without another glance at her sister. Why did she try to deal with Del rationally? It never worked.

By the time she returned to the patio, the guests had gathered at the base of the steps. Cordelia waved her over and pressed a flute into her hands. Her father watched her with an expression of excitement and pride on his face. He stood beside her and placed his arm around her shoulders.

"Really, Reggie?" he whispered to her. "You're it?"

"I guess that's as good a way of putting it as any," she whispered back.

Cordelia lifted her hand for quiet, then spoke. "I realize that you all have come here tonight to celebrate the engagement of my daughter, Adelaide, but we've just received news about our other daughter, Regina, that deserves just as much recognition. Regina has been named the next fairy godmother."

A murmur passed through the crowd. Reggie felt the myriad gazes fasten upon her, and she tried to smile and give a little wave. Flames erupted in her cheeks and she wondered if she looked as uncomfortable as she felt.

"So lift your glasses to my daughter, Regina." Cordelia raised her flute. When the glass reached its apex, a colorful burst of sparks floated from the top of the rim. In a moment the air was filled with the miniature fireworks as all the guests joined her in the toast.

"Uh, thanks," said Reggie. *Eloquent as ever,* she chided herself.

The crowd's murmuring mushroomed and then diminished as the guests took a sip from their glasses. From the corner of her eye, she saw Sophronia swigging the fine champagne, and then asking for a refill. Without a doubt, Reggie was going to suffer for her mother's triumph tonight.

Reggie gulped her champagne, glad the moment was over. But the crowd's noise swelled again, and all gazes focused toward her. She looked down at herself. Nope. Nothing spilled, nothing hanging out. Then she realized people were staring at a spot behind her and pointing at the house.

Reggie turned. A man stood in the doorway. Sun-bleached, thick blond hair framed his head, and his gaze surveyed the crowd. His face was tanned and his sharp features gave him an aura of strength. If that wasn't enough, the tuxedo he wore clearly wasn't a rental. It clung to his broad shoulders and tapered to the perfect fit around his waist and hips. The crisp white linen of his shirt offered a stark contrast to the black of the coat, and a purple handkerchief offered a hint of color and whimsy to the otherwise formal attire.

Her breath caught in her throat.

Cordelia gasped beside her. "I can't believe he came. This is wonderful. Oh, Sophronia will die."

Reggie tugged on her mother's sleeve. "Who is he, Mother?"

"Jonathan Bastion."

A waiter hurried to him with a tray, and Jonathan took a glass from it, then turned to the crowd. "Looks like I missed something. May I add my felicitations, a little late, but no less heartfelt." He lifted his glass and took a sip.

The guests exploded into multiple conversations. His gaze surveyed the crowd until it landed on Reggie. He smiled, a smile that focused on her as if he had known her his whole life.

She stopped breathing entirely.

4

CORDELIA'S RULES FOR HER
DAUGHTERS

•

First Impressions Can Never Be Taken Back.

I SENT HIM an invitation, but I never believed he would come." In spite of the whispered tone, Cordelia was crowing. "This will be the party of the year."

Reggie couldn't tear her gaze away. He was still looking at her. "Who . . . who . . . who . . . ?" She sounded like an owl.

"Don't tell me you haven't heard of him." Her mother's voice held a rebuke.

"Should I have?"

"Jonathan Bastion?" Cordelia enunciated every syllable.

"Saying it slowly doesn't help, Mother."

"Bastion Wands?"

Oh. Now she knew. Bastion Wands were the top wand makers in the Arcani world. Her parents' wands were from Bastion, and they had bought several different models for her to try before they accepted she didn't have magic. She studied him. He looked like someone with ties to a multimillion-dollar company.

"He rarely comes into society. He focuses on his business and nobody sees him anymore. Not since that debacle with that woman," Cordelia said.

"What woman?"

"Didn't you read the papers? That Arcani do-gooder." The scolding was back.

"Not often."

"Really Regina. You need to be more aware."

"Yes, Mother. Now do you want to tell me about the debacle?"

But before her mother could give an answer, the man himself made his way toward them. Reggie's heart kicked up a notch and she could feel the beating in her throat.

Jonathan Bastion's stride cleared the way in front of him as if he were an old-fashioned locomotive with a cowcatcher on the front. He owned his space. His shoulders squared, he created a surge of power around him that no one dared penetrate. Reggie watched the ripple of curiosity and excitement that traveled over the crowd as he passed through. How could one man generate such interest?

As he neared them, his gaze took her in. Heat unfurled in her. When he finished his evaluation, his gaze met hers and his mouth quirked up on one side as if he had enjoyed his investigation. He transferred his glass to his left hand and held out his right to her mother. "Mrs. Scott, such a pleasure to meet you. I've read about your many activities in the paper. Philanthropy has found a wonderful patroness in you."

Cordelia clasped his hand. "The society pages exaggerate. I'm just a simple woman."

Reggie nearly choked on a breath. Mother? Simple? Please.

Cordelia didn't notice. "Besides, Bastion Wands has many of its own causes."

"Ah, but we don't have your panache. Perhaps someday we might work together on something." He disengaged his hand from hers.

A hungry ardor sparkled in Cordelia's eyes. "I would enjoy that. We should speak next week, after I've recovered from this party."

"I would like that." Jonathan turned to Reggie's father and exchanged a handshake with him. "You, sir, are lucky to have such a capable and caring wife."

Vincent Scott shook his head. "Her capability has cost me plenty. Just wait until you're married."

Jonathan laughed. "I wouldn't know about that yet, sir."

"Don't say I didn't warn you," Vincent said with a smile that clearly showed affection for his wife.

Cordelia gave her husband a light tap of reproof with her fingers. "Vincent, he doesn't know you're teasing."

"Sure he does. Bastion wouldn't be where he is now if he weren't smart," Vincent said.

Reggie watched in horrified fascination as her parents fawned over their newest guest. She wanted to slip away and melt into the background just as she had promised Del.

Too late. Jonathan's gaze landed on her. "And this is . . . ?"

Cordelia waved her closer. "This is my daughter, Regina."

Jonathan stared into her eyes for a moment. She wished she had something clever, something scintillating to say, but her mouth was dry. She offered a limp hand in lieu of words.

"I seem to recall a different name on the invitation . . ." Jonathan took her hand in his. It engulfed hers in a warm, firm grip. She almost snatched it back as a jolt of awareness zipped up her arm and down her spine.

"The party is for my other daughter, Adelaide's engagement," Cordelia said.

"I'm very happy to hear that." His gaze hadn't wavered from hers.

His blue gaze gripped her almost as surely as if it were a vise. She drew in a breath, then wondered why she still felt starved for air. Finally, he released her hand. For an instant she let it float on the air in front of her until she jerked it back to her side.

Cordelia stepped up beside him. "I believe you arrived just after my announcement. Regina has been chosen as a fairy godmother."

His gaze intensified. A secret-filled smile lit on his lips. "So that's the toast I missed. May I offer my sincere congratulations to you?" He lifted the glass in his left hand, tilted it to her, and then took a sip.

Reggie couldn't take her gaze from the spot where his lips touched the glass.

Cordelia waved for a waiter to refill their glasses. "Thank you. We are so proud of her."

Reggie raised her brows. Really? Since when?

"I imagine you would be." Jonathan's gaze delved into hers.

That gaze knocked her irritation with her mother from her mind.

"She has always surprised us. Her lack of magic never slowed her down. She runs a highly successful business," Cordelia said.

"I'll bet she does," Jonathan said.

For once, Reggie was grateful for her mother's skill in commandeering a conversation, even if her mother was spewing all sorts of nonsense. Reggie didn't think she could ever speak again.

Cordelia preened. "And now she's a fairy godmother—"

Just as the waiter refilled their glasses, Sophronia strolled up to them. She thrust out her glass for a top-off as if she had been a part of this group from the start. "Now, now. Don't be premature. Reggie still has to pass my assessment."

Jonathan's gaze lingered on Reggie for a moment, and then he turned to the interloper. "If I am not mistaken, you are Sophronia Petros."

"You know me?" Sophronia's surprise was genuine.

"Who wouldn't recognize such an illustrious member of the Council?" Jonathan said.

Delighted, Sophronia tossed her head. With a wave of her hand, she dismissed the waiter as if this were her party. Reggie nearly smiled at the woman's audacity. If Reggie were capable of smiling right now. "Mr. Bastion, it is such a pleasure to finally make your acquaintance."

"The pleasure is mine. So am I correct in guessing you have something to do with Regina's new appointment?"

"Well, I didn't pick her for the job, but I am her arbiter." Sophronia gloated under his attention.

"How fortuitous. I'm sure she'll have no trouble qualifying with your help." Jonathan blazed his smile directly at Sophronia.

Reggie didn't know whether to laugh or gawk in awe. Here was a man aware of his own power, and he was using it on Sophronia. For the first time since he arrived, Reggie could breathe normally. Jonathan Bastion *was* clever beneath that polished exterior. In fact he was nearly perfect. And she wasn't. Therefore, he could have no interest in her. She relaxed as if a burden had been lifted from her shoulders.

Sophronia said, "Of course this party is for Adelaide, not for Reggie. We shouldn't make such a big deal about the whole godmother thing because people will think that Cordelia's toast was an afterthought."

Cordelia shot an annoyed glance at Sophronia. "I couldn't throw a proper celebration for Regina because she didn't tell us."

"Really?" Jonathan raised his eyebrows. "How long have you known, Regina?"

"Reggie. Please call me Reggie." She was pleased to hear her voice sounded natural. "Only Mother calls me Regina."

"Because Reggie isn't your name." Cordelia clicked her tongue.

Reggie smiled. "I know Mother, and I love that you don't compromise. It makes me feel special." She was back in her element. She glanced at Jonathan, who was watching her intensely. Oh, he could still steal her breath if she let him, but she knew her own limitations, and he was so far beyond anyone she could aspire to. She was back in control. "I found out this morning. It's pretty new to me."

"Hardly any time at all. I imagine you must be a bundle of nerves." His attention focused on her again. He leaned in closer. "If you are, it doesn't show."

His breath tickled her ear, and despite her resolve to remain impervious to his appeal, her stomach flipped. She tamped down a flash of impatience with herself. Maybe she should get out more if a pretty face held such sway over her. Although he was magnificent.

A waiter approached. "Mrs. Scott, your daughter wishes to speak to you." He nodded and left.

"My daughter? But . . ." Cordelia looked at Reggie. "Adelaide. How silly of me. Will you excuse me?" Her skirt twitching, she walked across the patio and into the house.

The other guests had migrated back to the lawn and tables or clumped in groups on the terrace. Relief filled Reggie. They were done with her. Her change in status wouldn't erase years of not knowing what to say to her or how to act around her. Their discomfort lingered. It didn't surprise her. Even when she had had no magic, she'd noticed. She hadn't been stupid.

Vincent gave Reggie a quick kiss on the cheek. "I am proud of you."

"Thanks, Daddy." Her father loved her, though he was probably more comfortable when her life didn't intrude on his. To be fair, he was distant and peripheral with her mother and Del too. He liked his work and his comfort. She learned a long time ago, as long as their lives didn't interrupt his, he was happy.

"I see Castor over there. I must speak with him. Nice to meet you, Bastion. You should come to the club one of these days." Vincent wandered off, dropping off the champagne at the bar and picking up a stronger drink.

Typical vague words. Reggie sighed. Her father wasn't bad, just clueless. Well, about their lives.

Sophronia sidled up to Jonathan. "Many of the other Council members are here. I would be happy to introduce you to them. A man in your position—"

"Thank you, Sophronia, but I never talk business in social situations. Right now I'd love a tour of the gardens from this lovely young woman." He took Reggie's hand and entwined his fingers with hers.

Reggie tried not to mirror the shock that appeared on Sophronia's face. She didn't know if she succeeded. Once again his hand engulfed hers, and a charge skittered through to her nerve endings. Her skin tingled. *Control, Reggie, control.*

Sophronia's smile hardened. "Of course. I completely understand. Have fun, you two." She pivoted on her heel, dumped her glass on the tray of a nearby waiter, and headed straight for the bar.

"I hope I didn't just get you in trouble," Jonathan said, giving her hand a reassuring squeeze.

"Don't worry. If you didn't, I'm sure I would have soon enough."

Jonathan laughed. "That bad?"

"You have no idea." With steely resolve, Reggie worked her fingers loose from his. As wonderful as the contact felt, she couldn't think if he touched her. "I totally get that you didn't want Sophronia hanging around you, and I was happy to help you get rid of her, but don't feel like you have to hang out with me."

He gazed into her eyes. A slow crinkle appeared at the corners as a crooked grin slid into place. "Who says I don't want to?"

That was it. Any aplomb she could fake was lost. She couldn't speak. Her mouth flopped open like a fish gasping for air. She probably looked as attractive as one too, she was sure.

Jonathan chuckled. "Come on. Show me that garden." He took her glass from her, and passed both his and hers to a waiter.

For a moment she stared at him, unable to comprehend what he wanted. Then she cleared her throat and said, "The tour begins here on an oversized patio made of the finest concrete disguised to look like marble."

Jonathan laughed. "Are you sure you should be sharing family secrets so soon?" He took her hand again.

She stared down at their linked fingers. "I, uh, don't think you can topple governments with this one."

Jonathan contained his satisfaction. Good. Reggie was nervous. The more he kept her off balance, the easier his task would be. "Don't worry. I won't tell a soul. Now take me into the garden."

She glanced around and cringed slightly. He had already noticed the many stares they were receiving, and now he knew she noticed them too. He didn't wait for Reggie's lead. He took a step and steered her from the patio onto the lawn. He felt the wiggle of her fingers as she tried to tug her hand free, but he didn't release it. Instead he stroked his thumb back and forth over the inside of her wrist. She inhaled sharply. Just the reaction he was hoping for.

At the edge of the lawn, a flagstone path wound in two directions. She pointed to the left. "That way is the tennis court."

"Do you play?" he whispered in a tone that he knew wouldn't make her think of tennis.

She swallowed hard. "A little. I don't have much time for games."

His conscience stirred. She wasn't like the women he was used to. There was an innocence about her. And a vulnerability he had never come across before. He shook himself. It mustn't matter. "Let's go that way." He pointed toward the right.

"That leads through the garden," she said.

"Perfect." He pulled her in that direction.

Solar-powered lighting guided their steps. As the winding path took them past several rosebushes, Reggie said, "These are my mother's prizewinners. Really they're not hers. She cuts them occasionally, but the gardeners take care of them. I always thought it unfair that she'd bring home ribbons and prizes for the flowers when they did all the work."

He chuckled. "Do you think your mother will mind your telling me this?"

"Probably, but I don't think she's fooling anyone. I mean,

really. Can you see her on her knees digging in the dirt?"
She shrugged.

"No, I can't." She amused him. Her honesty was charming. He couldn't remember when a woman's words had entertained him as much. "Relax. I won't spill this secret either."

"Good, because I wouldn't want to hurt you."

He laughed again, and this time she chuckled with him, a warm, genuine sound.

She took the lead along the path now. "Here, let me show you my favorite corner of the garden."

Around the next bend in the path stood a tall cottonwood tree. Gravel surrounded the bottom of the tree and a stone bench faced a fountain that spouted from the bougainvillea-covered concrete block walls surrounding the property. Soft lights illuminated the water. It was a pretty corner.

"Let's sit."

"Here?" She winced, probably because her voice was unnaturally high.

"Sure. You said it was your favorite corner of the garden." He took a place on the bench.

For a moment she didn't move, and then she sat beside him.

He moved closer to her. "I can see why you like it here. It's almost as if you are in a different world. You can't even see the house."

"The bushes block it. And the fountain drowns out all but the loudest noises."

"Privacy. I've learned to enjoy it when I can find it." He leaned back.

"I expect you've had your share of publicity," she said.

"You have no idea. Seven years ago I couldn't go anywhere without having my picture taken." The familiar bitterness rose in him, but he ignored it. "I suppose I brought most of it on myself. My behavior was less than stellar. I had a lot of growing up to do." That was certainly one way of putting it.

She tilted her head and looked at him, but said nothing.

Something about her gaze made him uncomfortable. Perhaps it was the honesty he found there. "I had just taken a position in my family's business, and I didn't know how to handle the attention," he said.

He had faced detractors who believed he didn't have the knowledge or the capability to hold the position of responsibility his father had given him. His business acumen had proven them wrong, but that same ruthlessness had spilled into his social life as well. He had been as famous for his business sense as for how quickly he dumped the beautiful women he'd dated. He had learned his lessons in both areas.

"And now?"

"And now I run the business and try to keep the rest of my life private." He smiled at her. "I expect you will find out about publicity soon enough."

"Why?" She looked genuinely puzzled.

"You're a fairy godmother, remember?"

Clearly she hadn't, because her face took on a look of horror. "You don't think . . ."

"Reggie, everyone will know who you are. The newspapers have been filled with the controversy surrounding the first candidate. You're bound to appear on the front page."

"Oh God." A shiver shook her. A few of the pebbles at her feet started rattling. "The bakery keeps me so busy, I haven't really had time to follow the story."

"I'm sure you'll do fine."

"Are you kidding? I don't know how to do magic. I only got a wand this morning." The pebbles at her feet were dancing now.

He wondered if she realized how upset she was. "Well, I'm somewhat of an expert on wands. Why don't you let me take a look?"

Her face lost that panicked look, and the pebbles stopped doing the jig. "Really?"

"I'd be happy to."

She held out her hand, focused on her palm, and took a deep breath. "Wand."

A moment passed and then another. Reggie's face screwed up with her efforts. And then a slender rod appeared in her hand. Her expression was jubilant. "Hah. I've only done that once before. I'm happy it wasn't a fluke."

Her candid enthusiasm elicited another chuckle from him. "May I?" He reached for it.

"Wait. I don't know if it will let you touch it. It shocked someone earlier when they tried to take it from me."

"Interesting." He eyed the wand. "Did they have your permission?"

"Well, no."

"Hmmm. May I try anyway?"

She handed him the wand. No shock flew from it. He turned it over in his hand. Although he couldn't see it well in the darkness, he could feel the superb craftsmanship, the careful balance, and the distinct lack of power his touch generated in it. Interesting. "This isn't one of ours."

"Really?"

"It's geared to one owner. We can't do that. A wand is personal, but all Arcani can feel power in wands. I couldn't sense any in yours except when you held it. Do you know where it came from?"

"No. I had a choice of two. This one spoke to me." She took it back from him. At once the wand balanced in her hand, and he could sense the magical footprint that it emitted. Great power flowed through it and her. His heartbeat quickened.

She focused on the wand again and said, "Sanctum." The wand vanished, and she drew in a deep breath. "I actually like holding it, but I really have no place to keep it in this dress. I suppose that's something I need to consider when shopping."

His gaze swept over her. "You're right. You couldn't hide anything in this dress."

Her eyes grew wider. He leaned closer to her. "I like it." His hand brushed the hem of the dress higher.

Her mouth opened slightly. He couldn't ask for a better opportunity. He bent over her and pressed his lips to hers . . .

The crunch of gravel interrupted the moment. Reggie sprang back.

"Oh, sorry. We didn't know anyone was here," a woman said. She was pulling a man behind her.

Reggie jumped to her feet. "Don't worry. We were just leaving." She turned toward the path.

The man said, "Say, aren't you—"

"No. I think you've mistaken me for someone else." Reggie grabbed Jonathan's hand and pulled him away from the spot.

"Did you know them?" he asked as soon as they were out of hearing.

"I may have gone to school with her."

"May have?"

"I didn't have many friends."

There was no self-pity in her voice. Nevertheless, he found it an odd thing to say.

"So why didn't you want to talk to her?"

"She wouldn't have remembered me."

So Reggie did know her. He wondered what the story was behind her school days.

"Besides, didn't you just tell me you value your privacy?" Reggie led him farther away. "They probably would have recognized *you* if we'd stayed any longer. Everybody seemed to know you when you arrived."

They had circled the entire lawn when the path branched again. The stones to the right would return them to the party. He pulled her to the left. "What's this way?"

"The pool."

They emerged from the garden and stepped onto the concrete surrounding a large natural-shaped pool. Big enough to do laps in, the dark-bottomed pool sparkled in the moonlight. At the far end, a six-foot waterfall cascaded into the water below. A slightly elevated Jacuzzi bubbled and spilled its warm overflow into the pool as well.

"Nice," he said. For an instant the image of Reggie slicing through the water sans clothes jumped into his mind. He glanced at her. She was shorter than the women he had dated in the past, but that red dress hugged curves he suddenly wanted to explore with his tongue.

Wait. Concentrate. He couldn't lose focus. He didn't have the time or the freedom to think about a diversion right now, no matter how pleasant it might be.

She smiled and her face lit up. "I always loved this pool. Come on. I want to show you a secret." She led him to the waterfall. A narrow space opened behind the curtain of water. She walked behind the water and disappeared from view. He stooped to follow her.

The artificial waterfall covered a grotto. Green and blue lights gave the spot an undersea glow. The grotto was built to look like it was a cave, but rocks jutted out from the fake rock wall to form a seat.

"Do you mind if I sit? I can't quite stand up straight here."

Her eyes widened. "I didn't think of that. I'm so sorry. You must be uncomfortable, and the bench is probably wet. It always is."

"I don't care." He sat, and then she yelped as he pulled her down beside him. "I'll dry us off after. Now there was something else I wanted to do. Oh, yes."

He placed a hand on her back, the other on her thigh, and pulled her to him. He kissed her then, surprising himself with his own ardor. Her lips were soft and pliant, and when her mouth opened, he took advantage of the gap and explored with his tongue. She tasted of champagne and sugar.

His hand slipped around her rib cage and brushed the side of her breast. He cupped his hand beneath it. It was the size of a peach, and warm and heavy to his touch. His other hand slid higher up her thigh until it grazed the lace of her panty.

She gasped and pushed away. Casting her gaze down, she said, "I know you must think me a prude, but I don't . . . I can't . . ."

"Shhhh." He placed his finger on her lips. "I'm not thinking anything besides how delicious I find you." To his own amazement, he realized he was telling the truth. He hadn't planned on actually feeling attracted to her.

She looked up at him as if she didn't believe him. The lights gave her face an otherworldly glow, and damned if he didn't find her even more fascinating.

"I'd better get back." She stood. "Del should be making her appearance soon and I can't miss it."

"Show me the way out, mermaid."

She threw him another confused look, but didn't say anything. She led the way from behind the waterfall, and he followed her out of the grotto.

When they stood beside the pool again, he said, "Two more things. First . . ." He pulled out his wand from his coat. "Turn around."

She did so.

"Desiccate." He waved a stream of hot air over her dress. The material dried instantly. Then he passed the wand over his own tux.

"Thank you. What's the other thing?" she asked.

"This." He leaned forward, kissed her quickly and asked, "Will you go out with me tomorrow night?"

She gulped, opened her mouth, then nodded.

"Excellent. Now let's get you back to the party before they come looking for you."

As soon as they returned to the patio, her mother spotted them. Luc LeRoy was standing with her. She waved them over. "There you are, Regina. Del is making her entrance in five minutes."

Reggie's brow creased for a moment. "I'm ready."

"Your lipstick is smudged. You have just enough time to fix it. I need to make sure the staff isn't making noise." Cordelia bustled off.

Luc LeRoy leaned toward them. "Five minutes is just time enough for Mr. Bastion to remove the lipstick from his mouth as well." He winked at them.

Jonathan laughed as Reggie's face flared with color. He grabbed a napkin and wiped away the remnants of their kiss.

Luc nodded at her. "And now I believe your mother is waving to you."

"Oh, right. The grand entrance. Excuse me." Reggie left them.

"She is quite charming," Luc said. He held out his hand. "We have not been properly introduced. I am Luc LeRoy."

"Jonathan Bastion."

"Who would not know the famous Jonathan Bastion? I am having a dinner party later this week. I would be pleased if you would join me. Reggie's parents have already said they would attend with Reggie." Luc cocked one eyebrow.

"Thank you, Mr. LeRoy, but I—"

"Don't say no yet. Think about it. I shall be in touch with you. It should prove an illuminating evening, an opportunity you won't regret. It was a pleasure to meet you, Mr. Bastion." Luc gave him a curt nod and disappeared into the crowd.

Jonathan wondered what the man had meant with those cryptic words. He had no desire to attend LeRoy's dinner party, but if Reggie were there, it might suit his plans. He would have to see. In the meantime he could only be pleased with the progress he had made tonight.

If he could ignore the niggling guilt his conscience pricked him with.

5

❧

CORDELIA'S RULES FOR HER
DAUGHTERS

•

*Actions Might Speak Louder Than Words, but They
Don't Grant You the Same Deniability.*

REGGIE DRAGGED HERSELF out of bed. She couldn't
party until late in the night and wake at five o'clock to get
the bakery ready to open at seven. She had left the party as
early as possible, but it had still been one A.M. before she
fell into bed.

And it hadn't helped that her dreams had been filled
with images of Jonathan Bastion.

A quick shower, a clean white bakery coat, and two cups
of coffee later, she was nearly as happy to see the morning
as she usually was. She loved summertime—the sun rose
so early. Tonight she would go to bed at a decent hour—

No, she wouldn't. She had a date tonight.

Her heartbeat quickened at the thought. The idea of a
second late night didn't trouble her. Not today. She nearly
danced out of her apartment. She'd be extra tired tomor-

row, but that didn't matter. She'd catch up on sleep later in the week.

As she descended the stairs leading from the three apartments upstairs to the bakery proper, she heard Joy and Tommy already blasting their music in their rooms. They loved their music loud and with a strong beat, but the warring cacophony between country rock and heavy metal sometimes made living in the same building with those two an experiment in surviving an earthquake's epicenter.

Reggie looked over the list of the day's plans. Her bakers had already measured out their ingredients for the morning's baking, so they were in fine shape. In the afternoon a shipment of flour and sugar would arrive. A quick survey of their supplies showed no major shortages, but she wrote a note to order more yeast.

Half an hour later, Reggie had finished mopping the floor and the front room was ready for the day. Joy and Tommy were already kneading, mixing, and pouring, and enticing smells were coming from the ovens.

As Reggie stocked the refrigerated display cases, she noticed movement by the front door. Nate was here. A little early, but that didn't matter. She waved to him, placed the last of the éclairs onto doily-covered trays, and went to let him in.

"Good morning," she said as he stepped inside. Once again the door had opened for her before she unlocked it. She smiled at that proof of magic.

"Morning." His voice was gruffer than usual. Despite the warmth of the morning, he was dressed in his usual style—gray knit hat pulled over his head, gloves, a light brown leather coat with the collar turned up, jeans, and a blue muffler wrapped around his face.

"You sound like you need coffee."

"I didn't sleep well." He took his usual seat at his usual table. "You're terribly chipper, and I do mean terribly."

She laughed. "It took two cups for me this morning."

"I wasn't sure you'd be here today," he said. His blue gaze focused on her. "I thought you'd be busy doing your fairy godmother stuff."

"I don't know what that fairy godmother stuff is. Besides, I can't just abandon Tommy and Joy. I need to find someone to help. You don't want a job, do you?"

His husky laugh sounded almost like a bark. "No thanks. I have a job."

She shrugged. "Just thought I'd ask. Want your usual?"

He nodded, grabbed a paper, and opened it.

Reggie bustled to the coffeemaker and poured him a cup. Really, she was far too happy this morning. She had to restrain herself from skipping around the floor. The prospect of one date shouldn't put her in such a mood.

When she placed his cup in front of him, Nate looked up at her. "You really are too peppy this morning."

"I know. It's a sickness. I'm taking pills for it."

He laughed again, a throaty, rasping sound. "Here. This will bring you down to earth." He pointed at an article in the paper.

She glanced at the headline. COUNCIL SEEKS FAIRY GOD-MOTHERS FOR QUESTIONING. "That will definitely slow me down. What does it say?"

Nate glanced at the article, then said, "The Council doesn't know where the fairy godmothers are. They haven't answered any summonses, nor have they been forthright with questions about Kristin Montgomery and Tennyson Ritter."

"The other godmother, right? And the guy who discovered the *Lagabóc*? Why do they want them?"

"Says here that they are spreading rumors about the

overthrow of the Council. The Council thinks they're planning to grab power."

"Maybe you'd better fill me in."

"There isn't much to tell. It's more a scandal than real news. The Council found Kristin Montgomery, your predecessor, unfit for the job. Instead of surrendering her wand, she fled, along with Tennyson Ritter."

Reggie understood that impulse. She touched the handle of her wand tucked safely in an inner pocket of her coat. She'd only had it a day, but she loved how it fit in her hand.

Nate shook his head. "You'd think a guy like Ritter wouldn't just abandon everything he'd worked for."

"Maybe it's not what the Council thinks. Maybe he knows Kristin's right and the Council is wrong." Reggie pointed to the article. "Maybe they know things we don't."

He shot her an incredulous look. "Are you always this optimistic?"

"Not by a long shot. But I have learned that optimism makes life better. It can really stink, you know?"

He didn't say anything for a moment. "I know."

Tommy came out of the kitchen carrying a plate. "Good morning, Mr. Nate. I heard you, so I made you an egg croissant."

"Thank you, Tommy," said Nate. "I think I might be getting too predictable."

Tommy grinned. "Yes, sir. Every morning. Coffee and an egg croissant. Bye, Mr. Nate."

"Wait. What are you baking special today?" Nate asked.

Tommy's face lit up. "I'm trying a new recipe. Green chile cheese muffins."

"Save me a couple, will you? I'd like to take them home."

"But they won't be ready for a long time." Tommy's eyes widened in surprise. "You don't stay that long."

"That's okay. I'll stay today." Nate's gaze fell on Reggie.

Was Nate flirting? No, he couldn't be. Could he? But she had a date tonight. She shouldn't encourage him if he was flirting. Could she?

God, she was so bad at this. She hadn't dated in school while she had been in special ed; and once she went to a Groundling school, she had been too busy catching up on what she didn't know. "I'll get you some more coffee." She turned from the table.

"But his cup is full," Tommy said.

"So it is. Well then, let's let him eat. I still have the cases to fill." Reggie retreated behind the counter and Tommy returned to the kitchen.

She was twenty-seven years old. Why couldn't she think like an adult? She didn't need to feel guilty about having a date tonight. Hell, she didn't even know if Nate was actually flirting with her. He was sitting behind his paper, his face obscured by the open pages, eating, she presumed. He hadn't glanced at her again.

"Reggie!" Panic filled Tommy's cry.

She ran into the kitchen and saw Joy tiptoeing on the top of the step stool reaching for something just out of her reach. She had grabbed a lower shelf that would not hold her weight, and the step stool was sliding backward.

Without thinking, Reggie grabbed her wand and waved it toward Joy just as the step stool lurched out from under Joy's feet. "Float!" she yelled.

The step stool skidded into an oven with a bang, but Joy didn't hit the floor. Instead she bobbed in the air a few feet above the tile.

"Oops," said Joy. She tried to control her expression, but her face turned red and tears filled her eyes. "I'm sorry."

"No, no." Reggie ran to her and looked up at her. "I was just worried that you might get hurt."

Joy wiped a tear from her cheek. "I didn't get hurt."

"No, but you almost did," Tommy said, frowning. "You can't reach up there."

"That's why I used the stool." Joy wiped away another tear.

"That's why you ask me to get it. I'm taller," Tommy said.

"Knock it off, you two. Nobody's hurt, and that's all that matters." Reggie looked up at Joy. "You are okay, right?"

"Yes." But the sad frown on her face said otherwise.

Nate appeared in the doorway. "Everything okay?"

"Joy's floating," Tommy said.

"I can see that." Nate didn't come farther into the room. He caught Reggie's gaze. "Did you do that?"

"I think so." Reggie walked around Joy. "While you're up there, kiddo, you may want to get what you needed."

Joy pulled her top lip between her teeth and reached for a small sack of poppy seeds. "Got it. I can come down now."

If I can get you down. Reggie looked at the wand in her hand. "I'll try, but be ready to jump if you need to."

"Okay." Joy watched the floor intently.

Wrinkling her brow, Reggie pointed her wand at Joy. "Gently," she whispered. With a slow flowing gesture, she moved the wand downward.

Joy glided to the floor and landed softly on her feet. "Hey, that was fun. Can I float again?"

Reggie let out a deep breath. "Not now." Her arms felt rubbery as if she had been holding Joy up herself.

"You used magic, Reggie," Tommy said. "I thought you didn't have magic."

"I didn't until yesterday." Reggie took another deep breath. She was tired. "Tommy, good job in calling for help, and Joy, next time remember we have a bigger step stool for those things up high."

"I know, but that one's heavy, and I liked floating," Joy said.

"But I may not be here next time." Reggie hugged Joy. "You know better. I'll add it to the rules." She pointed to a bright yellow rectangle on the wall. A list of rules graced a poster.

Joy liked rules and never deviated from them. "Okay, but will you let me float another time?"

Reggie smiled. "Maybe." *When I'm stronger,* she thought. Joy and Tommy were already back at work as if nothing had happened. Reggie turned to Nate.

"You seem more shaken up than they are," he said. They walked from the kitchen together.

"I just feel drained. Does magic always take that much out of you?"

"You get used to it, but there is a cost. You must know that."

"I do, at least I did, but I didn't fully understand it until now." She knew that magic required the energy of the person casting the spells, and that too much magic could even cost an Arcani his life. But she had been surrounded by people using their magic her whole life. They had never seemed tired afterward. "I suppose it's like getting into shape."

"That's a good analogy. So, how did you do that?" Nate pointed to the kitchen. "I know that wasn't one of your standard spells."

"I don't know. I didn't think. I just did."

Nate nodded. "Makes sense. Most magic is about instinct."

Reggie flopped onto a chair. "There's so much I don't know. And how am I supposed to learn everything and still run the bakery? Tommy and Joy need me." She dropped her head into her hands. "I can't be a fairy godmother."

"Oy." A voice from the doorway boomed into the room.

Reggie looked up. A small man, not more than three and a half feet tall, with a gray beard stood just inside. She said, "I'm sorry, but we're not open yet."

"I'm no' here for your goodies," said the man. If she wasn't mistaken, his accent was Scottish. He strode in as if he owned the place, examining the fixtures, the tables, the space. As he wandered about, Reggie noticed one of his sleeves was empty. "Ach, it'll do, but I dinnae know if I can live down the shame."

"Excuse me, but who are you?" she asked.

"Alfred. My friends call me Alf." He eyed her and squinted. "You can call me Alfred."

Reggie glanced at Nate, who shrugged. "Okay, Alfred. What can I do for you?"

"It's no' what you can do for me, but what I'm doing for you." The man closed his eyes as if smelling something distasteful. "Those meddling women sent me."

"What women?"

"Those three. The old gals. Them you call fairy god-mothers." Alfred peered into the cases. "Pastries. My life is a scandal."

"I'm sorry, Alfred, but I still don't understand," Reggie said. "Why are you here?"

"Are you daft as well as stupid? I can't verra well build with only one arm. I'm useless. But the women thought I'd be helpful here. At a bakery." He said the word as if it were a curse. "But I tell you now, I willnae shave my beard. My shame goes only so far."

Reggie was beginning to put it together. "You're here to help with the bakery?"

"Haven't I been saying that? The women told me you'd be needing help now that you've got yourself a new, fancy job—"

"You're a gnome," said Nate suddenly.

"And I'll thank you to keep it quiet. Groundlings come in here too. Anyone could hear." Alfred searched the room for possible eavesdroppers. "Besides, there's no need to be bandying my status about. I can't build anymore and I couldn't stand their pitying looks any longer."

"Whose looks?" asked Nate.

"My colleagues. The other gnomes." Alfred nearly spat, then remembered where he was. "What was I supposed to do? I'm still in me prime. The godmothers said I could work here."

"You can't just waltz in here and expect me to put you to work." Reggie crossed her arms over her chest.

"I'm no' dancing, and I dinnae see you doing any work." The gnome mirrored her stance, except with one arm.

"But—"

"Look. The women said you needed help. I need a job. Dinnae fash yerself."

"But I thought gnomes ate rocks and dirt."

"We do." He scowled. "But I've developed a bit of a sweet tooth. I know my way around pastries." Alfred froze, then narrowed his gaze. "Just dinnae be telling my friends. Working here is shame enough."

Joy came from the kitchen. "I need you to taste this." She held out a cookie. "It's good, but I think it's missing something."

The gnome's face transformed. A bright smile split his lips. "You must be Joy. An apt name I must say. You bring joy itself when you walk into a room. I'm Alfred, but you can call me Alf."

Joy giggled. "Hello, Alf."

Reggie raised her brows. She had never seen Joy so open with a stranger before.

"May I?" Alfred took the cookie and bit into it. He savored it a moment, then nodded. "You're right. Almost perfect, but I think a sprinkling of—"

"Coconut," they finished together.

"You have the gift, girl," said Alfred. "I want you to come to me any time."

Joy nodded and returned to the kitchen.

The gnome faced Reggie again, and his expression transformed back into its surly mask. "I'll need an apron. And a bluidy net to hold my beard," he said with a grumble.

Reggie said, "Look, Alf, I don't think—"

"It's Alfred to you," said the gnome, pointing at her. "I'll start today. Those cases still need to be filled. The customers arrive in a few minutes. The apron? Come on. We dinnae have time for you to be flirting with your boyfriend. Och, never mind." Alfred pulled out a gnarled stick with a bright ruby on the end of it. He waved it and an apron appeared on him. "That's better. If I waited for you, I'd be naked. No wonder the women sent me to whip this place into shape." He ambled behind the counter and disappeared from view.

"Now wait a minute . . ." She broke off as she realized Alf had disappeared into the kitchen. When had she lost control of the morning?

Nate's eyes glowed with amusement. "Looks like the bakery problem has settled itself."

She heard Tommy's laugh a moment later, and then she saw a tray filled with finished baked goods float toward the counter. She gasped. "You can't use magic. A Groundling might see you."

"I know that," came the burr from somewhere under the tray. "But we dinnae have much time thanks to your dawdling." In the next moment, the tray was empty and the case was full.

Reggie dashed behind the counter and nearly tripped over a series of steps that weren't there earlier.

Alfred glared at her. "Dinnae kick those. How else am I supposed to reach the counter if I can't use magic?"

Carrying a white paper bag, Alfred walked around her. He took it to Nate. "Tommy told me to give these to you. They're still hot, so open the bag when you get home." He handed the bag to Nate.

She had to agree that the gnome had everything under control. But his attitude . . . Dealing with that would have to wait. The bakery was about to open and the first customers were already walking toward the door.

Pulling out his wallet, Nate came to the counter. He pulled out a few bills. "So now you only have the fairy godmother thing to worry about."

"Hardly." She placed the bills into the till, and counted out his change. The door tinkled signaling the first customers of the day.

Nate hesitated. "You've been more than kind to me. I want to help. You close here at three o'clock. I'll be back then."

Before she could say anything, Alfred said, "Flip the sign on your way out."

Nate waved his hand in acknowledgement.

Reggie could only draw in a deep breath before she turned to help the first customer.

6

CORDELIA'S RULES FOR HER
DAUGHTERS

•

Never Forget Who Might Be Watching You.

At three o'clock Reggie swiped her brow, flipped the sign to CLOSED, and locked the door. She had to admit that Alfred was an incredible worker. His surly personality hadn't turned any customers away. On the contrary. He became a draw, insulting Groundling and Arcani alike, and they enjoyed it. The only time he had smiled was when he spoke to Joy or Tommy, who both loved him. After only one day.

"Humph." Alfred snorted. "What do we do with the extras?" He pointed to a tray one quarter filled with a mixture of éclairs, Danishes, and breads.

"You're welcome to take anything you like home."

"As if a gnome would want to eat such rich food," Alfred grumbled, but she saw him slip a cheese Danish into his pocket.

"The Restart Mission will pick up the rest at three thirty."

"Pretty meager pickings, if you ask me." He reached into his pocket and returned the Danish.

"We sold a lot today. The mission knows that we give what we can." She removed the Danish from the tray, wrapped it, and handed it back to him. "Some days we have more than others."

Alfred's entire face turned ruddy. "It's no' for me. It's for my mother. She doesnae have teeth anymore. Can't chew dirt like she used to."

"She's welcome to it." Reggie didn't know whether he was fibbing or not, but it didn't matter. "You're welcome to more."

"And be laughed at in the Great Hall? Not bluidy likely." But he pocketed a second Danish.

She hid a smile. "You were wonderful today."

He squinted at her. "What did you expect? I know how to work."

"Of course you do. I was just thanking you." She had made no progress in melting his brusque exterior, but in all honesty, she found him as amusing as the customers had.

"Dinnae thank me. It's my job. I work here now." He let out a deep sigh as he drew his hand down his face. "At a bluidy bakery."

"Well, I believe in acknowledging—"

"I'm going to see if Tommy and Joy need anything." Alfred walked away from her toward the kitchen. "Answer the door. Your boyfriend's back."

"I don't have—" But Alfred had disappeared. Reggie bit back her frustration. Alfred was rude, abrupt, and horribly disagreeable, but he was a good worker, and he was wonderful with Tommy and Joy.

She looked at the door. Nate was waiting on the other side. She waved, and he pushed the door open. She sighed. Once again the door had unlocked itself.

"Are you ready to do some work?" Nate asked.

"What do you think I've been doing all day?"

"I meant magic. Are you ready to learn?" Nate's voice was still gravelly through the layers of the muffler. Apparently his morning voice was not the result of a lack of coffee.

"I guess so." In truth, the late night, the early morning, and being on her feet all day were taking their tolls. And she still had a date to get ready for. However, she did need to practice magic if she was going to impress Sophronia. Nor could she ignore Nate's kind offer of help. She withdrew her wand from the inner pocket of her coat. "What's first?"

"How about transfiguration?" He pulled out his wand—a thick length of wood with golden cording up the side—and waved it. A long-stemmed rose appeared in his hand. "Let's start with something simple. Can you turn this into a snake?"

"What? I don't think so."

"Are you afraid of snakes?"

"No, but I can't have animals in the bakery."

He chuckled. "Right, I forgot. Health inspector probably wouldn't approve. How about a necklace then?"

She could see his logic. The form of the long rose stem would have lent itself well to a slim snake, but its form could also serve as the basis for a chain. It would be a little more difficult to go from organic material to metal, but she supposedly had lots of power. Maybe.

She knew how it was done. In theory. She had seen her mother and sister change things into clothing when they wanted just the right color. She focused on the rose. She could use its length, the shape of the leaves, the red of the bud.

"Don't think too hard," Nate said. "Just do it. Like you did this morning with Joy."

She cleared her mind . . . or tried to. Unfortunately the tousled blond hair and blue-eyed visage of Jonathan Bastion popped into her mind. She had a date tonight. A tiny smile curved her lips.

"You're not concentrating," Nate said.

"Sorry." Reggie drew in a deep breath, and lifted her arm, pointing the wand at the rose. She directed her energy. "*Transmutá*."

Her wand grew warm in her palm. She felt energy gush into the slender rod. Then the energy flowed from the tip into the flower. The bud shimmered for a moment, dropped a few of its petals, then flopped over Nate's glove.

Reggie let out the breath she had been holding and panted slowly. Her arm dropped to her side. The wand lost its warmth.

"You did it," Nate said. "Sort of."

She cocked an eyebrow.

He held up a slender chain. The links were green rather than silver or gold and leaf shaped, and a metallic red bud dangled at the end, but it was definitely not a flower anymore.

"It's more of a fob than a necklace, but not too bad."

But not great either. Reggie put her wand back in the pocket and took the chain from him. "Too bad I don't have a pocket watch."

"A valiant first attempt. How do you feel?" he asked.

"I'm not sure. I doubt I could do any push-ups right now, but otherwise pretty good." She picked up the petals from the floor.

"Good thing we can get our hands on some food to replenish you." Nate walked to the display case. "Éclair or muffin?"

"Scone. Blueberry."

Before her mouth could start to water, the air in the room

compressed. With a light pop, Sophronia appeared, accompanied again by Keith the Guard. She took in the scene in front of her. "Do you really have time for a tea party?"

Without regard for the new arrival, Nate brought the scone to Reggie. "Here. Eat this. It will give you strength."

Reggie took the scone, but didn't take a bite. "Hello, Sophronia. How can I help you?"

"I see your champion is here again. And still disguised." Sophronia examined him. "I never did catch a name."

"I didn't throw you one," Nate said as he took a position behind Reggie's shoulder. "You don't need my name. I'm nobody."

"I'm afraid I do." Sophronia beckoned Keith forward, and the Guard stepped closer. "My safety requires it. As a member of the Council—"

"Yeah, yeah, member of the Council, blah, blah, blah. We know. You do realize that Reggie's position is more important than yours?" Nate crossed his arms.

"*If* she passes *my* judgment." Sophronia smiled smugly. "Her associates might influence the way I judge her."

"That wouldn't surprise me." He shrugged. "Nate. Nate . . . Citadel."

Reggie realized she had never learned his last name either. How odd that she trusted him, yet knew so little about him.

Sophronia waved her hand dismissively. "These petty battles do no one good. Now that we've resolved this one, let's talk about why I am here."

Reggie took a bite of her scone. She'd need fortification if she had to discuss business with Sophronia.

From his tunic, Keith removed a scroll sealed with a wax medallion and placed it with a slap in Sophronia's waiting hand. She passed the rolled parchment to Reggie.

"What's this?" asked Reggie.

"Since the trouble with the last godmother, the Council has decided to make a list of requirements to guide you through the process."

"To protect themselves, you mean," Nate said.

"Well, yes." Sophronia lifted her brows. "You don't expect us to be so foolish as to let just anyone claim the powers of the godmother. So we've made a list of the tasks we require."

Reggie placed the rest of her uneaten scone on a napkin and brushed off the crumbs on the front of her jacket. She broke the wax symbol that sealed the scroll and unrolled it.

Bold black letters greeted her view:

REQUIREMENTS:

1. Demonstrate the ability to transport.

She hated transporting. The few times her mother had transported with her, the squeezing sensation had left her stomach upset for the rest of the day.

2. Demonstrate the ability to transform self.

Into what? she thought.

3. Proof of ability to hear wishes.

She had no idea what this meant.

4. Give proof of ability to grant wishes.

If she had no idea what number three meant, how did they expect her to provide proof for number four?

5. Sign the Oath of Allegiance to the Council.

This one gave her pause. They didn't trust her? She looked up at Sophronia. "I'm supposed to take an oath?"

Sophronia smiled. "Yes. It's a new idea the Council has implemented. The Guards have taken one for centuries, and now the Council feels it's the right time to require the Oath for everyone else. You'll be the first. You'll make history."

Reggie swallowed her distaste. She understood that the Council didn't trust the first godmother, but why should they question her loyalty? Something didn't feel right about the Council's demands. Reggie read further.

6. Make a weekly report to the Council.

Reggie's brow wrinkled. They wanted to keep tabs on her? "I'm supposed to give an account of my activities to the Council?"

"Well, you'll have to report to me," said Sophronia. "You can't appear in front of them until you've been presented, which you won't until you pass. I'll take your testimony to the Council."

"Have any other godmothers ever testified to the Council?" Nate asked.

"No, but these are extraordinary circumstances." Sophronia brushed a piece of imaginary dust from her blouse. "We have to know that we can trust Reggie."

Reggie bristled. Tension brewed in her head. How could the Council think she was untrustworthy? She read further.

7. As proof of loyalty and allegiance to the Council, report all contact with the outgoing godmothers, and, if possible, turn them in to the Council.

Now the Council wanted her to become a snitch? She was ready to protest when she read the final task.

8. Council cannot confirm Regina Scott as godmother until she delivers the wand of Kristin Montgomery.

Reggie's mouth dropped open. The wanted her to hand over the wand of the other fairy godmother? The one who was missing?

Nate pointed at number eight. "That's a little *Wizard of Oz*-ish, isn't it?"

"Don't be so dramatic," Sophronia said. "Besides, it isn't your concern. It's Reggie's."

"What makes you think I can find her if you can't?" Reggie asked.

Sophronia shrugged. "That's not my concern. The Council felt it a fair test of your abilities."

Fair? The entire document smacked of paranoia and deceit. Reggie shook her head. "I don't know that I like this."

"You feelings are irrelevant. If you want to become a fairy godmother, these are the requirements set by the Council." Sophronia held out her hand. "Unless you want to give up and hand over *your* wand right now."

Reggie froze. Why did she feel like she was being coerced into making a moral decision without being given all the information she needed?

Maybe because she was.

"Come on, Reggie," Sophronia said. "This isn't that hard. You knew you'd have to prove yourself to the Council. Now we've given you clear guidelines how to do that. It's your choice. You can be a fairy godmother with all the power that entails, or you can stay here in your little bakery and be the caretaker for your two little retarded friends."

Reggie gasped.

"Who said that?" came a roar from the kitchen. Alfred bounded from the doorway to the middle of the room. His face was drawn into a fierce scowl, not the annoyed one he wore earlier. Anger flashed in his eyes. "What idiot said that?"

"Good heavens, Reggie." Sophronia clasped a hand to her chest in a dramatic gesture. "This is quite the menagerie you're running here."

"I'll menagerie you, you brainless harpy," Alfred said. "Tommy and Joy may be slow in some things, but they can outperform you in many. Including manners."

"Hear, hear," Nate said.

"Well, really." Sophronia looked affronted.

Reggie was shaken from her shocked state. "We do not use the word 'retarded' here. It's a hurtful, prejudicial, bigoted word that has no place in polite company."

"You're making too big a deal of this." Sophronia glared down at Alfred.

"Big? Is that another insult?" Alfred drew himself up. "I'll show you big."

Alfred bunched his fist. Keith stepped between Sophronia and the gnome. Alfred punched the Guard in the solar plexus, and the huge man doubled over, gasping for breath.

"Now that's big," Nate said.

Reggie raised her hands. "Stop. Everyone just stop." She felt every gaze fasten on her. She turned to Sophronia first. "I think you should go, Sophronia. Thank you for bringing me the Council's edict. I'll take everything into consideration and get back to you." She glanced at the Guard, who was still trying to catch his breath. "I think he needs some help."

"Darn right he does," muttered Alfred with a note of pride in his voice.

"At least you're being sensible. I can report that much to the Council. I can't however say as much for your friends." Sophronia snapped her fingers at the Guard. "Straighten up, fool. Don't think I won't report your behavior to the Council." A moment later, they both transported.

"Good riddance," Nate said. He turned to Alfred. "Excellent shot."

"Thank you." Alfred nodded, his expression only now losing some of its belligerence.

"Nate, you're not helping." Reggie faced Alfred. "While I appreciate your defense of Tommy and Joy, this is not a place for fighting."

"I know that, missy." But a hint of contrition graced his visage. "But she was asking for it."

Reggie agreed. She couldn't pretend that she didn't enjoy seeing Sophronia and her Guard taken down a notch. But that didn't make it right. "Nevertheless, you can't punch everyone who says something unfortunate."

"I know that too." Alfred's familiar impatience with her was back. "I'm going to see how they are. I hope they dinnae hear anything."

"But you did."

"I'm a gnome," he said, as if it explained everything. "Acute hearing. You must have learned that in school."

She shook her head. "I wasn't allowed to learn about the Arcani world."

Alfred scrutinized her for a moment. "Idiots." He pointed to the scroll. "If you're going to be busy with that fairy godmother stuff, we're going to need more help here. I'll bring some people tomorrow." Without waiting for her answer, he left the room.

She sank into a chair. "Why do I feel that I don't have a choice in the matter?"

"Because you don't." Nate leaned against the back of a booth. "Do you want to be a fairy godmother?"

"I thought I did. Now I'm not so sure. I don't like this." She waved the scroll. "I've never heard of the Council having so much control over the godmothers. It doesn't sound right."

"Looks like you need to do some research."

"An excellent idea," came a new voice from the edge of the room.

Reggie looked up, and for an instant she smiled as she recognized the three godmothers. But the smile died, and she frowned at them.

Lily came forward, her face an expression of compassion. "I can understand how hard it must be to trust us right now."

"So we won't ask you to," Rose said.

"Sure we will," Hyacinth said. "But only after you're sure. 'Cause we have a big favor to ask of you."

Lily lifted her hand, then looked at Nate. "You were here the other morning."

He nodded.

"And you know who we are?" Lily watched him.

"Who doesn't? Even before the newspaper articles, you weren't exactly unknown," Nate said.

"Then if I may ask, who are you?" Lily smiled.

"Nate Citadel."

Hyacinth eyed him. "I've never heard that name before."

"I keep to myself." His voice was calm.

"He's helping me." Reggie had so many questions, she didn't want to waste time with introductions. "Is it true? All the things the Council says about you?"

The three women looked at one another, then Rose shrugged. "I like his eyes."

"I suppose we'll have to trust him. Unless Reggie wants to send him away . . ." Hyacinth raised her voice hopefully.

Reggie shook her head. She was losing patience. "My question."

Lily spread her hands in a gesture of confusion. "On the one hand, we *are* fugitives of a sort. We have broken contact with the Council."

"On the other, we really are trying to save the Arcani and Groundling worlds," Rose said.

"Gee, that doesn't sound melodramatic," Hyacinth said. "We want her to believe us, not think we're crazy."

"But it's the truth." Rose pursed her lips.

"Yeah, but give her a chance to catch up," Hyacinth said.

"Ladies, please, you'll just confuse her more." Lily shook her head. "We need your help, and I'm afraid you're the only one we can turn to."

Reggie took a deep breath. "I'm listening."

"There is a movement gaining momentum among the Arcani," Lily said. "A group that wants the Arcani to rule the world and all Groundlings."

Reggie furrowed her brow. "Wouldn't that lead to conflict between us?"

"Probably," Rose said, her voice somber. "That's why we need your help. The Council doesn't believe us."

"That's why you've broken contact with them," Nate said.

"Yes." Bitterness laced Lily's voice. "We tried to convince them, but they were more concerned with their own status than the truth."

"So instead of one enemy, we're fighting two." Rose sounded tired.

"We need the *Lagabóc*," Hyacinth said.

Merlin's book of laws for the Arcani. Even Reggie had heard of it.

"Not the original. That would be impractical," said Rose quickly. "Tennyson's copy. He was studying it when the difficulties happened."

For many years the *Lagabóc* had been considered merely a legend, until Tennyson Ritter found it. Now Tennyson was on the run with Kristin Montgomery, the first godmother. "Is that what all the trouble is about?"

"Not exactly," Hyacinth said. "You've heard of the Great Uprising?"

As Reggie shook her head, Nate leaned forward. "Sixty some years ago, one of the godmothers tried to lead a rebellion against Groundlings. She failed."

"She did," Lily said. "But she had a son. Lucas Reynard. He's taking advantage of the Time of Transition and planning to complete his mother's work."

"Wasn't she in Europe?" Nate asked.

"Yes. We eventually imprisoned her in France. That's where her son was born." Rose sighed. "It's a sad story."

"I wish you'd stop feeling sorry for the kid. He's a grown-up now, and he tried to kill us. Twice." Hyacinth pressed her lips together.

"He tried to kill you?" Reggie asked in shock.

"Yes. And Kristin too," Lily said.

"Is Reggie in danger?" Nate asked. His eyes narrowed.

"We don't think so, but we can't know for sure. We've been cut off from most communication." Lily patted Reggie's hand. "Don't worry. We have our sources though."

Reggie shook her head. "Wait. Is this Lucas here?"

"Yes," Lily said.

"Then why haven't we heard about him?" Reggie drew her brows together. "Why isn't the Council aware of his actions?"

"Well, he didn't exactly broadcast his intentions." Hyacinth puffed out a blast of air.

Lily sent Hyacinth a chiding look before speaking to Reggie again. "Apparently Lucas didn't inform the Council when he arrived here. He wanted to establish a base for himself before making his move."

"And he wanted to take his revenge on us," Hyacinth said. "We destroyed his house before the Council ever learned of his presence."

"Don't you think he left?" Nate said. "Before you could inform the Council?"

"The Council didn't believe us." Rose looked offended. "They accused Tennyson and Kristin of wanting power and us of aiding them. Of all the preposterous, outlandish—"

"Easy, Rose." Hyacinth smiled in approval. "Don't get yourself riled up."

"We don't know where he is now." Lily sighed. "But I don't think he's left. Not when he's already undermined our reputations and Kristin's. The Council here thinks we're the threat. Lucas has the perfect opportunity to recruit followers and take advantage of the situation he's created."

"We're so sorry to put you through this, but you're a godmother now," Rose said.

"This is a lot to take in," Reggie said.

"Do some research, dear," Hyacinth said. "You have to see for yourself if we're telling the truth."

"And now it's time for us to leave. I'm sure the Council has someone watching this place." Lily glanced out the window.

There was a way to detect magic. Her parents always said magic left a footprint. Reggie concentrated. She could feel magic coming from the kitchen where Tommy and Joy were baking for tomorrow, but she couldn't feel a footprint from any other magic. "I don't sense anything."

Rose shook her head. "They wouldn't put a spell on the bakery. You're too receptive to it now."

"Come on, girls. Mustn't tarry." Lily watched the door.

"We'll be back. I know we're asking you to take a lot on faith, but we are telling the truth." Hyacinth moved to the center of the room.

Rose fixed her gaze on Reggie. "You can find the *Lagabóc* at the Academy. Tennyson said—"

But a loud crash from outside caused Lily to jump. "Now, ladies." The three women gathered together, and a moment later they vanished.

Reggie rubbed her face. The tension that arrived with Sophronia had blossomed into a full-blown headache. "So now I need to do research on the Council, being a godmother, and the Great Uprising? Where do I start? I didn't attend an Arcani college. Hell, they didn't even let me in the regular Arcani history class. I was a Groundling, remember? They didn't want me learning too many of the secrets."

"I can help," Nate said.

She stared at him in surprise. "Why would you want to? Look at the trouble I've caused just by being chosen as a godmother."

"Let's just say I understand what it feels like to be outside the norm." Nate's fists clenched for an instant. "Finding this information isn't going to be easy."

"I know."

"I have a friend who can help us. He's got access to all kinds of databases."

She hesitated. "Do you think that's a good idea? Letting someone else know about this?"

"I'd trust him with my life. If you trust me, you can trust him."

"Who is it?"

"Jonathan Bastion."

Reggie couldn't breathe for a moment. *Jonathan? Oh my God. I have a date tonight.* She had almost forgotten. No, she *had* forgotten for a while. "I know him."

"Then you know we can trust him. I'll put him on it as soon as I get home." Nate walked to the door. "Try not to worry. We'll figure it out. I'll see you tomorrow." Nate left the bakery.

She stared after him. How had she gone from practicing magic to looking up conspiracy theories? Life was complicated, but this was insane. How was she supposed to balance the bakery, being a fairy godmother, the Council, and Jonathan Bastion?

She groaned. What had she been thinking accepting a

date from Jonathan? Too much was happening in her life to go on dates now. Okay. She'd go on this date tonight, and tell him she couldn't see him until life calmed down. Yes, that was exactly what she'd do. A simple solution.

Too bad the feeling of disappointment in her belly wouldn't be as easy to get rid of.

7

CORDELIA'S RULES FOR HER
DAUGHTERS

•

You Are Never Too Busy to Take Time for Yourself.

WHEN JONATHAN KNOCKED on the door of the apartment at eight thirty, his stomach fluttered. He hadn't been nervous for a date in . . . forever, it seemed. But she was a fairy godmother and that made this date different. He needed to win her over, to impress her. He needed her to—

"Hi," Reggie said as she opened the door. "You said casual. I hope this isn't too."

She was wearing a pink T-shirt with STAR BRIGHT BAKERY printed in white on it. It molded to her, curving over her breasts like a caress, nipping in at her waist, then flaring over the top of her jeans. With a bit of regret, he noticed she wore some sort of tank top beneath it, which meant that there were two layers of material between him and her skin. His stomach tightened anyway as he considered the challenge. He quirked one side of his mouth up.

"You look perfect. Sorry about the late start, but I had something I had to take care of."

She waved a hand. "That's fine. It gave me a chance to wash the bakery out of my hair."

Her hair fell in a riot of curls over her shoulders. A wide hair band attempted to hold it back, but the dark brown tresses defied containment and some shorter pieces curled over her temples and cheeks. He lifted a strand and it wrapped around his finger as he felt its silkiness. He lifted it to his nose. "Smells like strawberries."

"Guilty." Pink settled in her cheeks. "I don't usually do more to my hair than shampoo it and pull it back. I straightened it for the party."

"I like it this way."

She narrowed her gaze as if she didn't believe him, but she didn't contradict him. "Do you want to come in? I'd give you a tour, but there isn't anything else to see."

The apartment was tiny, but neat and clean, and had an ambiance that spoke of comfort. The kitchen and living area opened onto each other. A breakfast bar served as the eating area and a divider of the space. A plump sofa faced bookshelves packed with paperbacks, and a tiny television stood on top. Clearly she didn't watch much TV. Besides the front door, two other doors were visible on one wall, but the building didn't seem to have space for another room in that direction. He pointed to one. "Bedroom?"

"Bathroom, and the other one is my closet."

"Then where is your bedroom?" he asked.

"You're standing in it." She pointed to a wall covered in paneling. "Murphy bed."

He grinned. "I didn't think you'd invite me in here so quickly."

The pink in her cheeks darkened, but she smiled back. "I have some wine, if you'd like."

"That would be great." He took a seat on the sofa and watched her retrieve two wineglasses from her cupboard and place them on the counter.

"I'm glad we're not in a hurry," she said, "because I wanted to talk to you first." She opened the refrigerator and pulled out a bottle of white wine.

Uh-oh. "Does this have to do with Nate?"

"Oh good. He called you already." She popped the cork and poured. Leaving the bottle on the counter, she picked up the glasses and sat beside him. "It does have to do with Nate in a way."

He took the glass from her and tasted. "Nice wine."

"Mother taught me." She sipped, then took a larger swallow. "I don't know how much Nate told you . . ."

"Just that you wanted my help in researching a few things. I'd be happy to help." It would even the debt he would owe.

"Thanks, I appreciate it." She took another sip. "A lot has happened to me in the past two days," she said as if her mouth were so full of words these tumbled out.

"I can imagine."

"And today my arbiter visited." She placed her wine on the coffee table, jumped up from the sofa, and started pacing.

"I heard." He didn't know where she was going with this information, so he waited for her to continue.

"This whole fairy godmother thing . . ." Her hands punctuated her speech by waving at no one and nothing. "I thought it was an honor. I thought it would be wonderful."

"It's not?" A tremor of unease squirmed inside him.

"It is, but . . ." She grabbed a scroll from the countertop and shoved it at him. "It's become political. They want me to swear my allegiance, to find and turn in the godmothers. I need to know the history of the godmothers—what they did, who controls them, just everything. That's part of what I need to know before I can deal with the Council. I can't ask the outgoing ones because they're in hiding. They've only popped in on me twice and only for a few minutes at a time."

As her voice rose, a breeze sprung up in the apartment. The drapes fluttered and the cupboard doors rattled. He felt his arm hairs stand up and a prickle scratch at his neck. The light fixture above them swung on its chain, and the lights in the kitchen area flickered. She didn't seem to notice.

Her words continued their cascade. "I don't know anything. I don't know magic. Or what spells I can do, or what spells I can't do, or how much magic I can do before it drains me, or how I grant wishes or anything. And now the Council wants to control me and make me into some kind of political statement."

In the next moment, the lightbulbs exploded and sparks showered over them. Reggie cried out, and the apartment grew dark. But not entirely. The streetlights shone in through the window.

He sprang from the sofa and caught her in his arms. He clasped her to his chest. "Shhh."

Within his embrace, she drew in a trembling breath.

"I'm here. Let me help." He kissed the top of her head, and whispered soothing sounds until she lifted her face toward him.

It may have been the darkness and the odd illumination from the street, but an aura surrounded her face and beckoned to him. He bent his head and brushed her lips with his.

Her lips were cool and plump, like a ripe plum hinting at the sweetness within. He didn't expect his body's reaction. A fierce hunger stirred in his belly and he locked her against him. A rumble deep in his throat gave voice to energy coursing through him. And startled him.

He couldn't afford to lose control. He pressed away and heard the soft sigh of her exhale. And ignored its call to him. Releasing her, he withdrew his wand. "First. *Intactus*." He waved the slim white rod.

The glass shards flew back to their sockets and started glowing again.

"Second, I think you need some more wine." He led her to the couch, deposited her gently into the cushions, and handed her the glass. She gave him a sheepish smile and took a sip. She opened her mouth to speak, but he lifted a finger. "Not yet."

He opened the scroll and read the eight points, shaking his head. "This doesn't seem right. I can see why you got so upset."

She opened her mouth to speak again, but he lifted the same finger. "I've already told you I'd help, and I will. Happily. Trust me."

She opened her mouth for a third time, but then just looked at him.

He almost laughed. "Okay. Now you can speak."

"First, thank you. For the help and the lights." Her voice was calm and level, even if it held a note of chagrin. "But there's more."

"Go ahead."

Her cheeks turned pink again. "I like you. I mean I think I could really like you, but . . ." She ran her fingers through her hair until they bumped into the hair band. Then she just smoothed the curls, well, as much as they could be smoothed. "I'm so bad at this, and I might be presuming things . . ."

"You're not."

The blush deepened. "I don't think I could handle a relationship right now."

"Then we won't worry about a relationship right now.

We'll just let things flow as they will. What I think you need is some dinner and a little fun."

"But the Council—"

"Just for tonight. We can get serious tomorrow. Now what do you say about dinner?"

She smiled. "I am hungry."

"Then I have a treat for you. Let's go." He took her hands and pulled her up from the couch. Then for a moment he drew her close again. "But I want you to remain open to that whole relationship thing."

Her small intake of breath was answer enough.

AN HOUR LATER, Reggie's stomach was full. "I can't believe you took me to a taco stand."

"Why? The ambience not good enough for you?" He crunched on a rolled taco smothered in guacamole and cheese.

"Are you kidding? Roberto's is my favorite place. Okay, one of my favorite places. Their carne asada burritos are to die for." She patted her stomach. "And I ate all of it."

"You did magic, remember? The whole lights exploding thing?" He grinned at her and held up the last rolled taco. "One more. Sure you don't want it?"

"I couldn't. You're going to have to roll me out of here as it is." She lifted a napkin and wiped a smidge of guac from his mouth.

"You need exercise, which leads me to part two of our evening." He collected the paper wrappers, napkins, and empty salsa ramekins and tossed their trash. Then he held out his hand. "Come on."

They hopped into his car, a black Mercedes, and he whipped down Carmel Valley Road toward the ocean to the Pacific Coast Highway. "Where are we going?" she asked.

"It's June. The grunion are running and high tide ended about half an hour ago."

She laughed. "I've lived here all my life and have never seen the grunion."

"Then it's about time." He pulled the car into a parking lot by the beach. "You might want to take off your shoes and roll up your jeans."

They weren't the only ones in the parking lot. A few other cars were already there, and a couple more pulled in after them.

He peeled off his sandals. His feet were slender and long. She had never noticed anyone's feet before. Why his? And why did she find them so attractive?

He removed two flashlights from the glove compartment and passed her one. "You'll need this."

"We aren't keeping them, are we?" She tested the beam against the ground.

"No, you need a fishing license for that. We're just here to spot them." He went around to her side of the car and held out his hand.

She left her shoes in the car, and let him lead her to the beach.

The beach was relatively empty, but a few families wandered near the waterline. Here and there she could spot others near the water. The sand was cool on her feet in stark contrast to the heat of his hand holding hers.

The sand grew wetter as they approached the water. A family of five was running along the surf.

"Any luck?" Jonathan called out.

"Yes. It's a good night." The father bent over and scooped something up into a bucket. His young daughter squealed beside him.

"What do we do?" Reggie asked.

Jonathan leaned into her. "We wait until the next wave recedes. Then we flash our lights over the sand until we see one."

The next wave rolled over the beach. Her toes and ankles were covered with the cold California Pacific. As the wave drew back, she quickly shone her light over the exposed sand. A few feet from her a silver snake of a fish about eight inches long flopped on the land. "There's one."

They ran toward it and saw its almost opaque skin glisten in their beams. A milky substance oozed from the fish.

"Oh my gosh, that is so cool," she said.

Another wave deposited several more of the fish onto the beach. They ran from spot to spot. Their feet kicked up sand and water as they looked at the writhing fish. Every wave took the previous fish back out to the sea and dropped new ones. The bottoms of her pants grew soaked, but she laughed and grinned. She couldn't remember the last time she had felt such abandon.

In the next moment, she stopped. She shook her head to clear her vision and looked again. Above the head of the little girl still running beside her father a tiny crown appeared.

"Is something wrong?" Jonathan asked.

"Do you see that?" She pointed to the little girl.

"The family? Sure."

"No, no. I mean the little girl." The crown above her head twinkled then disappeared. "Oh, it's gone."

"What did you see?"

"A little crown hovering over the girl's head." She faced him. The night gave off enough light so she could just make out his features. "Didn't you see it?"

"No." He looked over at the child for a moment, then back at her. "Do you think the crown had anything to do with being a fairy godmother?"

"I don't know." Reggie looked back at the girl. Her

brothers had joined her. She must have been around six years old with one brother older, the other younger. A moment later a crown appeared over the head of the younger boy. "There it is again. Over the smallest."

Jonathan peered at them, then shook his head. "I don't see anything."

"But it's right there. No, wait, its gone now." She looked at Jonathan. "Do you think I'm going mad?"

"Right. Because tiny crowns are the first signs of madness." He jostled her with his shoulder. "No, I think this has something to do with your magic."

"I wish I knew more. Nobody has told me anything." She sighed.

"Next time focus on the crown. See what happens." Jonathan shrugged.

"Okay, but what if I don't see another one?"

Just then the crown reappeared over the girl. With a little gasp, Reggie focused on the golden image. She held her breath. For a moment she only heard the pounding of her own heart in her ears. Then slowly she heard a buzzing which grew more distinct.

". . . do this every day."

Reggie's breath exploded from her. She tugged on Jonathan's arm. "Did you hear that?"

"What?" He smiled at her indulgently.

"The little girl. I heard her speak."

"She didn't say anything. I was watching. What did you hear?"

" 'Do this every day.' You didn't hear that?"

"No." He thought for a moment. "I'll bet you only heard part of it. I bet she was thinking—"

"—I wish we could do this every day." Reggie finished in unison with him. She laughed. "I have got to test this."

She looked around the beach, wishing more people were

here. Right. Wishing. She almost laughed at the irony of her thoughts. Her gaze fell upon another family group. There a young boy stood to the side and watched as his mom and dad scooped up fish. He didn't participate. A crown flashed above his head. So she listened.

"I wish we could just get food at the store like regular people. I wish my dad could get a job."

Reggie sucked in a breath as her eyes filled with tears. "Oh no."

"What's wrong?" Jonathan placed his hands on her shoulders and forced her to look at him.

She blinked at the tears and cringed as one slipped down her cheek. "Not all wishes are happy, are they?"

Jonathan examined the little boy. "Tell me."

"His family isn't here for fun. They're here for food."

Jonathan didn't say anything for a moment, then he released her. "Wait here."

With long strides he ran in the direction of the car. He disappeared in the darkness, but she wasn't afraid. Instead she watched the family at the waterline. Only now she noticed the worn state of the boy's clothes and the haggard looks of his parents.

Not much time could have passed, only a minute or two, when Jonathan came back. But instead of coming to her, he approached the family. He was carrying a plastic bag.

"Hi," he said to the father.

The man straightened up and eyed him warily.

"Sorry to bother you, but I promised my kids we'd bring home some of those fish to fry up."

"Well, why don't you catch some?" said the man.

"I would, but really, I'd rather not touch those things. They kind of creep me out." Jonathan added a dramatic shudder. "I'll give you one hundred dollars for what's in your bucket."

The man hesitated only for a second. "Okay."

"Thanks, man." Jonathan pulled out his wallet and took out some bills. He handed the man the cash, then held out the bag. "Just dump them in here."

The man poured the contents of the bucket into the bag. A good two-dozen fish squirmed at the bottom.

"My kids will think me a hero. Thanks again."

"Sure. Any time." The man looked at Jonathan as if he were a little crazy.

Jonathan hurried back to her. Before she could say anything, he grabbed her hand. "Come on."

"What—"

But he didn't wait for her question. He pulled her up the beach until darkness had swallowed the family. Then he ran to the waterline and gently released the fish into the surf. "Be free and spawn again."

She giggled. "That was incredible."

"Actually it *was* kind of fun." He wadded up the plastic bag and shoved it into his pocket. "I will definitely have to wash these pants before I wear them again."

She laughed then.

"It's good to see you smile. I'm sorry you had to go through that."

"I suppose it's part of being a fairy godmother. Now I just have to figure out how to grant wishes. I doubt you'll always be there to grant them for me."

"It was my pleasure."

They walked slowly back to the car. He opened the door for her and sat her sideways in the seat so her feet hung out.

"Don't move." He walked to the trunk, opened it, and returned a moment later. Bending down on one knee, he lifted her left foot and wrapped a thick towel around it. Then he rubbed.

She nearly moaned with pleasure. She hadn't realized how cold her feet had become. Finished, he placed her foot in the car, then repeated the procedure on the other foot.

"I don't want you to think I'm spoiling you. I'm just making sure the inside of my car stays clean." His voice lilted with humor.

"Good to know. Otherwise I might fall for you." She froze. She did not just say that. Wanting to see his reaction, she raised her gaze toward him.

That one-sided smile of his greeted her sight. "Yeah. That would be a real problem. I would hate that." He placed her right foot in the car, then placed the towel on the roof.

"I just mean, what I said earlier about dating—"

He lifted his hand. "Relax. I know what you meant." He paused. "It's nearly midnight. I'd better get you home. Your bakery opens early." He walked to the other side of the car, dusted off his feet with the towel, and climbed in, throwing the towel into the backseat.

They didn't say anything during the quick trip back to her apartment. He helped her out of the car and walked her to her door. There he took her hand and turned her to face him.

"I understand your feelings, but I don't want you to fight what might happen between us."

He cupped her face and captured her lips.

At the first contact, she nearly forgot to breathe. She could taste where the salt spray had touched him. He was daylight, spreading liquid sunshine through her. Her nerves tingled as warmth unfurled in her belly.

Gently he released her. When he moved from her, she felt as if a part of her had broken off.

"Good night, Reggie." He disappeared down the stairs.

As she slipped inside, she realized her door had unlocked

itself. Then she realized she wasn't alone. Sophronia sat on her couch.

Sophronia's eyes honed in on Reggie. "Well, well, well. Jonathan Bastion. Who would have thought?"

8

CORDELIA'S RULES FOR HER
DAUGHTERS

•

*Sometimes You Do Things Because You Must; Desire or
Inclination Has Little to Do With It.*

Reggie closed her eyes and drew in a deep breath. "What do you want, Sophronia? It's late and the bakery opens—"

"The Council isn't happy with you. The fairy godmothers came today, and you didn't report it." Sophronia crossed her legs and bounced the top foot. "You can't imagine the verbal acrobatics I had to go through to get you another chance."

Oh, yes, she could imagine how much "help" Sophronia had given her.

"Why didn't you report their visit?"

"I was busy. After the bakery closed, you arrived, and after you left, they arrived. And after they left . . ." She hesitated. She had no desire to share her personal life with Sophronia.

"You had your date to get ready for." Sophronia uncrossed her legs and scrutinized her. A single raised eyebrow and an amused smirk gave her opinion of Reggie's appearance.

Reggie's hand flew to her unkempt hair, now curlier and messier from the time at the beach. She curled her bare toes away from the floor. Her sandals still dangled from her fingers. The rolled-up jeans, wet and sandy, slapped at her calves.

"Hmm. Very well, I believe you were busy. I know how long it can take to, um, pull yourself together."

Reggie bristled at the haughtiness in Sophronia's tone. "I wasn't—"

"The Council is willing to give you another chance, but let me make one thing perfectly clear. They expect you to report any contact with the godmothers immediately. Consider it top priority—*before* you undertake any unimportant tasks."

Irritation curdled in her gut. She clenched her teeth. It was too late to deal with this now. She was tired and five A.M. came too early. "Sophronia, I'm tired and . . . Wait a minute. How did the Council know the godmothers were here?"

"Please. You can't be that naive. We have someone watching you and the bakery. We didn't use magic because the godmothers would detect the footprint. We are keeping our eyes on you."

A mix of disquiet and revulsion wriggled up Reggie's spine. Had someone followed her and Jonathan on their date? She hadn't noticed, but suddenly their evening together seemed tainted and dirty. She'd done nothing wrong, and her reward was having her privacy invaded. "Call them off, Sophronia. Trust works both ways. You have to give me a little."

"So far you haven't given us any reason to."

"I didn't have the chance to report anything. I've been busy." Reggie pulled her hair band from her head and ran her fingers through her hair until they got caught in a tangle.

"Ah, yes. Your date. You might want to rethink your priorities."

She tugged her fingers loose from her hair. "Sophronia, I have to get ready for bed. Thank you for the warning. I'll consider everything you said."

"See that you do. I can't say I'll be successful with the Council next time." Sophronia stood and looked down at Reggie. Once again, the woman wore four-inch heels and Reggie was barefoot. Sophronia's smile was not friendly. "You're too innocent and green. Just remember you don't have much power yet. Good night, dear. Sleep well. I expect to hear from you soon."

Sophronia shimmered and vanished from the living room. Reggie wanted to scream. She was too tired to take in everything that happened this evening. All she wanted to do was crawl into bed and forget about the Council and Sophronia. She'd deal with everything tomorrow.

But the first thing she should learn is how to shield the building from unwanted visitors.

SHE WAS LATE. Tommy and Joy were already in the kitchen baking when she checked on them. She ran through the front room and pulled her cleaning supplies from the closet when she noticed activity by the front door. Alfred had his face pressed against the glass and looked ready to bang on the window. He wasn't alone. Nate stood behind him, and there was a group of . . . well, she wasn't sure. She hurried to the front door. As she fumbled for her key, the lock clicked and the door swung open. It couldn't have done that a minute ago?

"This is no way to run a bakery," Alfred said, pushing

his way into the shop. He was followed by three others, but she didn't think they were gnomes. "I'll need a key. Especially if you choose to sleep in every morning."

"I don't . . . Never mind." Arguing served no purpose. She wouldn't change his mind about her. "I have a spare key in my apartment. Take this one." She handed him the key she had just used. Or rather not used.

Alfred dropped it into the pocket of his clean white coat. His three followers likewise wore white bakery coats. Two of them were tall and the third was short like Alfred but much stockier. Alfred pointed to one of the taller ones. Up close Reggie realized he was a boy, a teenager. "This here is Brandon. He's a Groundling who stumbled upon us one day when he was a kid. Digging to China he was." Alfred chortled.

"Hi," said Brandon. He couldn't have been more than seventeen. "Are you really a fairy godmother?"

"Uh, yes."

"That is so cool." The teenager gave her two thumbs up and walked past her.

"Dinnae worry. He can be trusted. This will be his summer job until school starts again, and then he'll work here part time." Alfred pushed the short man forward. "This is Lump. He's a dwarf." Alfred placed his hand by the side of his mouth and dropped his volume. "Never mention the Chunnel to him. You dinnae want to know."

Lump nodded, but said nothing.

"And this is Frederick." Alfred indicated the other tall lad with his thumb. "He's my sister's son."

The tall, young man stepped forward and shook her hand.

"We think he's a changeling. He doesnae even like dirt." Alfred looked up at his nephew with some concern in his expression, then shrugged. "But what're you going to do? He's family."

Alfred clapped his hands and the three newcomers gave him their full attention. "I'll tell you what your duties are, and then I expect you to get to work." He led them into the kitchen. Before he disappeared, he glanced back at her. "By the way, your boyfriend is here."

Nate stood in the doorway and watched the odd proceedings. "Good morning, Reggie." He was bundled up in lightweight but his usual unrevealing attire.

"I think I've just been replaced." She pointed to the kitchen. She didn't know how she felt about her sudden unemployment. She scratched her head in consternation as she realized she wasn't needed.

"Probably a good thing. You've got other things to worry about right now."

"I suppose, but Joy and Tommy—"

"—are in good hands. Can you really doubt that?"

Reggie looked to the rear of the bakery and saw Brandon and Frederick carrying the trays to the display. Through the door she saw Lump heft a fifty-pound sack of flour and take it to the worktable where Tommy waited with a large bowl. Alfred was smiling at Joy, and Joy was grinning back. "No, I suppose not."

"Good news, really, because we can go to the Academy and do some of that research you wanted."

Reggie frowned. The thought of not spending a day at the bakery when it was open felt strange. She supposed she'd better get used to it. The bakery was safe in Alfred's hands, of that she had no doubt. As odd as it seemed, she knew the aunts wouldn't have sent her someone she couldn't trust. "Sounds good. I have a lot of things to look up." Her list of questions needing answers kept growing. Like how much influence the Council actually had over fairy godmothers and how much were Sophronia's lies.

They took Nate's sleek BMW to the *Academia Artis Magicae* located in the hills northeast of Poway. Hidden from Groundling view and discovery, the entrance to the Academy was shielded by a curtain of magic. Reggie felt the enchantment shower over her before they turned onto the entrance road. The curtain would warn security if a Groundling stumbled over the boundary. Several academies existed worldwide, but this was the newest, although its buildings had been built to look old. And now major construction was occurring on campus because of a strong earthquake that had struck the Academy a few weeks back. The library was once again open for use, but scaffolding still surrounded the building. She looked at the campus. It must have been beautiful before the destruction. It would be again if the activity of the gnomes and wizards was any indication.

"I've never been here before," Reggie said as they stepped out of the car.

"Really?"

"I was a Groundling, remember? They didn't allow us access. Too many secrets at the Academy." She started toward the library. "Do I need any sort of special pass or something?"

"No, the library is here for any Arcani's use, but most people don't come here unless they're students." Nate's long gait easily kept pace with her nervous one. "If you want to check something out, they'll ask you to fill out a form for a card."

"You sound as if you've been here before."

He paused. "I've done quite a bit of research here."

He wasn't any more forthcoming. Reggie tried to gauge whether the topic made him uncomfortable, but his eyes gave no hint to his mood, despite their usual expressiveness. "Well then, I'm glad you're here to help me."

Two hours later, she had a stack of books in front of her and five pages of notes. And she was angry. The information she had found tied her stomach in knots and left a foul taste in her mouth. "I need a break," she whispered to Nate, who had just returned to their table with a new pile of books.

Nodding, he walked to the librarian, said something, then returned. With a graceful hand, he wrote, *Occupied—do not remove,* on a sheet of paper, and laid it on top of the books. "Let's go."

Wincing slightly as she stood, Reggie heard some of her bones pop. She shook herself and walked to the entrance. Nate followed. Outside, she stretched her arms over her head.

The day was hot this far from the coast, and Reggie felt guilty for bringing Nate outside. At the bakery, the ocean kept the temperature mild, but out here his attire had to cause discomfort. She needed to walk off some of her frustration, but he didn't need to suffer.

"You seem agitated," Nate said.

"I am. I couldn't sit there any longer. I need to burn off some energy. Do you mind if I take a walk? You don't have to come with me. It's hot out here."

"But I want to. The heat won't bother me."

When she shot him a doubt-filled look, his eyes crinkled. "Okay, but I'm still coming with you. Now what has you so bothered?"

She started walking. With no particular destination, she headed over the quad toward other campus buildings. Once again his long stride easily matched her frenzied gait. "I've been reading about the history of fairy godmothers. When Merlin realized that Arcani and Groundlings couldn't co-exist together, he established the job of godmother to act as a sort of barrier between them. The role of fairy godmothers is to mix in with the Groundlings, occasionally granting wishes but also to make sure they don't discover the true extent of Arcani powers. On the other side, the fairy godmothers are also there to protect the Groundlings from Arcani who want to abuse or enslave them."

"Could you explain that a little more?"

"Maybe." She laughed at herself. "If I have this right, Merlin and Arthur tried to form a society where Arcani and Groundlings lived together. But some Groundlings got greedy and forced a few Arcani to use their powers until they died. At the same time, a group of Arcani felt that Groundlings were beneath them and little better than slaves. So Merlin established rules and laws for the Arcani."

"The *Lagabóc*," Nate said.

She nodded. "Which everyone believed was a legend until Tennyson Ritter found it a year ago."

Reggie took a wide berth around a collapsed building. "Anyway, Merlin didn't want to cut Groundlings off entirely from magic, but he had to guarantee the safety of the Arcani. So he created the fairy godmothers. We grant wishes, but don't really interfere in the Groundling world. If we did too much, the Groundlings wouldn't leave us alone."

"Makes sense," Nate said. "And as Groundlings developed technology, they needed magic less and less and started to believe in it less and less."

She glanced at him. "You've heard this before."

He shrugged. "I did go to the Academy." He sounded almost apologetic. "But I don't know much about the fairy godmothers themselves."

"Merlin set up a spell to choose the Arcani who would serve as fairy godmothers. When the new ones are born, years before the Time of Transition, their names are revealed to the previous godmothers, so they can watch over them. Meanwhile, the new ones live their lives as Groundlings until they are twenty-seven to give them a better understanding of the world. When the new ones reach the right age, the Magic sends wands to the outgoing godmothers for the Transition. They are created by the Magic and returned to the Magic when the godmother dies."

"Ahh. So that's why . . . uh, Jonathan was so interested in your wand."

"He told you about that?"

"We're good friends."

"Once the godmothers tell the new one who she is and present her with her wand, the name appears on stone tablets that hang on the walls of the Council Halls around the world."

"Which is how Sophronia knew to arrive so quickly after you were told." Nate paused beneath the shade of a tree. "So what has you so angry?"

Reggie felt a renewed surge of discontentment. She paced faster back and forth in the shade. "When Merlin set up the Time of Transition, he never intended the Council to have any control over the fairy godmothers. He trusted the Magic to select the right candidates. Well, after the *Lagabóc* was lost, the Council started to assert its power. The arbiter was an invention of the seventeenth century." She let out a puff of air. "We aren't supposed to be tested at all. That was never Merlin's intent."

Nate let out a soft whistle.

"And this reporting to the Council, the swearing of allegiance, that's brand new." Reggie's hands fisted. "Argh. I don't know what to think. I know the Council is concerned since Kristin Montgomery disappeared with Tennyson Ritter, but the Magic doesn't make mistakes."

"But it did sixty years ago, during the Great Uprising."

"Well, maybe. I don't know enough about that."

Nate eyed her. "Looks like you know what you want to do."

She nodded. "I need to read the *Lagabóc*."

"You realize it won't be easy to find."

"I know."

"They're still studying it. No one saw it for at least nine centuries if not longer. It was only found a year ago. The book has to be locked up somewhere."

"The original, but not all the copies."

"But those would be guarded as well. They're not going to let it out of their sight."

She glared at him. "Are you telling me to give up?"

"No, I'm just pointing out the difficulties." Nate rubbed his eyes.

"I need to understand more. I know it won't be easy, and I'm not asking you to help, but I'm going to steal Tennyson Ritter's copy of the *Lagabóc*." Reggie watched his eyes for a reaction.

Nate scrutinized her for a moment, then let out a breath. "I'm in."

His meaning escaped her for a moment, and then she shook her head. "I can't ask you to—"

"You didn't ask. I said I'm in." Nate chuckled. "Maybe next time I should pick my bakeries with more care."

Worry pecked at her. She pulled her lip between her teeth. She felt terrible. He clearly carried his own burdens, and now she was hoisting her problems on him.

"That was a joke," he said. "Not very funny, huh?"

"Not really." She let out a rueful chuckle. "I really do feel bad."

"Don't. I don't volunteer unless I want to." Nate nodded his head. "What's our first step?"

"I need to do more research on the Time of Transition and the Great Uprising. Then we can go home and plan." She had to admit the tasks that lay in front of her seemed less daunting with help. "And thank you. Knowing I'm not alone helps."

"Hang on to those thanks until you see how much coffee and pastries I'm going to require in return."

Her laugh was genuine then.

9

CORDELIA'S RULES FOR HER DAUGHTERS

•

Grace and Dignity Above All.

Jonathan stared at the computer screen with a sense of foreboding. The information he sought was proving elusive. Although he was willing to help Reggie, he couldn't if he didn't have the facts.

He pushed back from the desk and walked to the large picture window. The "June gloom" had burned off in the morning, and now, in the late afternoon, puffy white clouds dotted the sky. The ocean was a darker, more mysterious blue than the sky, and the white of the beach fairly glistened. Even from here he could see sunbathers on their colorful towels, along with children, picnickers, and the occasional dog.

He touched the glass. He couldn't remember the last time he had enjoyed a day at the beach. The evening, sure. Grunion hunting with Reggie had been more fun than he had allowed himself in years. But a *day* . . .

He went to the kitchen and got a glass of water and a chicken leg for a snack, then grabbed a cookie for good measure. He needed the energy.

She was complicating his life, sucking him into things he wasn't sure he had a right to be a part of or even wanted to be a part of, things that were beginning to seem bigger than either of them had first thought. He had problems of his own and didn't know if he wanted to take on hers too.

That was a lie. He didn't resent helping her, and that had been the biggest surprise of all. She was so different from the women he had known in the past. Selfless and caring, open and honest. Not that she wasn't capable of anger or masking her emotions. She'd had lots of practice with her family. He didn't know if he'd be as optimistic as she was if he'd had her experiences. She brought out a part of him he had forgotten existed. Or maybe had never known existed. Or maybe never had.

Enough. Too much introspection wasn't good for any man. His actions had a purpose. He wanted her help as well. He pushed down the guilt that always pricked him at that thought. It was only fair, he reminded himself.

He returned to the computer, and touched it with his wand. The screen popped up the Abracadabra logo, the search engine that served Arcani, accessible only by wand. He thought the name was hokey, but it worked well. He typed in "discovery and study of the *Lagabóc*," hit the return key, and bit into the chicken as he waited for the search to finish. As the first site came up, his eyes widened. He hadn't seen this page before. This one might actually be of some help.

AT FIVE O'CLOCK, Reggie couldn't deny it any longer. She was feeling achy and sore. Ever since she and Nate had returned from the Academy, her body felt . . . wrong. She had sent him home, made herself some tea, tried to read the notes she had taken, but she hadn't been able to concentrate. She had tried to nap on her couch, but her eyes wouldn't stay closed.

A loud pop from her neck nearly caused her to cry out in pain. Something wasn't right. The pops were coming more frequently now, each one accompanied by tenderness. She stood and nearly panicked. Either the room was larger or she was shorter. She ran to the phone on the breakfast bar, trying to ignore the pops that accompanied every movement. The countertop was level with her neck. She was short, but not that short. Winded and frightened, she dialed.

"Hello." Cordelia's smooth voice brought her some ease.

"Mom, something's wrong." Reggie heard her voice break.

"Regina? Where are you? You sound odd."

"I'm at home, Mom, and I don't feel good. Could you—"

"I'm on my way."

Reggie heard the phone click. As she replaced the receiver, she noticed that her shirt flopped against her body, and her pants were slipping off her. What the hell? She *was* shrinking.

A faint shimmer in the air announced her mother's arrival. Cordelia appeared fresh and vibrant in neatly pressed capris and a fitted blouse, but her face wore the tightness of a mother's concern. "Regina?" Cordelia looked around.

"Here, Mother." Reggie stepped forward and almost tripped as her pants pooled around her ankles. She stepped out of the jeans and tried not to let fear overwhelm her.

Cordelia didn't say anything. The frown deepened as she took in the sight. "You're shrinking."

Reggie felt her bra strap slip from one shoulder. Not that

it had anywhere to go. The now-oversized T-shirt held it in place. Another creak came from her bones and she grimaced. "Mom?"

Cordelia hurried to her and hugged her. An instant later, Cordelia released her and spun her around. She lifted the back of Reggie's shirt.

"Mom?" Reggie's voice raised a notch, but she had to admit that having the material lifted from her skin felt better.

"Wings. Regina, you are growing wings."

"What?" In a panic, she tore off the T-shirt, threw it to the ground. A moment later her bra and panties dropped to the floor. She snatched up the shirt again and clutched it to her, eyes wide with horror.

"Really, Regina. I gave birth to you." Her mother lifted her gaze to the ceiling. "You don't have anything I haven't seen before."

Surprisingly, Reggie took comfort in her mother's tone. Whatever was happening to her couldn't be that serious if her mother could chide her.

"You're transforming."

"Into what?"

"A fairy." Cordelia's voice was gentle and calm.

"Ohhhh." That made sense. In her research today she had learned that fairy godmothers did much of their work while the size of sprites. Her back cracked, and she let out a soft cry.

"Baby, it's going to hurt. All transfigurations do. The first time is the worst." Cordelia went into the kitchen and opened a drawer. "We all have to experience it. The Magic transforms us the first time, and then it's up to the individual to change again. Transfiguration isn't for everyone."

Cordelia pulled out a second drawer and rifled through it. "Do you remember when Adelaide transformed as a child? She turned into a collie."

She did remember. Del had cried while the change was occurring. When the transformation was complete, her sister had romped around for an hour until she decided she'd had enough. Del had cried during the reversal process as well.

"Adelaide hated it. Once she was a dog, she was fine, except that she was a dog, but the change itself and then the reversal was more than she ever wanted to experience again." Cordelia opened a cupboard. "Once when your father and I were dating, we turned ourselves into hawks and . . ." Cordelia stopped. She eyed her daughter. "Never mind. Let's just say that it hurts, but sometimes it's worth it."

"Can I take anything? Alcohol maybe?" Reggie bit back a groan as another crunch engulfed her body.

"Ibuprofen helps, but nothing takes away the pain." Cordelia flicked her wand and two small red tablets appeared. She grabbed a glass and filled it with water. "Here take these before you can't."

Reggie swallowed, then nearly vomited as another spasm gripped her. "Give me another."

Her mother just looked at her. "The good news is that next time it won't take as long." Cordelia opened the closet.

"What are you looking for, Mother?"

"A cloth napkin. Or something that I can cut into a little dress. That shirt you're clutching won't serve much purpose other than make you impossible to find in a few minutes."

Reggie looked down. The shirt's hem already touched the floor.

Cordelia pulled out one of the pink Star Bright Bakery T-shirts. "Can I cut this up?"

"Sure." Reggie had to admire her mother's presence of mind. Her mother's calmness helped her nerves too.

"The good news is your wings are beautiful." Cordelia brought the T-shirt to the sofa.

Reggie twisted from side to side. She could still only see the tips, but they were a magnificent shade of aquamarine and green.

"Where are your scissors?" Cordelia asked.

"In the first drawer in the kitchen." Her voice sounded like she had sucked in a helium balloon.

The continual twists and compressions and torques lasted another fifteen minutes. Finally she was seated naked in the middle of a large blob of material. She continued to hug her knees to her chest after the transformation finished in the fear that a few more kinks needed to be worked out.

"Mom?" Reggie looked up finally.

Above her, high above her, her mother smiled. "I think it's finished now. Here." She handed Reggie a rectangle of pink material with two flaps along the top half. "I'm not a designer, but this should work. Place the middle of the longest side under your breasts, wrap it around under your wings, then tie the flaps over your bosom."

Reggie did as she was told, and to her surprise the dress worked. Who would have thought an exaggerated T shape would make a rather cute dress?

"How's the length?" Cordelia asked.

"It's little long, but I'll manage."

"Nonsense. Let me fix it." Cordelia knelt on the ground and heaved the scissors toward her.

The ginormous blades were the most terrifying things Reggie had ever seen, and she recoiled. "Uh, thanks, Mom, but I think I'll wait."

Cordelia stopped. "Don't you trust me?"

"I do, I do, but try to see it from my perspective. Literally."

Cordelia chuckled and set the scissors aside. "I guess I see your point. Well, aren't you going to try them?"

"The dress?" She looked down.

"The wings."

"Oh, yeah." Reggie turned her head. They were magnificent. The blue and green shimmered together like jewels. How did they work? Did she simply have to concentrate on where she wanted to go and the wings would take her? Somehow she didn't think it would be that easy.

She flapped her arms up and down. That only succeeded in eliciting another chuckle from her mother.

"You're no help," Reggie said.

"No, I'm not." Cordelia sat back on her heels. "Would it help if I lifted you and you started from up high?"

Visions of her tiny body plummeting to the floor filled her imagination. "I don't think so."

She took a deep breath and took inventory of her body. She tightened her stomach, her shoulder blades, her glutes. She stretched her deltoids and then she felt it. There. A muscle she didn't normally have when she was big. Its movement came naturally—not easily, but naturally. She pulled the wings together, then apart. Again. Again and again, faster and faster. She lifted off the ground a few inches.

"Whoo-hoo." She pumped her fist in the air.

And promptly fell into the T-shirt still pooled on the floor.

"Maybe you should concentrate on flying rather than celebrating." But Cordelia's voice held admiration, not rebuke.

Reggie rose to her feet and started beating her wings. This time she rose into the air higher and higher until she was level with her mother's eyes.

"Amazing." Cordelia stood, and the slight shift in air movement battered Reggie, but she remembered to keep her wings moving, so she didn't fall.

Reggie flew higher. Here the air moved more, but she used the currents to flit across the room. Okay, so she wasn't graceful yet, but she was flying.

By the end of an hour, she had learned to swoop, dart, dive, and hover. She landed on the coffee table in front of her mother. "I can't believe I can do that."

"It was remarkable to watch." Her mother nodded approvingly. "But you shouldn't overdo it on your first try."

Now that she had stopped, she realized she was tired. "You're right." Then a thought panicked her. *I can't stay like this.* "How do I change back?"

"Your wand, Regina." Cordelia raised an eyebrow.

"Won't it be too big?"

"Just summon it, Regina." Cordelia crossed her legs and picked up a magazine.

Reggie held out her hand and concentrated. Her wand, diminutive and miniature, appeared in her hand. Relief allowed her to breathe again. Until that moment she had trusted the Magic to keep her safe, but now she knew magic was hers. Oh, she had a lot to learn, but she had magic.

The wand warmed in her hand. She smiled and touched the top of her head with the tip of her wand and said, "*Reverté.*"

Immediately a twinge of pain rippled over her nerves and a sensation of lengthening stretched through her body. During the hour filled with the euphoria and joy of flying, she had forgotten the pain that accompanied the change. She might trust the Magic, but that didn't mean she didn't fear it.

"Mother, are you staying?" Her voice wavered.

"Of course. I had nothing else I had to do this evening."

AT MIDNIGHT, SHE lay on soft cotton sheets, trying not to breathe too deeply. Her mother had put her to bed after she had changed back to her normal size. The change hadn't lasted as long, nor had the pain been quite as intense, but her body hurt as if she had run a marathon. Not that she had ever run a marathon, but she could imagine. A hot bath, a hot toddy, and a fresh nightgown later, her mother had left her in the center of the mattress with instructions to sleep.

The darkness was quieting, although the streetlights cast their customary shadows on the walls. Her mind was drifting off into that nether realm between sleep and awareness . . .

The phone rang.

She jerked, then rolled over and reached for the phone. "Ow, ow, ow, ow. Hello?"

"Did I wake you?" Jonathan's voice was far too alert for this time of night, and the delicious shiver it sent down her spine hurt.

"I'm awake." Despite the aches, she smiled in the darkness.

"You don't sound like yourself."

"I don't feel like myself. I had my first transformation today." She reached her free hand toward the ceiling, then thought better of it and let it fall back to the mattress. *Ow.*

"I understand. You should be sleeping."

She laughed. "I know."

He laughed too. "Right. My fault. Sorry. Listen, I just wanted to tell you that I found something interesting, but I can't make it tomorrow. I'll give it to Nate. Okay?"

"Sounds good." She yawned. "Ow."

"Ow?"

"Sorry. I just hurt all over."

"I know what you're saying. Get to sleep. I'll see you soon."

She heard the phone click at his end, and she dropped her end into its cradle. She didn't bother to roll back to the center of the bed. It would hurt too much.

What information had he found? It must have been important to call her so late. Or at least interesting.

Even more she wondered how a simple phone call could make her concentrate more on the man than the news he might bring?

10

❧

CORDELIA'S RULES FOR HER
DAUGHTERS

•

Style Is Not an Excuse for Bad Taste.

Rᴇɢɢɪᴇ ᴘᴜʟʟᴇᴅ ᴏᴜᴛ her second best dress, a little
black-and-white number her mother had bought her three
years ago. So what if it was slightly out of date. It was a
classic cut, and if her mother had wanted her to buy something new, she shouldn't have waited until today to tell her
she was going to a dinner party.

Irritation seeped through her. Her mother had accepted
Luc LeRoy's invitation on all their behalf. All Reggie
wanted to do was sleep—crawl into bed and lie uncon-
scious for more than five hours.

After last night's transformation, Reggie had been looking forward to sleeping in. Instead, at six o'clock, Alfred
had pounded on her door, saying her boyfriend was here
and just because he had taken over the running of the bakery didn't mean she could lie abed like a lazy dog. She

nearly groaned remembering. Too many cups of coffee later, she still hadn't felt awake enough to take in the information on the *Lagabóc* Nate had brought her. Luckily he had left the articles and papers with her. She could look at them at her leisure since she had barely been able to see them earlier. Her eyes had been bleary all day.

Her eyes still stung now. Rubbing her eyes, she crossed to the bathroom and then rummaged through her medicine cabinet to see if she had any eye drops. She didn't. For a brief moment she contemplated conjuring up some, but dismissed that thought when she glanced at the clock. She didn't have the time to attempt magic right now. It was already six thirty, and the party started in an hour.

As she extended her arms into the dress, she winced. Her muscles still ached. But she would get through this night. And she had left strict instructions with Alfred not to wake her tomorrow.

Her parents arrived while she was applying the last touches of makeup. They were driving because she couldn't transport yet, and besides, none of them had been to Luc's house before. Her mother, of course, made a comment about the dress's age, but Reggie ignored it and hoped the drive would be long enough to nap in the backseat.

No such luck. Her mother kept up a barrage of silly questions about her date with Jonathan the other night since she hadn't had a chance to grill her during the transformation. Reggie should have known her mother wouldn't leave her alone, but one date with Jonathan did not mean an engagement. Sheesh.

They pulled up to a beautiful house in Rancho Santa Fe. Two stories, built in a Spanish style, the house was huge. Reggie recognized Ian's car. He and Del must already be here. The circular driveway held a fair number of cars already. How many guests was Luc expecting?

As they climbed from the car, the front door opened, and Luc stepped toward them. He stretched out his arms. "Welcome, my friends."

Reggie nearly smiled at the showmanship. He, however, pulled it off. He oozed sincerity and enthusiasm. And it didn't hurt that he was so attractive. For an older man. In fact, she could see her mother perk up at the attention.

"Come in, come in." Luc clasped her father's hand and then led him into the house.

Reggie followed behind her parents. A woman wearing a black-and-white maid's uniform took her wrap at the door, and then directed her to the party. A conversational buzz hit her ears. About a dozen people gathered in the living room, talking, drinking, and noshing on finger foods.

"Wine?" Luc carried three glasses in one hand and a bottle in the other.

"Thank you," Cordelia said, taking a glass. She passed one to her husband.

Luc handed Reggie the third, and then started to pour. "I am loath to admit that your California wines rival France's for quality. However, if you try to quote me, I shall deny I ever said it."

Cordelia laughed. "We shan't tell a soul."

Luc gave Reggie his attention. "How goes your adjustment into your new life?"

"As well as can be expected, I suppose." Reggie sipped her wine.

"I can't imagine living without powers for so long. You must have found it difficult." Luc clicked his tongue in a very Gallic manner.

"You have no idea," Cordelia said.

Reggie lifted an eyebrow slightly as her mother answered for her. What did her mother know about it?

"We were so worried about her future, but now we can

relax," Vincent said. "As much as any father can relax, that is."

Funny. They hadn't sounded so anxious when boasting to Jonathan. While she could understand what her parents meant, she found their words unfair. She had never asked for their help, nor had she wallowed in self-pity. The bakery was her creation and a highly successful one. Just because it wasn't their idea of success didn't mean it wasn't admirable. She took a deep swallow of the wine, but said nothing.

Luc nodded his head. "To be ignorant and weak would be difficult to accept. But of course great things awaited your daughter." Luc nodded to her in acknowledgement.

She lifted her glass and downed the rest of her wine less in agreement to the previous sentiments and more in an attempt to drown them out. She had done well for herself. And now . . . well, now her life was way more complicated and difficult with her powers.

"Allow me to pour you some more." Luc filled her glass with the last of the wine in the bottle. He waved his hand, and a large man dressed in black appeared almost stealthily at his side and took the empty bottle from him. "Ah, Dimitri, bring another."

The man nodded and retreated from the room without a change in expression.

"Dimitri has been with me for many years. I fear he hasn't quite grown accustomed to the American friendliness." Luc shook his head as if he were talking about a simple child. "But he is an impeccable butler."

Reggie once again sought refuge in her wine. A butler? Yes, her family had had cooks and housekeepers, but never a butler.

Luc guided them farther into the room to mingle with his

other guests. Most of them she knew, at least by sight. Her parents engaged in separate conversations. Reggie spotted Ian holding forth with some old wizard whose name escaped her at the moment, and Del spoke with a group of wives whose main interest was fashion.

She glanced around and let out a long breath. This evening promised to be long and dull. She took another sip of wine, then realized she had drunk nearly half of this glass as well. Already she could feel the slight buzz from the alcohol. Tired and tipsy was no way to make a good impression. The wine was going straight to her head; time to slow down.

Dimitri appeared in the entry. His face unreadable, he waited until Luc noticed him. After excusing himself from his conversation, Luc walked to the butler. Their heads bent together until Luc nodded. He said something else to Dimitri, then returned to his guests.

"Ladies and gentlemen, I'm informed that our last guest is delayed slightly. He has asked us not to wait. So if you would bring your drinks, and come this way . . ." Luc led them into a large dining room where a long table was set with places for twenty-four. The window provided a view of the long fairway of a golf course in the deepening shadows of the sunset.

Reggie found her name on a place card and realized she was seated next to their host. Funny. The thought that Luc considered her important enough to sit beside him was vaguely disturbing. Dimitri surreptitiously switched the placard opposite her with one at the end. Briefly she wondered who her original tablemate was supposed to have been, but then Dimitri stepped forward. He waved his wand, and the soup course materialized.

"Bon appetit," Luc said.

The meal began. As the guests tucked in, table conversation became the accompaniment to the eating. Luc spoke with her and the wizard seated across from her. She knew him. He was one of her father's cronies. In fact, as she looked at the faces of the guests, she realized these Arcani all claimed some level of importance in the local sphere of their world, whether political, economic, or social.

The sun had set by the time the salad course arrived on the table. Reggie had to admit the food was delicious, but the small talk taxed her. She fielded questions about her new position, but her imprecise answers generated wrinkled brows and frowns of confusion. The doubtful looks her tablemates cast her revealed their qualms about her abilities. She wasn't surprised. She had more than a few qualms about her qualifications too. Still, Luc rescued her more than once from an awkward pause, and he regaled them with stories of magical mishaps in Europe.

As the fish course vanished with a flick from Dimitri's wand, the doorbell rang. Luc's face brightened. "Ah, our final guest is here."

With a brief nod, Dimitri left and reappeared a minute later, followed by the late arrival. Reggie looked up and her heart rate accelerated.

Jonathan walked to the empty spot at the end of the table. "Forgive my appalling rudeness. I'm so glad you didn't wait for me."

"Nothing to forgive, Jonathan." Luc gestured to Dimitri, who tapped the charger in front of Jonathan. The soup appeared on it, steam rising from its surface. "Everything was kept warm for you."

"You are one hell of a host," Jonathan said and lifted his glass in a silent toast. Then he caught her gaze and winked.

A smile blossomed at his attention. She lifted her wineglass, ignoring her own earlier advice, and drank. Her mother, seated next to Jonathan, had already launched into conversation with him, but even the prospect of her mother's prying couldn't erase the giddiness she felt at Jonathan's arrival.

The fancy meal progressed through two more courses. More than once laughter from Jonathan's end of the table captured her attention, and more than once she looked toward him to find him already watching her. His gaze was electric. Her blood warmed each time his eyes met hers. The simple cock of an eyebrow felt like a shared joke, his crooked smile a touch.

At the end of the dinner, Luc stood up. "I thought we'd have dessert in my collection room. I have many interesting artifacts I'd like to share with you. Don't worry. Everything is protected. You won't spill coffee on anything."

The guests chuckled appropriately as they moved from the dining room. Jonathan maneuvered himself to her side. Up close he looked even more beautiful, but a hint of tightness surrounded his mouth and eyes. "Have you recovered from last night, Reggie?"

"Almost," she said. "It only hurts when I move."

He laughed, and the tension eased from his expression.

"I didn't know you were coming," she said.

"I wasn't sure I was. Luc invited me the night of your sister's party, but I hadn't decided until yesterday." He leaned over to her. "Knowing you'd be here was the deciding factor."

She didn't trust the thrill his words caused. "You knew?"

"Luc told me, but I still wasn't sure I could make it. As it was, I was still late. Luckily, Luc said he didn't mind." He took her hand. A frisson of excitement gamboled along her nerves. His thumb brushed over her knuckles as they walked. "And I did want to see you again. Especially to see how you were doing today."

"Better now that you're here." Whoops. Too bold. She shouldn't have had that wine with dinner.

"Then I'm glad I decided to come."

They followed the party into a spacious, but windowless room that almost looked like the interior of a museum. A small, but beautiful tapestry lit by precisely placed spotlights hung on the wall. An ancient sheet of parchment hung beside it, and next to that was a remarkable painting of a wizard consulting an astrolabe. An intricately carved staff stood in the corner. A bookshelf along the opposite wall housed several antique volumes. Another large painting depicted a woman holding a red sphere, and a third painting depicted a carefully rendered witch burning, beautiful in its artistry, yet horrible to look at. Reggie shivered at the fear and agony in the Arcani's eyes.

"Terrible, isn't it?" said a voice beside her.

Reggie jumped and whirled to see Luc frowning sadly as he gazed at the painting.

Jonathan squeezed her hand. "I'm surprised you display it."

"I debated long and hard with myself, but in the end I decided one cannot dismiss the truth because it is unpleasant. That's what great art is—truth—and the truth can make us uncomfortable." Luc's gaze still focused on the painting. "When Caravaggio had earned enough money from the Groundlings and could afford to retreat from their world, he created his true masterpieces."

Reggie's eyes widened. "Are you telling me this is a Caravaggio?"

Luc turned to her and smiled. "Of course. You can see his contempt for Groundlings in this work, can't you? And you can feel the pain of this poor Arcani. Look at the eagerness and ecstasy in the upturned faces of the Groundlings. They are beautiful, and yet it isn't redemption in their expressions, but an anticipation that is monstrous."

Reggie looked at the painting again, shivered again, and turned away. Jonathan placed his arm around her and she drew strength from the comforting touch.

Luc moved with them as they walked to the next painting. "Now this one is more fanciful. It's called *Merlin's Gifts: The Ruby Sphere,* by a student of Botticelli. The fairy godmother in the picture has just found the ruby sphere and feels the power flow through her. Unfortunately the two companion pieces, *The Living Staff* and *The Tapestry of Power,* were lost in World War II. Together they formed a triptych of the legend of Merlin's Gifts. I had a staff carved and found a tapestry to place on the wall to complete the image." He gestured at the two items in other parts of the room.

"What a charming idea," Reggie said. "And the last painting?"

"A fanciful depiction of Merlin by some pre-Raphaelite artist. Actually this was a Groundling work, but I found it an interesting distortion of our history." Luc smiled. Turning to the center of the room, he took out his wand, waved it once and said, "*Tables du café. Cinq.*"

Five quaint bistro tables emerged scattered around the room like a café. Four chairs surrounded each table, and a pot of coffee and four cups and saucers appeared on the top of each table. Cream and sugar accompanied the settings.

"Please take a seat and enjoy your coffee. Dimitri?" Luc pointed at the butler who observed from the doorway. "The dessert cart if you would."

The silent man nodded, and a moment later, he clutched the rail of a well-laden trolley, filled with an amazing array of sweets, cheeses, and fruit.

The guests' babble rose in approval as they settled themselves at the tables. Luc joined Reggie and Jonathan and another woman who couldn't keep her gaze from Jonathan, Reggie noticed with acrimony. He seemed to notice as well, for he made a show of covering Reggie's hand with his on the tabletop. Beneath the table, hidden from view, he placed his leg against hers. The contact nearly caused her to jump up, but instead she gnawed on her lip for a moment, then following an impulse, she rubbed her ankle against his. His answering grin told her he appreciated her action.

When Dimitri made his rounds and everyone had selected their choice and poured their coffee, Luc stood. "My friends, thank you for sharing this evening with me. I may be a stranger here, but if I can find friends such as you, I shall not remain a stranger for long.

"We Arcani can count on one another, can we not? Something the Groundlings cannot seem to do." Luc shook his head. "How petty their squabbles are. I've always believed they could use a stronger hand in guiding their actions. But please enjoy." He sat again and sipped his coffee.

That little speech was decidedly odd. Reggie watched him as she stirred her coffee.

"So how do you propose to help the Groundlings?" Jonathan asked.

"Yes, LeRoy," came a voice from the neighboring table. "How do you propose to help them?"

Luc shrugged. "Sometimes I think they'd be better off if we told them what to do, if we ruled them."

"Like a monarchy?" came another voice.

"Why not?" Luc said. "They seem to have a strong affection for kings."

Jonathan raised an eyebrow. "You can't think they'd stand for that."

"Again, I ask why not? They crave leadership, prefer not to think for themselves, don't stand up for what's right. Their own great Mark Twain agreed with me."

Reggie held her silence. That wasn't right. Groundlings might become complacent, but if necessary, they were capable of great things.

"Yes, but they outnumber us." Vincent spoke up. "I don't think we should overlook that."

"But we have magic." Ian spoke from another table. He looked enthused by the conversation. He would, the prat.

"Indeed we do," Luc said.

"And they are weak," said another voice from another table.

They weren't. Reggie frowned. Groundlings had a great capacity for love. Sure, they were also capable of great idiocy, but she knew Arcani who fell into that same category.

"I don't know. Groundlings were able to dominate a lot of Arcani. History tells us so. Just look at that painting." Another man pointed at the Caravaggio.

"Oh, please," said another. "That Arcani should have just blasted them. Or at least transported."

"And yet, we have to hide from them, make sure they don't discover us, and if we take risks, the Council makes sure we follow the rules." The speaker nodded to the Council member who was present. "No offense intended."

"None taken. I believe in the value of discussion," the old wizard said.

"Groundlings aren't bad. Don't we intermarry regularly?" said a third voice.

"Which is followed by more rules and regulations." A woman spoke this time.

"Please, friends, forgive me. I did not mean to spoil a lovely evening with political discourse," Luc said with a laugh. He lifted his cup. "Shall we leave it for another time?"

With good-natured laughter, the guests returned to their desserts. Reggie couldn't miss the relief on Del's face. How was she going to function as Ian's wife if she wasn't interested in politics? Ian certainly thought himself prime candidate for the next Council.

She scooped a delicate spoonful of chocolate mousse into her mouth. A tiny bit remained on her lip. Before she could lick it off, Jonathan leaned over and swiped it with his finger. For a moment the urge to suck his finger into her mouth gripped her, but she stifled the desire.

He popped his finger into his mouth. "Mmm, delicious."

She squirmed on her chair. She had felt his action as intimately as if they had kissed. Really, she was reading too much into his actions. And thinking like a crazed teenager.

Dessert finished, the party moved back to the living room where more wine was poured and conversations continued. Before she could decline it, Luc pushed another glass of wine into her hand. The stinging of her eyes had returned every time she blinked. Too little sleep and too much wine. That explained her wild thoughts. She stifled a yawn.

"You want to get out of here?" Jonathan asked.

"You can tell? My mother will be mortified," Reggie said, as she tamped down the desire to rub her eyes.

"Wait here."

Jonathan found her parents in the room and told them something. Glancing at her, Cordelia looked thrilled. Jonathan returned a moment later. "Come on, I'm taking you home."

She left her half-empty glass on the table and stood. Whoa. A bit too much wine indeed. Any effect the coffee might have had was completely gone.

They said their good-byes to Luc, and Jonathan led her to his car. She climbed onto the leather seat and sank into its softness.

As Jonathan maneuvered the car over the twisting roads toward the freeway, Reggie felt her eyelids close. She fought the sensation, but she couldn't overcome her lack of sleep, the wine, and the comfort of the leather, the contentment of being with Jonathan. The last thing she remembered was Jonathan's soft chuckle and gentle music coming from the speakers as he changed the selection on his iPod.

Too soon, or much later, she stirred, but his soft whispered "shhh" relaxed her, and she snuggled into his arms.

His arms?

Her eyes flew open. He was carrying her up the stairs to the apartment above the bakery.

"Hey, sleepyhead." He smiled into her gaze and kissed her forehead. "As long as I have your attention, where are your keys?"

"I . . . you . . . no, put me down."

"Uh-uh. I have you right where I want you."

Anticipation surged through her, and her senses quivered. They reached her front door, and it flew open in front of them.

Her mouth opened in shock, and then she breathed again. "I've been having trouble with doors and locks lately."

He laughed. "Never mind." He carried her in and stood in the center of the small room. With a single glance and a little twitch of his finger, the bed lowered from the wall.

"I've been thinking about this bed since I saw it," he said. A crafty glint sparkled in his eyes.

Reggie didn't know what to say to that, so she did the only thing she could think of.

She kissed him.

11

~⧉~

CORDELIA'S RULES FOR HER DAUGHTERS

•

Boredom Is Not an Option.

Hᴇʀ ᴋɪss ᴜɴʟᴇᴀsʜᴇᴅ a sweet fire in his blood. His surprise quickly vanished in an onslaught of yearnings untamed and unfettered by civilization. She was such a contradiction in words and actions. Fierce and meek, smart and naive, innocent and sexy. He concentrated on the last one. She was sexy as hell right now.

Without breaking the contact of their lips, he released her legs and slid her down his body, making sure she felt his every response and using her to heighten his own sensation, until she stood in front of him. She placed a hand on his chest and broke off the kiss, still leaning into him and letting out a sigh of such satisfaction his desire flamed higher.

But he waited for her cue. He stared into her dark coffee gaze. She didn't flinch, and reached up a hand to unfasten the first button on his shirt. Something in her timid yet eager movement stirred a primitive ownership response in him. He wanted to claim her.

He reached behind her, found the dress's zipper, and eased it down, slowly, feeling every ratchet. She shivered, and her fingers fumbled on the buttons. He grinned. Yeah, he hadn't lost his touch. When the zipper fell open, he brushed the material from her shoulders. The dress slipped all the way down to the floor.

Her gaze dropped to the dress, and he could see color bloom in her cheeks. He traced his fingertip around the lace of her bra. The palest pink, the cup hinted at transparency, teasing his vision. He tilted her chin so she looked at him.

"Beautiful."

Her eyes widened for a moment, then she finished unbuttoning his shirt and pulled it from him. She stepped backward and lay upon the bed. "It's hardly fair if I don't get to see you."

"Yeah, but I like this advantage." He knelt beside her and held himself above her. His gaze raked over her. With a lithe and practiced movement, he unclasped the restrictive material and tossed her bra to the side. The unimpeded view fulfilled the fantasy of the earlier tantalizing glimpse. He bent his head and licked a spot between her breasts.

Her breath hissed with her sharp intake. She reached for his waistband and undid the belt and button there. He caught her hands so she could do no more. "I'm not finished exploring you yet."

With one hand he trapped both her wrists above her head. His mouth savored the skin of her neck, nibbling gently. His free hand cupped one breast and rolled her nipple until it was a hard pebble. He needed to taste it. From the small indentation at the base of her neck, he blazed a hot, breathy trail down her chest to her breast and then sucked the tip into his mouth. He released her hands, and she buried her fingers into his hair, holding him to her. His tongue toyed with her nipple while his hand followed the curve of her waist lower and lower still until he slipped into the elastic of her panties. She twisted restlessly beneath him.

His exploration hadn't nearly sated him. He needed to feel more of her. His fingers delved deeper under the lacy pink fabric, brushing over the curls he found. Deeper still, into her folds. Warm and wet, she pressed against the contact, seeking more. He obliged, teasing the tiny bud to a fullness not present moments ago. Her breathing became more and more uneven.

His own constriction was becoming uncomfortable. He knelt again and pushed his pants and boxers from him in one move. His erection jutted free. From the pocket of his trousers, he pulled a condom.

"Planning?" she asked.

"Hoping," he said. He ripped open the foil envelope and unrolled the sheath over his length.

She wriggled out of her panties and wrapped her legs around his. Propping himself on his hands, he lowered his hips. Once again her touch was at once timid and bold, as she took hold of him and guided him to her. He slid in, relishing the slick pressure that encased him. She arched beneath him, taking him in another inch. The air rushed from his lungs on a long sibilant.

She pulled his mouth to hers and stole his breath again. He braced himself on his elbows and buried his forearms under her shoulders. Holding her head between his hands, he returned the kiss as he pulled almost completely out of her. With the next pause for air, he eased back in. She moved with him, bending, arching, driving, meeting him move for move.

As she increased her tempo, he slowed it down, making sure their loins rubbed together with every conjunction. She grew more frantic, but he trapped her head and controlled the pace.

She squirmed, writhed, raised her hips from the bed to follow his motion. "Please, please." Her voice was airy, susurrant.

"Almost." He tormented her with a few more slow deliberate strokes. Beneath him, her body glistened with sweat, allowing his belly to slide over hers.

She clutched his shoulders as he drove in hard, again and again. Her pulsating contractions gripped him as he moved inside her, out, and then in again. His own breathing grew ragged as she tightened around him. Faster, and faster, until he could not hold back any longer. He pushed himself deeply inside as his body released the sweet fire that had built within. Effervescence danced through him, bubbling in his ears, bubbling through his veins.

Her wide, dark gaze never wavered from his. A sheen of moisture flooded them.

"Reggie?" He peered into her gaze, suddenly unsure of himself.

"I've never . . . I didn't . . ."

"You weren't a virgin, were you?" Regret pricked him. He wasn't rough, but neither could he say he was gentle. "You should have told me."

She laughed. "No, at least I don't think so."

Now he was confused. "What do you mean you don't think so?"

"I've only done this once before, and it certainly didn't

feel like that." She smiled, even as a tear leaked from her eye.

"Once, huh?" He wiped the tear from her cheek.

"Well, none of the kids at school ever wanted to date someone in special ed, and when I went to a Groundling school, I was too busy trying to catch up with everyone else. And then when the bakery started, I didn't have time." She shrugged.

He relaxed and rolled off of her. "In that case, I give you a B plus."

"What?" A mix of outrage and hurt edged her voice.

"Don't get me wrong, this was good, but I have to leave room for improvement. With the right instruction, you're just going to get better. If I'd already given you an A, what scale could I use?"

"Beast," she said with a laugh. "And I suppose you're going to be my instructor."

He rolled back over her. "Only me." He kissed her again before she could make another wiseass remark, and a purr was his reward.

But as he laid back, arms around her, he couldn't stop his thoughts. Reggie had reacted exactly as he had hoped, exactly as he had planned. If he were a gentleman, if he had any decency left, he would leave her alone. But how could he? Perhaps it had been too long for him. Perhaps his self-imposed exile had left him celibate for longer than he wanted, but sex with Reggie had felt better than any he'd experienced in the past. He didn't want to read more into it. She was too fine a woman, too fine a lady to get involved with him. She deserved someone better than he. But he had made his decision. And he blamed himself for that too.

"I never thought this was how Luc's party was going to end." Reggie interrupted his musing.

"This was much more interesting than the party." Jonathan stroked the skin of her shoulder. "But I think I know what you mean."

"Yeah. Tonight was the second time in two days that I've heard talk of taking over the world." Reggie closed her eyes for a moment, then they flew open again. All traces of languor fled her. "Oh my God."

"What's wrong?"

Reggie sat up in the bed and clutched the bedcover to her, which wasn't easy since he still lay upon it. "The aunts were right. Oh my God."

"What are you talking about?"

"Luc. He's the guy the aunts were talking about. He's trying to take over the world." She abandoned the bedcover and ran to her closet. "The aunts told me that Lucas Reynard is the son of the woman who started the Great Uprising. It makes sense. Luc is Lucas."

He drew his brows together. "I was there this evening too, you know, and I didn't hear anything about taking over the world."

"No, not overtly. All that talk about Groundlings, their place in the world. Our place in the world." She pulled a robe over herself and faced him, fists on hips. "He was feeling us out."

Jonathan turned on his side and propped his head on his elbow. "Well, I don't know what he was feeling, but it clearly wasn't what I was feeling."

She blushed and whirled around. "Could you put something on? I can't have this conversation with you if you're naked."

"Aw, you're no fun." But he rose from the bed and wrapped the counterpane around his waist. "Okay, you can turn around."

She did, and her eyes widened. "You're barely covered."

"Think of it as a long kilt." He moved toward her, kicking the comforter as he walked. The blanket rode low on his hips, and he knew she watched his every step.

"Except you're not Scottish."

"No, I'm not." He slipped his arms around her. "Tell me what you suspect about Luc."

She rested her cheek against his chest. "I think he's looking for supporters of his ideas among us. I think he showed us his paintings and started that talk to see who agreed with him or might be open to persuasion."

He fell silent for a moment. "You don't have any proof."

"No, I don't, but didn't you get a strange feeling from Luc's words? From his artwork?"

He had to admit she was right. "Okay, I believe you. Tell me more."

"The aunts told me that this Lucas Reynard is trying to take over the world."

"Really?"

"Not in those words. They said someone is trying to impose Arcani rule over Groundlings." She pushed away from him. "It sounds like a bad movie even coming from my mouth."

"No, it doesn't."

She started pacing. "He's French."

"A lot of people are French."

"I know. It's not proof, but it feels right." She looked at him. "I don't know enough about Arcani history to be sure about anything."

"I'll help you find out more about him, but you can't do anything about it tonight."

She glanced at the clock and groaned. "It can't be one. I am so not a night person."

"You could have fooled me." He grinned wickedly.

Her blush returned. "Do you want to stay?"

He shook his head. "I can't. I have an early morning appointment."

Disappointment clouded her features for a moment. "I understand."

"No, I don't think you do." He crossed the room and kissed her. "But I really do have to go."

She nodded.

He gathered his clothes and peeled off the quilt. She averted her gaze. There it was again, that odd mix of innocence and worldliness. She had responded with such abandon to his lovemaking, but now she was too shy to watch him dress.

A few minutes later he stood, clothed and ready to go. In the next moment, he swept her off her feet and placed her in the bed. "You need to sleep."

"I still have to get my nightgown on." She pointed to her bathroom.

"Uh-uh." He pulled the belt from her robe and spread the material wide, revealing her body to his gaze. "I prefer to think of you sleeping this way."

He kissed her then, while his palm took one last feel of her breast. He broke away, leaving her slightly open-mouthed and panting. "That's much better. Good night, Reggie."

He let himself out, locked the door behind him with his wand, and climbed into his car.

Dawn was coming soon. He wasn't going to get much sleep himself. But she wouldn't forget him now, he had achieved that much.

He tamped down the guilt as he shifted gears. He hadn't imagined he'd like her so much when he started with this plan. She intrigued him as no woman had before. Maybe he could just tell her. She'd probably just . . .

Right. She'd probably have the same response that any normal person would. No, he had chosen his course and he would continue on it. He would help her. He could find information on Luc for her. Anything she needed.

Anything except the truth.

12

❧

CORDELIA'S RULES FOR HER
DAUGHTERS

•

A Reputation Once Lost Is Seldom Regained.

T HIS IS A picture of the original *Lagabóc*, the one Tennyson Ritter found." Nate placed the picture on the table.

The book was a thick volume, bound in bejeweled leather. Its thick, wavy pages were yellow with age or perhaps origin, Reggie didn't know. She had trouble enough focusing her bleary gaze on the photo.

Despite her orders, Alfred had once again pounded on her door at seven, saying he was not an answering service and she could greet her guests herself. Nate had waited for her with copies of articles and papers about the *Lagabóc*. Refilling her coffee too many times still had not made her feel alert. And her muscles ached from the unaccustomed activity of the previous night.

However, her dreams had been wonderful.

Even now a smile curled her lips as she thought about

last night. And then she realized she hadn't heard a word of Nate's discourse on the *Lagabóc*. "I'm sorry. What were you saying?"

"The original is at the Primary Council Hall in London. Presumably locked up and under guard." Nate laid another photo on the table. "Now this is a picture of one of the copies. They made seven."

This book looked like the original except that the cover wasn't leather, and the jewels were merely printed. In addition, its pages lay flat. Paper versus vellum.

Reggie picked up the picture and examined it through her stinging eyes. "And presumably they gave these to each of the seven lower Councils so they could have a copy?" The Council had smaller chambers in seven cities of the world—Luxor, Egypt; Madras, India; Kyoto, Japan; San Diego, California; Budapest, Hungary; Buenos Aires, Argentina; Québec City, Canada.

"No. The seven were given to scholars to study, one at each Academy, so, yes, there's one in each Council city. But that means that one of them is at the Academy here. Ritter's copy." Nate pointed at the picture. "I don't know where they're keeping it."

"Well, at least we know it's at the Academy."

"We know more than that. Here's the interesting part." Nate placed a campus map in front of her. He circled several buildings. "All these buildings are having work done to them."

"Because of the earthquake."

"Right. They're too damaged to hold something that valuable and important. Everything's been moved out of them. Now here—" he tapped on a small square "—are the history offices. Ritter's office is here. He was known to work either in the library or his office."

"So the book must be in one of those two spots."

Nate nodded slowly. "I can't be sure, but I think these two spots are where we should concentrate our search. The only other place they might have kept the copy would be the History Building, but it was destroyed, and there's been no report of the loss of one of the copies."

"But with Tennyson on the run, they would have searched his office. They might have found it and taken it somewhere else," she said. She reached for her mug, but then changed her mind. More coffee wouldn't help.

"I doubt it. They would have reported that they retrieved Ritter's copy. Heck, they would have broadcast it to prove they aren't incompetent. I think they're silent because they don't want anyone to know they've lost a copy. In any case, we won't know until we get there." Nate gathered the sheets and replaced them in the folder he'd brought.

Great. Now she had to take on the job of burglar. She rubbed her face.

Alfred showed up at her elbow. "You've been sitting here for an hour. We could use the table for paying customers. And that's another thing. How long are you going to be expecting freebies?"

"We're leaving," Nate said with no rancor in his voice. In fact he sounded amused.

Nothing like feeling wanted. Reggie looked at Alfred. "Can we talk about this later? I have to concentrate on something else."

"Sure. You've got *important* things to do." Alfred took their cups and plates. "Because we're just dancing around rainbows making lemonade from the sunshine. Take your time then. We dinnae have to earn a living."

She scrunched her eyes shut. She couldn't argue with him now. "We're going." To Nate she said, "I need to get a few things. I'll be right back."

"I'll meet you at the car," Nate said.

Before she even left the bakery, she noticed their table already held new customers. Her mood wasn't helped by knowing Alfred was right.

Forty-five minutes later, she and Nate pulled into a parking lot at the Academy.

Reggie felt the butterflies bump into the knots in her stomach. She faced Nate. "I can't ask you to do this with me. It's essentially stealing."

Nate turned off the ignition and looked at her. "As I told you before, you didn't ask, and I'm going."

She placed her hand on top of his gloved one. For an instant, he froze. She smiled and squeezed his hand. Even through the glove, it was harder and rougher than she expected. For a moment she wondered if his attire hid massive scarring, and then she looked back at his eyes. "Thank you. I don't think I can do this alone, but I couldn't expect you to break the law for me."

He shrugged. "You need me. I'm able to do things you probably couldn't."

"True. I doubt my powers extend to stealth and evasion yet."

"Probably not." He slid his hand free and climbed from the car.

She wondered if she'd crossed a boundary by touching him, but his voice sounded as friendly as before. She opened the car door.

The bright sunshine stung her vision. Glancing at her watch, she saw it was now nine A.M. Reggie blinked against the brightness. She could barely think straight. She couldn't stay up every night and wake up early. "Where to first?"

Nate considered for a moment. "The library will have fewer students at this hour. So let's try to think like criminals. Are we better off having fewer possible witnesses, or waiting until the library is busier so that the librarians don't have the time to check on us? Either way, I'm not exactly incognito."

He wasn't. He was tall and broad, and his odd attire did stand out in a climate where the normal fare was tank tops, shorts, and flip-flops. "Let's go with the library first. Maybe we'll get lucky."

They entered the building together. The air-conditioning was a welcome relief against the already hot morning of inland San Diego County. Nate was right. Few students roamed the bookshelves at this hour.

"Nate, it's good to see you again," said the woman behind the front desk. "Do you need more spell books from the stacks?"

Reggie wondered briefly why Nate would need spell books, but now was not the time to ask.

"You know me, Nancy. I'm always looking for unusual findings."

"How is that book coming? It's been, what, seven years?" the librarian asked.

Nate was writing a book? Reggie realized just how little she knew about him.

"Slower than expected, that's for sure." Nate shrugged. "This is my assistant, Reggie."

The librarian looked at her. "Do I know you?"

Panic jolted through her. Reggie lowered her gaze and shook her head. "I don't think so."

"Your face looks so familiar. Were you a student here?"

"No."

"I know." The librarian snapped her fingers. "You were here with Nate the other morning."

Overwhelming relief swamped Reggie, and then a modicum of humiliation. If a simple question garnered this reaction, what would she do if she were really in trouble? Subterfuge did not suit her.

The librarian waved them in. "Happy hunting. You never know what your research will turn up. Perhaps today will be your lucky day."

"Maybe I'll find another *Lagabóc*." Nate accompanied his line with a little chuckle.

"I doubt we'll be that lucky again in our lifetimes," the librarian said. She sighed. "A find like that only happens once."

"Have you seen it?"

"The original? I can only dream about that." The librarian's voice held a lustful and envious tone. "I did get to see the copy we have here."

"That's right," Nate said, hitting just the right tone of recollection. "You have a copy here."

Oh, he was good. Reggie's curiosity about Nate grew. How had he become such a talented prevaricator?

"Yes, but not for general perusal," the librarian said with a slight bitterness. "They haven't finished studying it. Ours was supposed to be under the care of Tennyson Ritter, but now . . ." She shrugged. "You know I really ought to ask what's happened to it, but with the earthquake, Aldous Montrose's death, and now the scandal with Tennyson, I really don't know where it might be."

"So you don't have it here, hidden under your desk?" He pretended to peek over the counter.

The librarian laughed. "Stop playing around. This is supposed to be a library, you know." She lowered her voice. "I'll bet they have some interesting spells in that one. They'd be lovely for your book."

"Don't even tease me, Nancy. They'd never give me access to the *Lagabóc*. I'm just a hack."

"Don't say such things. All books have value. I expect you to give me an autographed copy when yours comes out."

"You'll be the first."

The librarian reached under her desk and handed him a piece of paper. "Here's the key to the lock. The stacks should be fairly empty today. Unfortunately, these students don't know the treasures they could find in there."

"Thanks, Nancy. I'll tell you if we find anything interesting." He led Reggie past the bookshelves.

"Do you think she knew me?" Reggie asked.

"I don't think so, but she might have seen your picture in the *Quid Novi* three days ago."

She hadn't bothered with the paper in days. Not with everything that had happened. Not that she had ever bothered with the paper before. When had she had the time? "Why? I haven't done anything yet."

Nate widened his eyes. "Your sister's party?"

"Oh, right." She felt sheepish. Her picture had appeared in the society pages after the announcement of Del's engagement. However, she had escaped front page exposure. At least as far as she knew.

They passed the last bookshelf and reached a wall. A door labeled ARCHIVES AND SPECIAL COLLECTIONS—AUTHORIZED PERSONNEL ONLY. Pulling out the paper slip, he read it, touched the door with his wand and said, "Pumpernickel."

The door clicked open and sprang outward.

"Pumpernickel?"

Nate shrugged. "They change the password daily."

They entered a quiet, darkened area with more bookshelves than she had ever seen in one place before. "Wow."

He consulted a map posted on the nearest wall, then walked toward the far end. "The elevator is over here." He led her to a sleek stainless steel door.

"Why do they have an elevator?"

He pushed the button. "They have five stories of books

back here. Not everything is on the Internet. Especially our stuff."

"So you must know this library inside and out. After seven years. I didn't know you were writing a book." Reggie hoped her voice sounded casual.

"I'm not, but I needed an excuse to search the library."

"Oh." Then why was Nate conducting research? She waited for him to elaborate, but the elevator arrived. He stepped in, and didn't offer any more information.

Her curiosity flared now, but she couldn't think of a polite way to probe further. He valued his privacy, and she wasn't about to reward his help with unwanted questions. Tamping down her nosiness with a sigh, she followed him inside. "By the way, good job in bringing up the *Lagabóc*. I don't think she suspected anything."

"I hope not. It'll be too easy to put us together with it once it's missing." Nate focused on the numbers flashing over the door. "But we might be lucky. If Nancy doesn't know where it is, it may not be missed for a while."

On the other hand, if no one knew where it was, what chance did they have of finding it?

When the lights hit "3", the elevator stopped and the door slid open. Nate held the door for her. "If the *Lagabóc* is in the library, it's probably on this floor."

The air smelled of history. As he led her past rows of books, she couldn't help but notice the age of the volumes. Some were thick with elaborate covers; others were slender, delicate, paper-backed treatises. She could only wonder at their contents as they hurried past shelf after shelf.

At the center of the floor was a glass room. Seven volumes lay on pedestals in the enclosed space. An eighth plinth stood empty in the space. Nate walked to it and peered at the sheet that rested on its surface.

"Just as I thought. Nancy would have known if it were here."

"What?" Reggie examined the empty spot.

"That spot is reserved for the *Lagabóc* copy, but the paper has Tennyson Ritter's signature on it and says he is currently studying it."

Reggie stared at the paper. In her pocket, her wand jumped. When she pulled it out, it was warm. She pointed it at the empty pedestal.

"What are you doing?" Nate grabbed her wrist.

"I don't know." Reggie focused on the paper. The urge to write struck her. Her hand started to move in the shape of letters. *Where is the* Lagabóc *now?* she wrote in the air.

The sheet lifted off the stand and floated behind the glass. The original writing disappeared, and new words formed on the paper in the same handwriting as the signature.

Not here. Look in my office. Tennyson Ritter.

Nate stared at her. "How did you do that?"

"It just seemed the sensible thing to do, to ask the paper." Nate continued to stare at her. "Did I do something wrong?"

He shook his head. "I've heard of magic memory, but I've never seen it used before."

"Magic memory?"

"If an Arcani touches something, a memory remains behind. But you'd have to be a powerful Arcani to recall it." Nate's intense gaze never wavered. "I've never heard of anyone doing what you just did."

"Oh." She looked at her wand. "I just thought . . . it might work. . . ."

Nate nodded. "That's a little scary. Come on. We're wasting our time. The *Lagabóc* isn't here."

They returned the way they came, through the maze of

the stacks. They sneaked past Nancy while she was busy with a student. In the sunshine once again, Reggie blinked rapidly. She followed Nate around the demolished history building to a small structure. The building looked like a house, but a bronze marquee proclaimed it the Department of Arcani History. When Nate pointed his wand at the plaque, a mouth formed on the metal. "History Department. Where may I direct you?"

"The office of Tennyson Ritter," she said with a little awe. None of the buildings at her community college ever spoke to her.

"Down the hall, last door on your left, but he isn't here right now," said the sign.

"Oh. Thank you," she said.

"You're welcome." The mouth morphed back into the smooth surface of the bronze.

They climbed the three steps to the entrance. A long counter formed a reception area, but no one sat behind the desk.

Reggie glanced up the hall. At the end to the left is what the sign said. Said. She shook herself.

A rustling from a room off the reception area signaled that someone was coming.

"Go." Nate shoved her down the corridor in the direction of the office and leaned on the counter.

Reggie stumbled forward a few steps. She almost turned around, but heard, "Hi, can I help you?"

"I'm looking into making a sizeable donation." Nate's voice was slick; well, as slick as Nate's voice could be.

"Really?" The secretary's voice became degrees friendlier.

Reggie nearly laughed. Nate *was* good at this sort of thing.

She continued down the hallway, waiting and listening at every door along the way for anyone to surprise her. None opened. When she reached the end of the corridor, she found the office. TENNYSON RITTER stood out in black letters on the glass of the door.

She turned the knob, and as expected it was locked. She looked askance at the door. For a week no door had stayed locked for her. Now when she needed a door to open, it stayed locked.

Drawing her wand, she faced the door. Only then did she feel the footprint of the magic surrounding the jamb. Someone had sealed this door shut. It made sense. Tennyson was a fugitive. Whoever was investigating wouldn't want anyone rifling through his office.

She glanced around to make sure no one was watching. In the distance, she heard Nate charming the receptionist. She faced the door and concentrated. "Open."

Nothing.

Her wand sat cool in her palm.

Now what? She wasn't good enough at magic to pull this off. That's why she needed Nate here.

No, no self-defeatist talk. Rousing herself, she drew a deep breath. She had performed memory magic in the library. She had surprised and impressed Nate. If she could pull that off, why couldn't she unlock a door?

The magic in the library required no thinking. She had just done it.

"Okay, wand, let's do this." Reggie pulled her lower lip between her teeth.

For whatever reason, peanut butter came to mind— spreading it, getting it off the roof of your mouth, using it as glue for chocolate chips to a banana. She swirled her wand into a jar of imaginary peanut butter and wiped it over the door. Then she scraped it off. "Open."

The door cracked ajar.

"Yes," she said, then clamped a hand over her mouth. She froze to see if the conversation at the front of the building had stopped. The murmur of Nate's voice and a giggle from the girl floated down the hall.

Checking once more that no one watched her, she slipped inside the office.

Chaos greeted her eyes. Papers lay all over the floor, desk, and couch. Partially pulled-out books littered the shelves, drawers stood open, and a poor plant withered pitifully in the corner.

"This would have been a lot easier if the aunts had just told me where to look." She looked at the mess. Certainly the search, if that's what this had been, looked thorough. How could anything have been missed? But maybe . . .

She closed her eyes and cleared her mind. Holding her wand loosely in her hand, she let anything and everything wash over her, opening herself to influences and hunches. She had no idea if what she was doing was right, but instinct had served her well so far.

Her wand jumped. Her eyes flew open. The yellow wood pointed toward the desk. Really? Like they wouldn't have searched that the most thoroughly?

Still, she went to the desk and looked at the top. Random loose papers, none of which looked like anything that belonged in the *Lagabóc*, littered the surface. She rapped the top of the desk. Not that she knew what she was listening for. A hidden drawer could sound like a bongo drum for all she knew.

She sat down behind the desk and examined it. Nothing. The drawers slid in and out with ease, the edges had no hidden switches, and the wood sounded like wood. Her wand didn't move or point to anything anymore.

Frustration crept through her. She placed her elbows on

the desktop and dropped her face into her hands. Staring down at the top, she noticed the intricate, carved braid that encircled the leather writing area. In the middle of each side, a symbol appeared—a crescent moon, a leaf, a sun, and a water drop. Each drawer pull repeated one of the symbols.

Could it be that simple? She looked at the order of the symbols on the desk and the way they were arranged on the drawers. If one looked at the desk top as the face of a clock, the moon came first.

She pressed the symbol on the bottom left drawer and heard a definite click. Next came the leaf on the top right drawer. Another click. The sun came next, bottom right, and finally the drop, top left.

As soon as her finger left the last symbol, a light burst out from the top of the desk. She pushed back, and watched as a book appeared in the beam. It looked solid. She reached out into the shaft and plucked the book from where it floated. The light disappeared.

The *Lagabóc* weighed heavy in her hands. She wanted to yell out in celebration, but settled for mouthing the word "yes" and shaking the book. Her celebration didn't last long. Someone stood in front of the door. She could see a silhouette through the glass.

"What the hell?" said a male voice.

Reggie froze. There was nowhere to hide in the room. And she was holding the *Lagabóc*. This did not bode well.

"Who unsealed this door?"

Reggie saw the doorknob turn. Holding her breath, she squeezed her eyes shut, tensed, and tightened up every part of her body.

13

CORDELIA'S RULES FOR HER DAUGHTERS

•

Manners Never Go Out of Style.

From down the hall, Nate watched in paralyzing dread as the man entered the office. Reggie would be discovered, and he would be unmasked. How could he explain himself then? No one would believe a beast. How could he have risked so much?

He waited to hear shouting, or voices, or something, but a moment later, the man emerged again. Alone.

For once he was grateful for his concealing attire because his face registered his shock and confusion, but no one could tell. Where was Reggie?

"Marie, did you see anyone in this hallway?" The older man strode toward them, a frown on his face.

"No, professor. No one has come in except Mr. Citadel here." The receptionist indicated Nate.

Nate glanced down the hallway, expecting to see Reggie come out of the office, but the hall remained empty.

"Someone has broken into Tennyson's office. Call security. You know no one is allowed in there."

"Right away, professor." Marie grabbed the phone and dialed.

The professor still frowned as he turned to Nate and drew back in surprise. Nate knew his long black coat, the hat, and the face cover didn't engender confidence; he looked more like a terrorist than someone respectable. The professor narrowed his gaze, no doubt wondering about his identity. "Who are you?"

"Nate Citadel. As I was saying to your secretary here, I was interested in setting up a scholarship for a history student in my father's name."

The professor's face became more genial at once. "Really? Mr. Citadel, was it? Do come into my office where you can be more comfortable."

Hardly. "I'm afraid I can't right now." He took one more glance down the hall. "I have another appointment, but I wanted to know whom I should talk to. Apparently you're the man. If you could give me your card . . ."

"My pleasure." The professor fussed in his pocket for a bit, then pulled out an old wallet. He removed a dog-eared card from inside. "I am not officially head of the department yet, but I expect the appointment soon. We've had a loss recently."

"I heard about that. During the earthquake." He was having trouble concentrating on the professor's words when his attention was elsewhere. Where was Reggie?

"Yes, a tragedy, really. We are still recovering from the event. But if you would like to call—"

"I will, sir. You can count on me." Nate tucked the card in his pocket and patted it reassuringly. He took another glance up the hallway. "Trouble?"

"Just a door that shouldn't be unlocked. I don't know yet if anything was stolen." The professor shook his head. "You mustn't think too poorly of us, Mr. Citadel. The trouble we've had in the past weeks is not a reflection on the Academy. The earthquake—"

"I know that, sir. None of the chaos is your fault. In fact, I applaud the efforts already undertaken." Nate spied the security guards arriving outside the building. "I will be in touch. If you will excuse me . . ."

As the guards came in, he ducked to the side of the entrance. Probably better if the security detail didn't get a good glimpse of him. When they passed, he waved to Marie, then left.

The day was hotter now, and his beastlike appearance added to the stifling effect of his clothes. Despite the discomfort, he set off at a slow jog toward his car. The advantage of his animal existence was the strength and stamina it gave him. He had slept little last night, but he barely felt it. His senses were heightened, and he had faster reflexes. If he didn't muffle them with the layers of clothes. But how could he walk among people as a beast?

His instincts weren't serving him now. He had no idea where to look for Reggie. What had happened to her? He had seen her go into the office, but she hadn't come out. At least not through the door. Damn it. Was there another exit he'd missed? Was she still there? Had he left her behind? God, he was not cut out for espionage work.

He reached his car and pounded on the roof in frustration.

The door to the BMW flew open. He leapt back and took a defensive stance. He growled low in his throat.

"I did it." Reggie sprang out of the car. "Oh Nate, I did it." She ran to him and hugged him.

For an awkward moment, he didn't know what to do with his arms. No one had touched him in years, and this was the second time she had today. He didn't want anyone touching him. He grasped her upper arms firmly and pushed her away from him. "Did what?"

"Sorry." She stepped back, but wore a big grin. "I transported. I didn't get far, just inside your car actually. It was the only place I could think of. I wasn't sure I could and I was afraid I might throw up afterward, but I did it. The last time I transported, my mother took me and I hated it. It's still a weird feeling, but I did it. Only now I feel so drained. And hungry."

She was babbling, but he didn't mind. "That's because you've done too much magic. I don't think you should try anything else until you've rested and eaten."

"You're right." She sat back on the leather seat. "I really want to try again, but I keep forgetting that magic has a cost. Do you mind if we go home now?"

"I think that's a good idea." He climbed into the driver's seat, turned on the engine, and blasted the air-conditioning. The cool air would take a while to reach him, but he'd be more comfortable in a few minutes. He let the engine idle. "When do you want to come back?"

"Come back?" She looked at him. The grin reappeared on her face. "We don't have to come back." She reached behind her and picked up a large text from the floor of the backseat. "I found it."

He gaped at it for a moment. He wanted to take the book from her grasp and start reading it immediately. This book held more secrets than any of the others he had examined in his years of research, and if the rumors were true, it also held some powerful spells. He swallowed hard, then shook his head. "I thought they searched the office."

"They had. It was a mess. But Ritter had rigged some sort of magical secret compartment where he kept the book." She stroked the cover.

"You were able to find it?"

"Only because I still don't think with magic. Magic was used to hide the book, but no magic was required to retrieve it. I mean you didn't need magic to trigger the magic." She paused. "I don't think I'm explaining this well."

"No, you're doing fine." He put the car in gear and pulled out of the lot. The faster they left, the safer he'd feel. A lot of people would be searching for that book once they realized it was gone. If they ever realized it was gone. And it didn't help that he was thinking of taking it himself.

By the time they reached the bakery, he was ready to burst with impatience. He needed to look through that book. His hands clenched into fists as Reggie carried the prize to the building.

She stopped halfway. "Aren't you coming?"

He didn't know if he should. He was having difficulty tamping down the animal side of his temperament. Reggie didn't deserve his deceit, but he had to see that book. He nodded.

His nature struggled against itself as he followed her upstairs. The gap between them widened as the internal battle raged. He shouldn't be here. She trusted him.

"Come in." She left the door open.

He stopped in the opening, but didn't enter. It wasn't too late to leave. The windows in Reggie's apartment were open and a brisk breeze was blowing through it. The air smelled of the ocean and cooled the room. She placed the *Lagabóc* on the coffee table and dashed to the refrigerator. She leaned in and pulled out some cold cuts, tomatoes, avocadoes, and mayonnaise. She plopped these on the kitchen bar and threw a bag of rolls beside them. "Do you want a sandwich?"

"No." It was one thing to eat behind a newspaper in the bakery, quite another to sit down and share a meal with her. His decision made, he stepped into the apartment and acknowledged the regret that accompanied his action. He sat on her sofa and eyed the book. "May I look at it?"

"I don't see why not. We've already stolen it. It can't hurt now to read it."

His heart pounded. Checking to see she wasn't watching, he opened the copy with deliberate care; he feared he might tear the pages in his eagerness. He flipped to a random page. Then another. Then another. He couldn't prevent the groan that sounded in his throat.

Reggie looked up from her sandwich making. "Are you okay?"

Frustration flowed through him, and anger swelled in his chest. "Did you know this book was written in Old English or something?" He reined in the temptation to rip the tome into pieces. Tossing it on the table, he clenched his fists and tried to keep his voice calm. "I think there's Latin in here as well."

"I guess we have to wait until someone can translate the text for us." She bit into her sandwich.

"Oh, do you know anyone?" He hated the sarcasm in his voice.

"No, but I'll bet the aunts do. And they know where Tennyson Ritter is, who knows Latin and Old English." She joined him on the couch, still eating.

"And you're just going to hand it over to him?"

"No. I've already decided I want to meet Kristin and Tennyson before I make any decisions. I'm not that naive." She took another bite, chewed and swallowed, while he bit back his impatience. "But the Council has been the only one lying to me. So far."

She flipped through a few pages of the *Lagabóc*. The colorful illustrations and the precise calligraphy glowed on the pages. "They sure knew how to produce beautiful books back then. Can you imagine how lovely this would look in the original?"

"Hmmm." How could she focus on such unimportant things?

"Thanks for your help in . . . uh, acquiring the book." She turned a few more pages. "You're a quick thinker. I couldn't have come up with a lie that quickly."

He narrowed his gaze. "Are you calling me a good liar?"

She laughed. "Well, I don't want to do that, because I truly admired your ability to come up with a story. Like you're writing a book. That was an inspiration. The librarian totally believed you. And whatever you told the receptionist in the History Building worked too. I'm pretty sure you weren't regaling her with the tale of how we were trying to steal, uh, acquire the *Lagabóc*."

"So you like that I'm a liar."

"No, I like that you are clever. I couldn't come up with a story on the spot, so I'm pretty much stuck with honesty." She nodded. "Honesty is overrated, you know. I always hated those books and movies where the hero proclaims he cannot lie, so he tells the bad guy the truth when a good lie would get him out of trouble."

He chuckled. He couldn't help it. She was unlike anyone he had ever met before. "So honesty is not the best policy."

"Don't get me wrong. Honesty is important, but really, could we have gotten the *Lagabóc* if we were honest?" She lifted a finger as if launching into an oration. "Of course not. Lying . . . ahem, storytelling has its place. The best I can do is not blurt out what's on my mind. Especially to my mother. Although the skill has come in handy with Sophronia as well."

He laughed then. "You are a hidden cynic."

"Maybe. But I'm an optimistic cynic." She closed the *Lagabóc*. "Funny, I thought I'd feel better after stealing the book."

"That's because you *are* honest, and even though you claim to admire dishonesty, you don't like it." And with that observation, a pang of guilt flashed through him. He still wanted the *Lagabóc* for himself.

Wait, he wasn't thinking. That was the major weakness with his animalism. He became too emotional, too dependent on instinct, and forgot the part of him that could reason. "What if I made a copy?"

"What?" She coughed once, then cleared her throat. "You want to make a copy?"

"Yeah. Now that we have the *Lagabóc*, wouldn't it make sense to have an extra just in case?" And he could always find someone later to help him translate.

"I don't know. If it got into the wrong hands . . ."

"No one knows we have it, and I'm not telling anyone."

She smiled. "Me neither." But she frowned at the book. "It seems wrong somehow to copy it."

Her reluctance rolled off her. He suppressed his own qualms. "I suppose you're right. On the other hand, I don't think Merlin meant for it to be just in the hands of a few. He meant the laws for the entire Arcani world."

"You're right. And if the Council gets it back, the aunts would still need one." She pulled out her wand and paused. "I don't think I can—"

"Maybe not, but I could." He pulled out his wand, and tapped the book once. "Duplicate."

Nothing happened.

"Do you think maybe they placed some sort of restricting spell on it?" Reggie asked.

"It's possible." He closed the cover and examined the book. It was a fine facsimile. The cover wasn't leather and the jewels weren't real, but it looked imposing and significant. He placed his hand on the book and felt the pulsating power of a spell. "There's definitely some magic on this copy."

"Too bad we don't have a Xerox machine." She took the last bite of her sandwich.

He stared at her. "What?"

She laughed. "See, I still don't think in Arcani terms. A Xerox machine might work."

He stared at her for a moment until understanding dawned. "Of course. A copy machine. I've seen them on TV. I would never have thought of one. Do they really work?"

Now it was her turn to look surprised. "Yes. Haven't you ever used one?"

"There's no need. Copying can be a simple spell." He looked around for space in her tiny apartment. "Where do you want it?"

"Oh, no. They're huge, and clunky, and I do not have room in here for one, but there's a copy place just up the street." She grabbed the *Lagabóc*. "Do you want to come with me?"

Forty minutes later, they once again sat in Reggie's apartment with two copies of the *Lagabóc*, one Arcani, one not. Nate wondered how often Arcani forgot to take the Groundling world into account. The copier had not even slowed at the spell on the *Lagabóc*. Perhaps Merlin had been right in forcing the godmothers to undergo twenty-seven years without magic. Reggie was able to think beyond the limits of the Arcani.

Reggie placed her hand on the book. "So now what? I

can't call the aunts, and until I speak to them, I'm responsible for these." She patted the cover.

"I could send a bubble, but I don't know where to send it."

"A bubble?"

"You know, a dictosphere."

She shook her head. "I have no idea what you're talking about."

"You don't see them anymore, except rarely. Hell, you stopped seeing them thirty years ago. They were what Arcani used to communicate. But with the improvements in Groundling telephones and then cell phones, not even Arcani use magic to communicate." At the eager glint in her eyes, he held up his hand. "But you have to know where to send them. I suppose I could leave one here for when the godmothers come back, but that's pointless. They'll be coming to visit you, so you can just speak to them in person."

She sighed heavily. "So what do I do?"

"Does the bakery have a safe?" he asked.

"It does, but that won't work. I'll be giving Alfred the combination today, and he'd notice something in there." She tapped her finger against her upper lip. "I don't know whether to be clever and leave it someplace nobody would think of looking, like the bookshelf, or to be paranoid and hide it with magic."

"Nobody knows you have it, except me, so I suppose you can just stash it." He looked around the apartment. She didn't have a lot of furniture. "How about in the freezer?"

"That might just work." She opened the freezer, shuffled some of its contents, and nodded. "Perfect. I'll put one here and the other behind the bookcase."

He brought her the Academy's copy, which she placed in a plastic bag and laid inside for a deep freeze. Then he gathered the loose pages of the copy they had made, replaced them in the bag the store had given them, and slid it behind the bookcase. "Done."

"Now we wait. I don't know when the aunts will return."

He stood and crossed to her. "Don't worry. If it helps at all I think you're doing the right thing."

She smiled at him. "Thanks, Nate. I couldn't have done this without your help." She reached out to hug him, but he stepped back.

"Sorry. I'll remember next time. Actually, I probably won't." She laughed at herself. "I tend to hug friends."

Friends. Damn, he had crossed that line, hadn't he? But that didn't matter. He had to remain focused. He'd make it up to her someday. Hadn't she said she admired dishonesty? "No problem. I'll see you tomorrow. Rest."

He let himself out of the apartment and walked down to his car. The BMW had been cooking in the sun, but the AC came on as soon as he started the engine. He unbuttoned his coat, but not to remove it. As soon as he could reach in, he withdrew a sheaf of papers, the copy of the copy of the *Lagabóc* she hadn't seen him make.

14

CORDELIA'S RULES FOR HER
DAUGHTERS

•

There Is No Sin in Presenting a Social Face that
Differs From Your Private One.

LATE THE FOLLOWING afternoon after a good night's sleep, not having had to steal anything, not having a dinner party, and not having anything more to do than take care of business, Reggie appeared in the bakery, her arms filled with notebooks, folders, and papers. She found Alfred, Joy, and Tommy drinking coffee in the café section.

Joy's eyes brightened when she saw her. "Reggie." Joy jumped up and ran to hug her, ignoring the papers and such in Reggie's arms.

"Hi, Joy. I feel like I don't have the chance to see you anymore." It was true. Tears blurred Reggie's vision as she realized this part of her life was over. After only five days, Joy and Tommy were handling the change better than she. "I've missed you."

Tommy came over and took the papers from her and placed them on the table. "We made something special for you." He nodded at Joy, who bounded away and returned a moment later with the most perfect little cake Reggie had ever seen. Slightly bigger than three cupcakes, it was chocolate and smooth across the top except for the decoration. A chocolate twig with its end wrapped in gold leaf represented a wand. From the other end of the wand, a waterfall of spun sugar sprinkled with stars. It looked magical.

"See, we made you a wand making magic." Tommy pointed to the topping. "Because you're a fairy godmother."

Her tears spilled out. "Oh, Tommy, it's beautiful."

"Bother," muttered Alfred as he took in the histrionics.

"Don't cry. We didn't want to make you sad." Tommy's face crumpled.

Reggie hurried to him and hugged him. "No, no. Sometimes when people are happy, they cry."

"That's silly," said Tommy.

"I know," she said as she cried and laughed at the same time. This was her good-bye party, wasn't it? She had accomplished so much here, and now she had to let it go. And she would do so, with pride at what she'd created and more pride for what Tommy and Joy had achieved. "I'm happy to be a fairy godmother, but sad that I won't be working with you anymore."

"But you can always come to visit," Joy said.

"Of course, and I'm not moving yet, so we'll still be neighbors." She kissed Tommy's cheek and then Joy's. "I love the cake. It's beautiful. You know, maybe we should consider making little celebration cakes like these for the bakery."

"I'll worry about new ideas from now on, but that one is fairly good," Alfred said.

She had to admit Alfred would be wonderful at this job. He'd already proven himself capable, and Tommy and Joy liked him. And he seemed to love them in return. He would protect them. "I've brought down my files on the bakery for us to go over. I have all the business licenses, addresses, everything you'll need to keep the bakery running." She waved at the piles of papers.

"Does this mean you're letting me take over? Officially?" Alfred squinted at her.

"Yes. It's time." Her heart constricted, but she knew she was doing the right thing. The bakery couldn't receive the attention it deserved from her. Her world had become too complex.

"Reggie, there's more." Joy took her hand and led her to the counter.

A huge bouquet of flowers adorned the glass top. She hadn't even noticed them when she walked in. "What are these?"

"They came a short while ago. For you," Alfred said. "If you ask me, they're taking up space."

"There's a card." Joy handed her the tiny envelope.

Flummoxed, she pulled out the card.

> *Just thinking of you.*
> *—Jonathan*

The air rushed out of her lungs. Even in the excitement of finding the *Lagabóc*, he and the memory of their night together had been there hovering in the back of her mind. She inhaled the scent.

"Ahem, we have work to do," Alfred said.

Reggie pulled her nose from the bouquet. "Yes, we do."

For the next two hours, Reggie explained, presented,

and relinquished her knowledge about the bakery. Alfred's questions were thoughtful and precise. Tommy and Joy added their thoughts as well. At the end of two hours, the cake was a memory, the coffee mugs were empty, and the four looked satisfied.

Alf nodded. "Is that all?"

"I believe so. If anything comes up, I'm still living upstairs." For now. A niggling suspicion in her gut told her that would change soon too. "If I think of anything else, I'll call you."

"Cell phones dinnae work underground, so I dinnae have one. If I need anything, I'll ask." He tucked all the papers neatly together and stood. "Tommy, Joy, I'll see you tomorrow."

"Good-bye, Alf," Tommy said.

Joy waved, and the two climbed the stairs to their apartments.

"You'll watch them and see that they don't hurt themselves, that they don't use too much magic?" Reggie's gaze followed the bakers upstairs.

"I'm no' a troll. I wouldn't let anything happen to those two innocents." Alfred scowled at her.

"They're my friends before my employees," she said, wiping a late tear from her eyes.

Alfred drew in a deep breath and his expression softened. "You did well by them. Now trust me to do the same. I will nae let them get hurt."

"I know you won't." Reggie smiled at the gnome, whose scowl returned.

"But that doesnae mean I will be soft on them."

"You shouldn't be. They have a job to do."

"You do too. Dinnae forget your job. Blasted fairy gobbledygook." He disappeared with a small pop.

Reggie sat alone for a moment, unsure of what to do next. How was she going to earn money now? The bakery had been her means of support. She might be an Arcani, but she still needed to do grocery shopping and pay electric bills and buy clothes. Arcani had to live in this world, and this world required money. She had a bit of savings, but she hadn't been planning on becoming a fairy godmother. Even Arcani couldn't create things out of nothing, and stealing was as illegal among the Arcani as among the Groundlings.

Whoops. She had already broken that rule, hadn't she?

REGGIE POINTED HER wand at the cupboard. "Glass."

A glass glided from the cabinet. She guided it to the sink.

"Water."

The faucet turned on, and water spilled into the glass.

"*Vení.*"

The glass floated to her.

She took a deep swallow then glared at the glass. Three hours of practice and she could get herself a drink. Big deal.

The magic she had performed this morning had not been impressive, but she realized that she needed to master the basics if she wanted to handle her magic. So she had been practicing the easy stuff.

And wondering what else could happen.

As if in response to her thought, a knock startled her. Water sloshed over the side of the glass as her hand jerked. She turned to the heavens. "I wasn't serious."

She walked to the door and opened it. At the sight of Sophronia, Reggie clenched her teeth and bit back a groan. She wasn't up to a visit. "Hi, Sophronia. What can I do for you?"

Sophronia pushed past her without waiting to be invited in, accompanied by a different Guard. He wore dark glasses and a suit. He reminded Reggie of the Secret Service. After he checked the lock on the door, he positioned himself by the window. He removed his wand and cast some sort of spell.

Reggie felt the magic as it encompassed the room. She pointed at the Guard. "He's new."

"Well, I couldn't keep Keith after that fiasco with the gnome. I wasn't safe." Sophronia waited until the Guard nodded at her. Spreading his legs slightly, he crossed his arms over his chest, his gaze surveying the neighborhood and her.

"What is he doing?" Reggie asked.

"Making sure no one can transport in or out. Making sure I'm safe." Sophronia's gaze darted over the apartment. "You don't have any visitors?"

"No. I was just practicing—"

"Good." As Sophronia brushed her bangs to the side, Reggie noticed her hands trembled.

Sophronia was frightened.

"What's happened?" Reggie asked.

"There's been a murder."

"What?" Reggie gulped in air. "Wh-who?"

"Tiberius Herald. He was found dead in his home."

The name triggered some recognition, but Reggie couldn't place him at once. "Who was he?"

"A member of the Council. He was due to step down during this Time of Transition."

Reggie remembered. He was the Council member who had attended Luc's dinner party the other night. She hadn't really known him, but her father had. In fact, she believed he had been at Del's party as well.

As shocking as the news was, Reggie knew Sophronia hadn't come simply to inform her. "I could have read about it in the newspapers. Why did you come to tell me?"

"Surely it's obvious. Use your brains, girl." Sophronia wrinkled her nose as if she smelled something nasty. "Someone is attacking the Council. Who would try to destroy us? There's only one answer."

Lucas Reynard, but Reggie knew Sophronia wouldn't believe her. Then a cold ribbon of disbelief ran through her. "You can't mean the aunts."

"Oh, I can mean exactly that." Sophronia shook with agitation. "They have defied all the Council's edicts, hidden themselves, and refused to cooperate."

Reggie didn't mention that the Council didn't have the right to ask the godmothers to report to them. Not according to the research she'd done.

Sophronia continued. "They know where those two fugitives are, Kristin Montgomery and Tennyson Ritter. The Council considers them all unstable, perhaps even dangerous. This isn't some game, Reggie. Have you seen them?"

"No. I would have told you."

"Would you? You didn't last time." Sophronia's face flushed red. "Don't you see? The Council has been attacked. One of our members has been murdered. How can you stand there acting stupid and denying us help?"

"I haven't seen them. My God, how can you think they killed someone?" Reggie's voice reached the same pitch as Sophronia's. The dishes in the cupboards rattled, and the coffee table bounced on the floor. The Guard stepped forward toward them.

Reggie held up her hand as she fought for control. She inhaled. The dishes and table settled down. "Relax, whatever-your-name-is. I'm not going to hurt her. I wouldn't know how." She faced Sophronia. "Does the Council really think the godmothers are capable of murder?"

Sophronia and the Guard eyed her warily. Impatience and distrust smoldered in their expressions. Clearly they did. And their assessment included her.

She shook her head. "This has to be some kind of mistake. The aunts wouldn't kill anyone."

"Do I have to spell it out for you?" If Sophronia's nostrils flared any wider, she would suck the sofa into her nose. "Herald left evidence. Before he died, he left a vapor message."

A vapor message? Reggie knew that was outdated magic. A pen and paper was much more efficient than writing in the air with the black smoke of a wand. But if he'd only had his wand with him in his dying moments . . . Reggie's sense of horror grew. "What message?"

"When the Guards found him, Herald was clutching his wand. When they checked it, it wrote out the words, 'The godmothers are . . .'"

"Are what?"

"We don't know. That's all there was. But the Guards also found evidence that Herald had had three visitors that afternoon."

"But that doesn't mean they killed him. He could have been writing 'The godmothers are innocent,' or 'The godmothers are in danger.'" Reggie didn't know why she argued so vehemently. Her mind refused to believe what Sophronia was telling her.

"My goodness, what more evidence do you need? Herald had three visitors. We know that. He tried to identify his killers. Don't be so stubborn."

Reggie tried to calm down. It didn't make sense. Everything she had discovered pointed to deception from the

Council. The godmothers had encouraged her to do research. They wouldn't have done that if she might uncover evidence against them. What of Lucas Reynard? Was she wrong about him? She hadn't researched him yet. Maybe Lucas Reynard was a lie the godmothers had fed her to get her to cooperate. Had she been wrong to believe the godmothers? Maybe Luc LeRoy was simply a Frenchman who was a convenient scapegoat. Doubt assailed her, leaving her unsure of everything.

"What do you want me to do?" Her tone mirrored her confusion.

"My senseless little charge, you're the new godmother. They have to come to you sometime. I had to warn you and find out if you knew anything." Sophronia had recovered her composure. She drew herself up. "Have you signed the Oath of Allegiance yet?"

"No, I haven't had a chance. I've been busy."

"You've used that excuse before. Watch out, Reggie, or the Council might think you're hiding something." Sophronia made herself comfortable on the sofa.

So apparently Sophronia wasn't going to suck it up her nose.

Sophronia touched the table with her wand and a parchment sheet appeared. "I have a copy right here. There's no time like the present." She handed it to Reggie.

Reggie stared at the paper. Fancy swirls and calligraphy decorated the parchment, but the words "Oath of Allegiance" at the top burned into her vision. Multiple paragraphs covered the rest of the document. "I can't sign this yet."

"Why not?" Sophronia asked in a completely fake innocent voice.

"I haven't read it. I never sign anything without reading it." Even to her ears the excuse sounded lame.

"Suit yourself, but I have to say it doesn't make you look good." Sophronia stood. "You are treading into matters from which you may not be able to climb."

Tell me something I don't know. Reggie sighed. "Sophronia . . . Sophie, the past few days have been overwhelming. So much has happened, and the entire situation has become complex beyond understanding. I need time. I need time to think about things, to read things." She pointed to the pledge. "And I don't need bullying."

Sophronia's eyes widened. "I? A bully? Your welfare is my utmost—"

Reggie held up her hand. "I have no doubt you're an excellent representative of the Council. I just . . . need time."

Sophronia studied her, then nodded. "I can see you're not yourself right now. The news must have been too much. It shocked to us all to discover the godmothers are capable of such betrayal."

"Thank you." Reggie didn't trust herself to say anything else.

"But be warned. The Council is running out of patience. They won't be as lenient as I have been." Sophronia stood. "It's time to go."

The Guard nodded. He waved his wand, and Reggie felt the enchantments lift from her apartment.

"I will be back tomorrow for the pledge," Sophronia said. "Make sure you sign it."

Before Reggie could reply, the Guard stood behind Sophronia, placed his hand on her shoulder, and they vanished from the room.

Reggie wanted nothing more than to hide under her covers for the rest of the day, but she knew she had to face reality. Her thoughts jumbled in her mind, and she needed to sort through them. She sat on the sofa and dropped her head into her hands, only to pop up a moment later and dash to the phone. She punched in a number, and after hearing several rings, the phone was picked up. Damn, it was an answering machine. Nevertheless she spoke into it.

"Jonathan, I need to talk. Please?"

15

CORDELIA'S RULES FOR HER
DAUGHTERS

•

Strength Comes When We Bear That
Which Cannot Be Borne.

THE LANDING OUTSIDE Reggie's door was dark. Jonathan drew his wand and repaired the bulb. The light did little to alleviate his worry. Her voice in the message had sounded odd. He knocked.

When she opened the door, the pained expression on her face struck him like a cold wind in the rain. Her eyes were rimmed in red, her hair jumbled everywhere; he had always thought "drowning in sorrow" a cliché until he saw her. He pulled her into his arms and held tight. "I didn't get your message until half an hour ago. I came as fast as I could."

Her arms twined around him, and she clung as if she needed his support. She inhaled deeply, and he heard the air hitch in her throat.

Giving in to the urge to protect her, he swept her up in his arms and carried her into the apartment, kicking the door shut behind him. His own heart pounded. What had happened here?

When he reached the couch, he lowered himself so she was seated on his lap. She hadn't said a word. His imagination supplied too many possible answers.

"Did someone hurt you?" He felt a deep, raging fury unfurl in his gut.

She shook her head. "No." The word was muffled against his chest.

One nightmare idea resolved, hundreds to go. He tightened his grip on her and kissed the top of her head. "How can I help? What can I do?"

"You're doing it," she whispered back.

He let her stay in his arms and didn't push her to talk. He could wait until she was ready. Patience had never been his strength, but he had learned much about it in the past few years.

After a couple of minutes she lifted her face to his. Although her face still showed evidence of tears, she wasn't crying now. "You probably think I'm losing my mind."

"Why would you say that?" He shook his head. "I think something has happened that affected you deeply. I can wait to find out what it is."

"I'm sorry I called you. I just don't have many people I can talk to right now, and I didn't know who else to turn to." She tried to climb from his lap.

He held her in place. "You did the right thing. And I should hope we're more than friends."

A light blush stole into her cheeks, giving her the first color he'd seen since he arrived. He said, "Can you tell me what's got you so upset?"

"I don't even know where to start." She drew in a deep breath. "There was a murder today."

He hadn't expected that news. "Someone you know?"

"Not really. We met him at Luc's party. Tiberius Herald."

"The old Council member?"

"Right. The Council thinks the aunts killed him." Reggie gazed up at his face.

The news had just become weirder. "Are they serious?"

At his reaction, she relaxed a little. "I didn't believe it at first either. I think I still don't believe it."

As she filled him in with the facts, he remained silent and skeptical. As she finished her eyes welled up with tears. Her voice dropped to a level hardly above a whisper. "Yesterday I stole the *Lagabóc* for the aunts. Before I found out any of this."

"I know." At her glance, he said, "Nate told me."

She nodded. "I felt justified because the Council hasn't been honest with me, but now I don't know what to think."

"What does your gut tell you?" he asked.

"That I'm in this alone." A tear splashed down her cheek.

"You're not alone. You have me." He wiped the tear from her cheek. "And Nate."

"But what if it's true? What if the godmothers have changed somehow?" Reggie stared up at him. The confusion and doubt in her expression rent his heart.

He cupped her face and touched his forehead to hers. "Do you believe that?"

"I don't know what to believe anymore."

"What you need is to get out." He placed her gently on the sofa and stood in front of her. He reached down his hand. "Come on."

She placed her hand in his and let him pull her up. "Where are we going?"

"Out." He led her out of the apartment and to the street.

There were few people walking, but enough activity at the restaurants and bars that they weren't alone. Music poured out of one club, and the drone of cars provided yet another note in this symphony of the night. Jonathan held her hand, but didn't try to draw her into conversation. He could wait until she needed to speak again.

A couple walked by, dragging a small girl beside them. The child shuffled her feet and a massive frown elongated her face. Jonathan shook his head. What were the parents thinking? It was after nine o'clock. That child should be in bed, not out with her parents.

Reggie had noticed them too. She stopped and gazed at the girl. Slowly, a half smile curved her expression. Reggie looked around and nodded. She touched the wand in her pocket, then twitched her fingers a little. A moment later a balloon drifted out of the top window of a catering business. A second balloon followed, then another and another until a rainbow shower of balloons cascaded over the people dining outside, the street, and most especially over the little girl, who laughed and danced in the unusual rain. Diners joined in with their own laughter, and the volume on the street grew as others spilled out of the bars and restaurants to witness the spectacle. Cars slowed to a friendly pace as they drove through a river of balloons, sending them skyward again.

Reggie laughed with everyone, as she batted a balloon upward again. The carnival-like atmosphere that descended over Del Mar was contagious. More and more people came out to join in the fun. People were chatting with strangers, sharing the whimsy of the moment, and for a little while anyway, peace and good will ruled. Oh, there were a few curmudgeons who grumbled, but Jonathan had never seen anything like the spontaneous fun that surrounded him.

A half hour later, the street was quieter, but people still smiled at each other as they picked up the remnants of balloons, which had been almost as much fun to pop as to play with.

"Aren't you worried about the mess?" Jonathan asked as she bent over to pick up another scrap of rubber.

"No. The pieces will all disappear in an hour, except for a few leftovers that will remind people of tonight when they find them later. I wouldn't let the rubber get to the sea. That's bad for the turtles."

"I should have known you thought of everything." He chuckled. "How did you do it?"

"Magic." She laughed. "I don't know. It just felt right. That catering business is short a couple of cases of balloons, but I'll send them money anonymously tomorrow."

"Oh, no. I'll replace the balloons. This evening is on me." He squeezed her hand.

"Really? Because I'm starving."

He laughed. "I'll bet. That was some show you put on. I can take care of that as well." He pulled her into a restaurant where they were seated at once.

An hour later, they headed back to her apartment. Their pace was slow, and traffic was light.

"You've got your smile back. I like that," Jonathan said.

"I haven't solved anything, but I feel better. Thanks for making me go out." She gazed up at him, and her face glowed.

His breath caught in his throat. Without thinking, he reached out and buried his hand in the mass of hair at the back of her neck. Drawing her closer, he bent his head. He could no more prevent his actions than stop his heart beating. He needed to touch her, to feel her, to taste her. He kissed her and felt her energy stir in his own blood.

A car honked at them, and they broke apart, laughing. Then Reggie stiffened.

"What's wrong?"

"I thought I saw someone watching us." She pointed to the other side of the street.

He scanned the area, but he didn't see anyone. He sent out his senses and felt the faint footprint of magic. "Someone was there."

"You felt it too?" She shivered. "Do you suppose it's the Council? The godmothers told me they would be watching."

He couldn't answer. "Let's get you home."

When they returned to her apartment, he didn't turn on the lights. Instead, he stood by the front window, hidden by the curtains. He searched the street.

"Do you see anything?"

"No, but I'm not an expert at this spy stuff." He turned away from the window as futility washed over him. He wasn't helping her. Nate could. Nate could probably sense the guy, if there was one, with his heightened perception. He froze. This was the first time he had ever envied Nate.

She flopped onto the couch. "I suppose I should just get used to the idea of being watched." She jerked upright a moment later. "Do you think they might have followed me to the Academy?"

He shook his head. "Nate would have known. His senses are keener than most."

She relaxed. "Maybe I won't be branded a criminal just yet then."

Without turning the lights on, he sat beside her. The ambient glow from the streetlamps was enough to see by. "That's not going to happen."

"You don't know that."

"You're not a criminal. You're trying to figure out what the right course of action is."

"I know what it is. It's just not easy going against years of being told how to comport yourself. Mother will not be pleased." She sighed. "Actually it feels kind of liberating."

"Want to let me in on your plans?"

"I don't know that I should. You're too important. Everyone knows who you are. It might be better for you not to get involved with me." She took his hand. "You know too much already."

"Wait, are you trying to protect me?" He stared at her in disbelief.

"Yes, I think I am." She stood and walked away from him. "It's probably best if we don't see each other anymore."

"Now you're breaking up with me?" Indignation and surprise vied for the top spot in his emotional response. Not to mention something else that simmered beneath, something he didn't recognize. Something that troubled him more than he cared to examine.

"I can't ask you to risk your reputation on me. No, I can't *let* you."

He crossed to her and grabbed her upper arms. "Don't you think you should let me decide for myself?" He crushed her to him and kissed her.

Beneath the onslaught of his lips, he felt her melt into him, opening her mouth to him, accepting him. He could feel the eager pull of her kiss in return, detect her heart's acceleration, sense the hunger build. She couldn't dismiss him as easily as she wished.

He pushed her away from him. "Tell me now you don't want me around."

"That . . . this doesn't matter. Don't you see? I have to meet with people whom the Council have branded as criminals, and just might possibly *be* criminals. I have to do this without alerting the Council or letting them think that I'm doing anything but following their directives. And I still want to know more about some Frenchman who may or may not be gathering followers in some huge conspiracy theory." She moved away, and then faced him, hands on hips. "You want me to say it out loud? I like you. I may like you more than I should, but can't ask you to risk everything for me."

"You haven't asked." He stepped to her and used his height to tower over her. "Have you considered that maybe I have a stake in your causes as well? Maybe I don't like the idea of the Council bullying you any more than you do? Maybe your cockamamie idea of some guy trying to take over the world isn't as far-fetched as you'd like to think it is. Or as much as I'd like to think it is. Maybe whatever is going on with you and the fairy godmothers is bigger than the both of us." He paused. "Martyrdom doesn't suit either one of us."

She drew in a sharp breath. "You barely know me. How do you know I wouldn't make a good martyr?"

"You're too practical. You want to be a fairy godmother. I saw your face as you dealt with that little girl tonight. You had fun. You enjoyed it." He cocked a grin at her. "If you martyr yourself, you won't be able to grant wishes anymore. You need to solve your problems."

He walked to the door, leaving her standing in the middle of the room. "Think about it. I'm going to help you whether you want it or not. And I'll see you tomorrow night."

He left the apartment, almost whistling as he skipped down the stairs. He shouldn't be in such a good mood. They were facing some weird and uncertain circumstances, but she had said she liked him.

It would be better if he could be completely honest with her.

He was getting ready to transport, when he saw a glint from a dark entrance across the street. Without thinking about the consequences, he transported to an adjacent doorway. He ducked into the shadows. As his eyes adjusted to the dim light, he watched the spot. Sure enough, someone was watching Reggie's apartment. The man wore black and carried binoculars.

Rage blasted through Jonathan, but as he stepped out to confront the lurker, the man jerked back. For an instant they stared at each other, and then the stranger vanished.

At least he knew the man was an Arcani. But that didn't tell him whom the guy worked for. Frustration mixed with his anger. He should have caught the guy. If he had, he probably would have strangled the guy, but that would have been better than what he had accomplished. Some stranger was watching Reggie. She needed to be told. No, she needed to be moved.

His steps filled with apprehension, he ran up the steps to her apartment, rapped on her door, then threw it open.

Reggie jumped and cried out. She stared at him. "Jonathan?"

"Pack some stuff. You're getting out of here." He walked to the window, but could see no one below.

"What are you talking about?"

"You were right. Someone is watching you."

Her mouth dropped into an O, and she trembled. "You saw him?"

"Yes, but he disappeared before I could ask him any questions." He left the window and opened the closet. "Do you have a suitcase in here?"

"I can't just leave."

"Yes, you can. I'm not going to let you stay here with some strange guy watching you. We need to find you a safe place to stay for a while."

"What about Joy and Tommy?"

"They're here for you, not them, but I'll call someone to make sure they're safe."

"You can do that?

"The advantage of owning an important business." He found a bag at the bottom of the closet. He tossed it at her. "You can pack in this for the night. We'll come back tomorrow for more stuff."

"But how will I find the aunts? Or how will they find me?"

"Don't worry about that now. Get packed. On second thought . . ." He grabbed her wrist. "I can zap up anything you might need. Hang on."

He yanked her to him and transported. His insides squeezed tightly, and the air rushed out of his lungs. Because he conveyed both of them, the time in the blackness lasted longer, but it was still hardly more than a second.

When his feet touched solid ground again, he released her. They were in a spacious living room with spectacular windows. The view at this hour showed only diamond dots of brightness. A few low lights in the room gave off a dull illumination. He turned on a lamp.

She grabbed her head and stomach. "I don't like doing that. It always leaves me feeling dizzy."

"Here." He walked to a bar, opened a mini-fridge, and grabbed a small soda water. He screwed the top off and brought it back to her. "Drink this. It will settle your stomach."

She took it and drank it as she looked at the surroundings. "Where are we?"

He paused. "Nate's house."

"Nate's? Why here?" She sounded disappointed.

"You'll be safe here. Nate doesn't get visitors." The thought of that man watching her continued to send jolts of fear and fury down his spine. Bringing her here was a good idea. "There's a bedroom at the end of this hallway you can use."

"Oh." She avoided his gaze. "You seem to know your way around."

"I've been here a lot."

"Oh."

He crossed to her, and slipping a finger beneath her chin, turned her gaze to his. "Our names are linked. They would look for you at my house."

"Oh," she said again, but the word was filled with understanding this time. "Won't Nate mind?"

"No. I'll explain to him."

"Where is he?"

"Don't worry. I'll find him." He smiled at her. "Now what will you need for tonight?"

"Not just tonight. I'll need something for tomorrow too. My mother would be appalled if I wore the same thing two days in a row." She smiled back at him.

He chuckled. "I'll make your mother proud. And then I'll go find Nate for you and arrange for security."

She shot him a questioning look. "Are you sure he won't mind?"

"Positive."

16

❦

CORDELIA'S RULES FOR HER DAUGHTERS

•

Wardrobe Is the One Thing Over Which
We Truly Have Control.

Reggie's eyelids fluttered open, and for a moment she couldn't remember where she was. The bed was more comfortable than hers, the covers more sumptuous than hers, the room brighter than hers. Then she remembered. She was in Nate's house. He hadn't returned before she went to bed, but exhaustion had set in, and she fell asleep at Jonathan's behest. Worried now, she climbed from the bed and found the thick robe Jonathan had conjured up for her.

She padded out to the living room, which was empty. The view from the window was spectacular. Del Mar lay below her, and beyond that the ocean stretched into forever. The sun glistened off the water like lines of horizontal lightning.

Wait a minute. Sunshine? Fog marked June mornings in San Diego. What time was it?

"Good morning, sleepyhead." Nate came in from an archway, through which she could see a kitchen. He was bundled up as usual, even in his own home. He carried a tray with a glass of orange juice, a croissant, and a cup of coffee.

"Is it still morning?" she asked. "How late is it?"

"Nearly noon. You must have been tired."

That was an understatement. When she thought back on the past few days, she was surprised she hadn't fallen into a coma. But that didn't excuse sleeping so long, especially when she was taking advantage of a friendship.

He placed the tray on the coffee table. "I didn't know what you'd want for breakfast, so I just guessed. The croissant is fresh from your bakery."

"I'm sorry, Nate. I didn't mean to impose on you. And then to sleep in so long—"

He lifted a hand. "Stop that. You have nothing to apologize for. Jonathan explained everything to me. I'm happy I can help. I'm just sorry I couldn't have told you that myself last night."

"You've done so much to help me already, I can't just—"

"Enough. Someday you can make it up to me if you feel the need to. Now have some breakfast. You want cream or sugar?"

"No, I'm good." She sat on the leather couch and picked up the coffee. "Thanks."

As she sipped the hot liquid, she realized this was the first time in days that she didn't need the coffee to feel alert. "I don't know what your mattress is stuffed with, but I slept better last night than I have for days."

"I'm happy to hear that. My guest room doesn't get much use. Good to know it serves its purpose." Nate moved to the window.

"That's an amazing view," she said.

"The selling feature of the house." He turned away from the window. "Can I get you anything else?"

"No, this is fine." She bit into the croissant.

"After breakfast, you might want to go back to your apartment and pick up a few things. I think you'll be here for a few days." He dug into his pocket and pulled out a keychain with a single key on it. "Here's a key. I have the house protected from transporting, but I'd be happy to add you to the open list if you think you'd prefer to come in that way."

Taking the key, she let out a chuckle. "Yeah, I don't think I'm ready for that yet. I've only ever transported by myself that one time when we were at the Academy."

"I'll add you anyway." He drew out his wand. Touching her with the end, he said, "Unlock," then pointed the wand at each of the four corners of the room.

Energy rained over her like a shower without water, and when it stopped, she was quite dry.

"There. The house knows you now."

"Thanks, but I still think I'll use the Groundling way." She jangled the key and dropped it into her pocket. "You use a different spell than my parents do."

He shrugged. "It works for me."

"My sister used to drive my parents crazy with her magic. They'd try to teach her the way they performed a spell, and she'd insist on doing it her own way. They would get into such arguments over the best words to use to invoke the magic." She drank some of the orange juice.

"What about you?"

"Once they knew I didn't have magic, they never did try to teach me anything." Her eyes widened. "I hope they don't start now."

"Magic is personal." Nate looked at his wand. "Most people wouldn't want a wand as thick as mine, but I couldn't handle a slim one. Neither life nor magic is straightforward. Don't let anyone tell you otherwise."

He was waxing philosophic. The more time she spent with Nate the more questions she had about him. But she wasn't about to reward his hospitality with curiosity. She finished her breakfast and picked up the tray. "I suppose I should get dressed and then get back to my apartment." She stopped. "I don't know how to get there. My car is back at the bakery."

"You can't drive anyway. They'll be watching again, and your car is too easy to follow," Nate said. "I'll take you."

His suggestion made sense, even if it put her more into his debt. "Someday I'll be able to do something nice for you too."

"Don't worry about it." Nate took the tray from her. "Go get dressed."

Reggie walked back to the bedroom. She shed the robe and the nightgown Jonathan had acquired for her and grabbed the underwear he had gotten her. At first she stared, and then she smiled. She had never worn red lace before, but it thrilled her that he thought it appropriate for her.

Ten minutes later, clad in shorts that were slightly loose and a blouse that was slightly not, she was ready.

Nate put his arm around her and gripped her tightly. "Hang on."

She closed her eyes. Transporting was not her favorite mode of travel.

Little more than a moment passed when they arrived on the landing in front of her apartment. He released her and waited for her to open the door. After a few deep breaths, she shook off the vertigo that accompanied the jaunt.

As she reached for her door, Tommy peeked out of his apartment. "Hi, Reggie. A lot of people have been knocking on your door today. It's been loud."

Tommy's broad grin cheered her, but couldn't shake the uneasiness his news gave her. She expected the Council had been among those searching for her. "Sorry about that, Tommy."

"That's okay. Alf got me an iPod. Now I can listen to my music and not hear anything else." He waved the wires of his new gadget. He turned to Nate. "You need to come to the bakery tomorrow. I'm making something new. Cheese puffs. They're not sweet."

"They sound delicious," Nate said. "I'll be sure to pick some up."

"I will save you some." Tommy popped his ear buds into his ears. "Okay. I've got to go back and start baking!" He shouted the last words.

Reggie bit back her smile and thumped him on the shoulder. "Bye, Tommy." She waved at him.

"Bye!" Tommy shouted, and he went down to the bakery.

Reggie opened her door and stepped in. Nate followed her and locked the door with his wand.

The first thing she grabbed was her cell phone. Six missed calls. She'd deal with those later. She grabbed a suitcase from the closet and threw a few things in, then glanced around her apartment.

Funny. Nothing had changed. She had expected something to at least look different, but her apartment was the same. Except that globe on the table.

Nate followed her gaze. "A dictosphere. Jonathan left one for the godmothers." Nate picked it up in his gloved hand. He touched his wand to it. "Looks like they got it because this one's for you." He handed it to her.

She held it in her hand for a moment. "What do I do with it?"

"Break it."

Really? She rapped the sphere against the table. It cracked open at once, and a smoky fog coiled from the broken orb. Startled, she dropped the pieces on the table. The cloudy vapor formed into three figures—the aunts.

"Hello, Reggie dear. We thought this would be the safest way to communicate," the figure of Lily said. New lines etched her face.

"'Cause only you can open this." Hyacinth's image frowned.

"We received Jonathan's message. We will meet you where he suggested." Rose's smile crinkled her nose.

Nate's eyes squinted in disgust. "Is she always that annoyingly upbeat? She's a wanted woman."

Reggie would have answered, but Lily's hologram spoke over the end of Nate's words.

"I know you have questions for us. Please trust us a little bit longer."

"We're running out of time here. See you later," Hyacinth said.

"Good-bye, dear." Rose waved.

The smoke dissipated, and the images and the sphere halves disappeared.

"Where do you suppose Jonathan arranged to meet them?" she asked.

Nate just looked at her.

"Right. Sorry. I'll just pack, shall I?" She threw a few more items into the suitcase, then swept some toiletries into a tote. "Are you sure I'm not putting you out?"

"No one else wants to use that room." Nate stood behind her drapes and peered out the window. "I think you should hurry. I feel a footprint, and someone's watching from across the street. They probably have some sort of spell telling them when someone's in here. Yup. He's pulling out his cell and his wand."

Her heart hammered in her chest. She reached out with her senses. There it was. The footprint was coming from outside, not the bakery. Tommy and Joy were not the source of this magic. She looked around quickly. "I have everything I need."

Nate retrieved the *Lagabóc* from the freezer and crossed to her. "You'll probably need this. Let's hope they didn't put a transporting barrier on the building." He put his arm around her and held her tightly against him.

She shut her eyes again as the squeezing started. Her breath left her, but a moment later they were back in Nate's living room. He let her go. She dropped her bags and took a couple of deep breaths. She hated the dizzy feeling she got when transporting.

"You okay?" Nate asked.

She nodded.

"There's food in the kitchen if you get hungry. Make yourself at home. My office and bedroom are down this hallway." He pointed toward a part of the house she hadn't seen. "I'd prefer if I wasn't disturbed."

"Ooooo. Very *Beauty and the Beast*. 'What's in the West Wing?' 'It's forbidden.'" She grinned at him.

Nate just looked at her in silence. Then he nodded. "Right. The movie."

Whoops. He didn't find her movie quote funny. "Don't worry. I won't bother you." She picked up her bags. "Thanks again for letting me stay here. Do you want me to make lunch?"

"No, I'll find something for myself. If you need anything, just knock." He retreated down the hallway.

Well, she hadn't expected entertainment. She was sure he

had things to do, even if she didn't know what his job was. She carried her bags to the bedroom she was occupying.

She was still deciding if she should unpack, when her cell phone rang. When she saw the number, she sighed. "Hello, Mother."

"Where have you been? Sophronia has called here twice looking for you. I've called three times. Don't you check your messages?"

"I haven't had a chance, Mother." Reggie was not in the mood for an exchange with Cordelia.

"Where are you? Sophronia said she went by your place today and you weren't there."

"I had to go away. Don't worry. I'm fine."

"Fine? You won't tell me where you are and you expect me to believe you're fine?"

Reggie could just picture her mother on the other end. Cordelia did not like it when she didn't have control. Over all things.

"Mother, I'll be in touch. If Sophronia calls again, let her know that I will contact her." Sometime, but not today. She wondered if the man they saw watching her apartment was working for Sophronia.

"Regina, I don't like this at all. Sophronia seems to think you're acting strangely, and she doesn't know if you're to be trusted. What have you done?"

Yeah, she was having a lot of issues with trust herself these days. "I have to go, Mother. I'll call you later." She ended the call and turned off the phone. Better to deal with an irate Cordelia when Reggie was ready.

She wandered through the house, found a book-filled room that she added to her list for further exploration, and then decided to practice magic. She went out on the deck and pulled out her wand. She tried to focus on simple spells, but her mind kept going back to the thoughts of some stranger watching her. To how she had stolen the *Lagabóc*, to how she had been chased from her home, to the murder.

Her hands trembled. In the trees and bushes around her, the birds grew quiet. Her agitation intensified. How dare the Council ask her to sign an allegiance pledge? How dare Sophronia belittle her and act so condescending toward her? Her discontentment grew. She had become a thief, given up her business, and now lost her home.

A wind swirled around her, stirring the leaves of nearby trees and lifting her hair. A potted plant on the deck turned over with a loud thump. Sure, now even plants didn't like her. But that she could fix.

She focused on the plant. Power flowed through her and over her. Energy gathered within her. She pointed her wand. A simple spell. All she had to do was tidy up an overturned plant. She could do this. Even if nothing else in her life was going right, this stupid plant would stand up straight. "Behave."

With a thundering boom, the pot exploded. Dirt shot into the air like a waterspout, the birds flew off screeching and squawking, and the planter evaporated. Shredded plant leaves cascaded down around her like confetti.

Her eyes widened in shock as she saw the damage she had caused. The railing behind the pot was definitely cracked, and the deck beneath the planter had a scorch mark.

A few moments later, Nate ran out. "What happened?"

"I broke your house." She pointed with her wand, and then realized what she was doing and hastily withdrew it.

He examined the spot. "A little angry were you?"

"I didn't mean—"

He just laughed. "I've done worse myself." He pulled out his wand. "*Reparo*."

The scorch mark vanished, and the railing reknit itself. He turned to her. "I'm afraid the plant and the pot are a loss."

"I'm so sorry. I'll replace them." She couldn't meet his gaze. Her cheeks burned. Embarrassment and mortification flooded her.

"What were you trying to do?" Nate's eyes sparkled with amusement.

"The pot fell over and I was trying to stand it upright again."

"What word did you use?"

"Behave," she said meekly.

A great belly laugh burst out of him. "You might want to remember that word in case you need to destroy something."

Her heart still raced, and the sting of tears pricked at her eyes.

He must have noticed her state. "Hey, it's okay. You just have to work on control. When I . . . A few years ago, I had some problems with my temper. That window with the great view? I've replaced it five times." He chuckled. "You're a fairy godmother now with all the powers that entails. It's all about control. And you won't learn it overnight."

Despite his understanding, her stomach churned. "So why can I do some really complex stuff and screw up the simple spells?"

"Maybe because you don't know they're complex, so you aren't afraid of doing them. Maybe you're concentrating so hard on the simple ones that you're overpowering them."

She sighed. "What if I never get it right?"

"You've been at this, what, a week? The things you have done are amazing. Give yourself a break." Nate pointed to the door. "Go inside, have a glass of water . . . or rum, or whatever. Take a bath or read a book. But really, it's okay."

She gave him a tremulous smile. "Control, huh?"

"A skill worth learning." He nodded.

"Thank you, Nate." She wanted to give him a kiss, but she didn't think he'd like that.

17

∼⊱⊰∼

CORDELIA'S RULES FOR HER DAUGHTERS

•

There Is No Substitute for Sleep as a
Restorative and Beauty Treatment.

JONATHAN PICKED REGGIE up at nine. Nate had made her dinner, which she chalked up as another addition to her debt. He wasn't there to serve her, even if he insisted that he was just making himself dinner and added more for her. He had eaten a tremendous amount. Nate had gone out soon after.

"What are you thinking?" Jonathan asked as they drove south on the Five toward some destination he hadn't shared yet.

She shook off her reverie. "How much people are going out of their way for me. Nate has been more than kind to me."

"He'd better, or he'd have me to answer to." Jonathan placed his hand on her thigh.

The simple yet intimate gesture sent her heart fluttering. Silly, she knew, but her heart reacted nonetheless.

They pulled off at a downtown exit and headed for the Gas Lamp district. The lights of Petco Park glowed in the downtown sky.

"We're going to a Padres game?"

He nodded. "It's the top of the seventh. The godmothers figured it was a great place to meet and I agreed. Even this early in the season, there will be enough of a crowd to hide us. And I have tickets and a great secret parking spot known only to hard-core fans."

They parked in a half-empty garage and walked to the stadium. Its façade had incorporated the old warehouses and buildings of the waterfront area, looking both modern and historic at the same time.

Jonathan was right. No one noticed them as they climbed to their seats. A row in front of them, the three aunts were watching the game, just a few of many fans enjoying the cool San Diego night at a baseball game.

Hyacinth wore a Padres cap and a large foam finger. "Are you blind? When's the last time you had your prescription checked?"

Reggie glanced at Jonathan, who sported a wide grin. "She must be a fan," he said.

Lily looked up when he spoke. At once her expression changed from relaxed to concerned. "Reggie, dear. I'm so glad you came."

Rose and Hyacinth turned around at the greeting. Reggie didn't know how to react. Was she happy to see them, or should she be frightened? She had so many questions and doubts. Their expressions mirrored her hesitation.

Jonathan showed her to the empty chair right behind the aunts. He sat beside her. "Well, ladies, I believe you have a lot to talk about."

Rose spoke first, twisting in her seat so she could face Reggie. "How are you, dear?"

"I'm okay, I guess."

"You're looking a little peaked." Hyacinth looked her up and down. "Like you're not sleeping."

"I'm not really. There's a lot going on." Reggie observed the surroundings. Few people occupied the stands around them, so high in the stadium. Halfway through the season, only die-hard fans attended these games, especially in these seats, but she didn't know how they could have this conversation without someone overhearing. The man beside Rose was already scowling at them.

"How is Alfred working out at the bakery?" Lily asked.

"He's perfect." Reggie sighed. "I'm not needed there anymore."

Lily patted her arm. "You're always needed, dear. Just in other ways now."

The man diagonal to Rose turned to them. He looked annoyed. "Are you going to have a conversation or watch the game?"

"We're going to have a conversation. Thank you for asking," Rose said with bright smile on her face.

The man gaped for a second, then turned back to the game.

Rose reached into her handbag, accidentally . . . maybe . . . bopping him on the head as she swung it around. "I have these unused tickets for the seats down there. You and your friend are welcome to them if you wish." She handed him the stubs.

The man gaped at them. "These are behind the plate, lady."

"I know, and I'm sorry. I do hate the way that net blocks your view."

The man's mouth dropped open, but he groped in the air for his buddy's shoulder. "Come on, Joe, we're moving. We're going to watch the rest of the game in style." The two men left, nearly stumbling in their hurry.

"See? I can be quite ruthless in my own way," Rose said with a smirk of satisfaction.

"Yeah, Rose'll surprise you." Hyacinth turned back to the game. "Come on, that was an out."

"And now before we continue . . ." Lily glanced around. With great stealth, she took her wand from her bag and made a circle. "*Quietus*. There, now we can talk without anyone overhearing us."

"Good thinking," Jonathan said. "I was just about to suggest the same thing."

Several seconds passed as Reggie eyed the three women without speaking. Reggie swallowed. "Tiberius Herald?"

They met her gaze without wavering or flinching. Reggie saw a fierce pride and nobility in each of their eyes, and she knew. A sense of relief swamped her. "You didn't do it. You couldn't have."

"Don't be too sure. If the cause is right, we can be cold-blooded, but not to poor, old Tiberius," Hyacinth said, and tears puddled in her eyes. Hyacinth never cried. "I've known the fool for eighty-five years. He was my friend."

"And in fact the only man we could trust on the Council right now," said Rose, pulling out a handkerchief and dabbing her eyes.

"I'm sorry I doubted you, even for one second," Reggie said. Even the greatest actor couldn't have portrayed the true loss reflected in Hyacinth's expression.

"You have nothing to be sorry about," Lily said. "Of course you had doubts. Any sane person would. I'm sure you were told many things and didn't know what to think."

That was certainly true. "Perhaps, but I still feel guilty."

"Well, get over it," Hyacinth said. "We're good now, and Tibi will be avenged."

Rose shrugged. "She did say she could be cold-blooded given the right motivation."

Lily smiled at Hyacinth. "The truth is we had gone to see him that afternoon. We were there, and the Council was correct in their interpretation of the evidence. We were the last to see him alive. Except his killer."

"We don't know who came after us. We do know they made sure to cast the blame on us." Rose huffed out a breath.

"Technically, we still don't have proof you're innocent," Jonathan said.

The four women stared at him.

He lifted his hands in front of him. "I'm just saying. I don't think you're guilty any more than Reggie does."

"Fairy godmothers have gone bad before," Lily said. "Lucas's mother did."

"So the Magic does make mistakes in choosing fairy godmothers." Doubt about her own abilities niggled at Reggie.

"Not really. Elenka was perfect for the job. Circumstances caused her to change." Rose shook her head. "The Nazis tortured her during the war, and afterward, the Communists weren't any better."

"She lived in Prague, you know. It was a beautiful city. Heartless, really, what the Nazis, and afterward the Russians, did to its people," Lily said.

"We don't have time for a history lesson," Hyacinth said. "We all make choices and have to live with them. We've made our choice, to stand beside Kristin, and now we face the consequences."

Reggie drew a deep breath. Hyacinth was right. "I have the *Lagabóc*."

The three women looked at her. Lily's eyebrows arched above her eyes. "So fast?"

"It didn't feel fast when I was stealing it."

"Tennyson will be so pleased." Rose clapped her hands together.

"About that." Reggie paused. "Before I turn it over, I need to meet them. You know them, but I don't."

"Completely understandable," Lily said.

"It's time you and Kristin met anyway," Rose said. "You'll be working together when all this is over."

"If it's ever over," said Hyacinth under her breath. When they all looked at her, she said, "Sorry. Sometimes it's hard to maintain optimism."

"That's why we keep you around. You keep us grounded in reality," Lily said. She faced forward. "Kristin, come meet Reggie."

Who was Lily speaking to? The *Quietus* spell would prevent anyone from hearing unless they were included in the circle.

Apparently they had been. A woman two rows in front of them turned around. Beside her, a handsome man turned as well. Reggie realized at once who they were. The two stood and made their way out of their row to the empty seats around them.

Reggie got to her feet to meet them. The woman was tall with rich auburn hair that floated perfectly around her face. Reggie's hand pulled at her own dark curls. It figured.

The woman stuck out her hand. "Hi, I'm Kristin. Sorry about the subterfuge. We didn't know if you'd want to meet us."

"Us" must have meant her and Tennyson. "I understand. I'm Regina Scott." Reggie shook her hand. The wary look in Kristin's eyes couldn't hide the hope for friendship and camaraderie her expression held. Kristin appeared aware of the awkwardness of the situation. Sympathetic, but cautious; eager, but not foolish. Just the kind of person Reggie could like. "Call me Reggie. All my friends do."

The two men hadn't spoken yet. They gazed at each other, sizing the other one up. Reggie nearly laughed. They were like two dogs sniffing. Jonathan held his hand out first. "Jonathan Bastion."

The other man's eyes widened, but he gripped the proffered hand and said, "Tennyson Ritter." Tennyson was taller than Jonathan and had dark coloring.

"Good. Now that that's over with, can we sit down and watch some more of this game?" Hyacinth said.

"It's a helluva way to start a friendship," Kristin said. "Bad guys and murders and plots."

"Oh my," finished Reggie. The two women looked at each other and smiled.

"I told you they'd like each other," Rose said.

"Well, of course they would. The Magic doesn't pick just anybody." Hyacinth sighed as she looked back at the field. "The game just isn't the same without Tibi to pick on. He loved the Padres."

Lily patted Hyacinth's arm, but looked at Reggie. "Tell us what's been happening."

Reggie filled them in on the demands from the Council, eliciting tongue clicks from Rose and mutterings from Hyacinth. Lily took in all the news stoically.

"Maybe I should be glad I'm not waiting for their approval," Kristin said. A note of sadness tinged her voice.

Tennyson lifted her hand to hold it, but as he did, Rose gasped. "You have a ring."

Kristin lifted her hand to show off the ring. Two fiery rubies accompanied a flawless pearl in the center. White and yellow gold twined together to form the band. "We bought it in England. It's official."

"I'm so happy for you," Lily said.

"When's the date?" Rose asked.

"We don't have one." Kristin brushed a lock of hair from Tennyson's forehead.

"Why not?" Hyacainth said. "We could use some cheerfulness right now."

"I told her the same thing, but she wanted to wait a little longer." Tennyson braided his fingers in Kristin's and kissed her hand.

"It's beautiful. And so unusual," Reggie said.

"I didn't want a conventional engagement ring." Kristin shrugged.

"So you're engaged?" Reggie asked. Was it her imagination, or did Jonathan suddenly relax a little?

"More than that really," Kristin said. "A ceremony won't do anything that I don't already feel and I haven't already committed to."

The look Kristin sent Tennyson stopped the breath in Reggie's lungs. Her heart pounded. She steeled herself against the impulse to glance at Jonathan. It was too soon for such strong feelings for him. It was. Even if she had to remind herself of that fact.

Jonathan said, "I hate to break up this party, but we don't know how much time we have."

Kristin's expression grew serious. "Did the aunts tell you our theory about Lucas Reynard?"

"That he is the son of the godmother who led the Great Uprising?" Reggie nodded.

"Right after our . . . troubles, we traveled to England to talk with Elenka's son. Like Groundlings, so no one could trace our footprints."

Tennyson leaned over to Jonathan. "Try getting a passport when you're Arcani."

Jonathan gave a half-smile in appreciation of the dilemma.

"Anyway, we found Ivan Dimitrov, the purported son of Elenka. We talked to him and he gave all the right answers, but something about the way he spoke was too perfunctory." Kristin shook her head. "So I tried a little something—"

"She is really scary," Tennyson said with pride in his voice. "I've never seen anything like it."

"You didn't hurt him?" Reggie asked.

"No, I just . . ." Kristin drew her brows together. "Actually I don't know exactly what I did. I just did it."

"That's what you get when you give a Rare One the powers of a fairy godmother," Tennyson said.

Kristin was a Rare One? A Groundling who had magical powers? Reggie had thought they were just legend. Of course, in the past few days she'd discovered several legends that were real. This one shouldn't surprise her.

"He wasn't hurt. He just doesn't remember talking to us," Tennyson said.

"Anyway, we found out that this Ivan is simply a supporter of Lucas Reynard who was given the role of decoy. And he was quite proud to be given the part." Kristin shivered. "Ivan Dimitrov was the name Elenka gave the Council as her son's identity, but Lucas Reynard is his actual name."

Reggie chanced a look at Jonathan. The crease in his brow showed how much this information troubled him. He looked at her. "Luc."

She nodded, then turned to the group. "I have my own theory about him. He's established himself under another name."

"Wait. You've met him?" Tennyson asked. His expression became intense.

Reggie hesitated. "I think so. He's using the name Luc LeRoy."

Tennyson sat up. "*Roi* means king in French."

"Figures," Kristin said. "The guy is a real megalomaniac."

"He had a dinner party," Reggie said. "He showed us his art collection. Interesting paintings that elicited some interesting conversation."

"About the Arcani ruling the world. Am I right?" Kristin asked. Her frown was fierce.

With Kristin's words, all Reggie's misgivings about Luc solidified. "You are."

Silence fell over the group for a few moments.

"Taking over the world doesn't sound so melodramatic now," Hyacinth said.

Tennyson addressed Reggie. "What were the paintings?"

"He had a Caravaggio of a witch burning," Jonathan answered.

"You were there too?" Tennyson looked surprised.

Jonathan nodded. "He also had a depiction of Merlin, and the center portion of a triptych depicting the Merlin's Gifts."

Tennyson glanced at Kristin, then looked at Jonathan again. "Did he have the staff and tapestry?"

Jonathan hesitated. "He had replicas of them."

"Those weren't fakes," Tennyson said. "We have to go get them. Do you remember where he lives?"

"Wait a minute." Jonathan eyed Tennyson. "Are you telling me those were the actual Gifts from Merlin? They're not just legends?"

Legend again. Reggie didn't know the story. Her lack of knowledge always seemed to be getting in the way.

Tennyson gave Kristin a pointed look. With a quick glance to make sure no one was looking, Kristin held out her hand. A red orb appeared in her palm. "It's not a myth."

Jonathan stared at the orb. "That's not the real Ruby Sphere, is it?"

Tennyson laughed. "I told you she was scary. Reynard will use the other Gifts to build his following. Let's go get them." He jumped to his feet.

"With what army?" Kristin said.

"We can't go now, Tennyson, although I admire your spirit," Lily said. "Since we don't have the numbers or the Council on our side, we have to be smarter. We really need to learn more."

Tennyson sat again. "You're right. Reynard has tightened his security for sure. I really need the *Lagabóc* to study up on the Gifts."

"Oh my gosh, the *Lagabóc*." Reggie straightened. "I have it."

"Here? And you didn't tell us?" Tennyson looked ready to shout at her.

Jonathan narrowed his eyes. "She isn't stupid. Back off."

"It's okay, Jonathan, he didn't mean anything." A secret thrill rushed through Reggie at his defense of her.

"Sorry, man." Tennyson nodded. "I didn't mean to sound so harsh. I guess we've all been on edge lately, and sometimes I forget that I don't have control over much these days."

"Now that we're all friends again . . ." Kristin's voice held a hint of humor. She leaned over to Reggie and whispered, "They're so cute when they get riled up. By the way, I think you made a good choice." She cocked her head toward Jonathan.

"Oh, he's not . . . I mean I barely know him."

But Kristin just raised one eyebrow, and Reggie blushed. Kristin said, "Hey, I was just there. I met this guy a month ago."

Reggie's mouth dropped open. "But I thought . . ."

Kristin shrugged. "I know. It isn't like me at all, but it's right."

Reggie looked at Jonathan, but dismissed the thought.

"So about the *Lagabóc* . . ." Tennyson said.

"Oh." Reggie cleared her mind of the extraneous thoughts and focused on the *Lagabóc*. She could picture it on the table in Nate's house. She filled herself with the desire to have the book with her. Now. Without thinking, she closed her eyes and willed it to her.

"Reggie?" Jonathan's voice broke through her trance.

"I must be getting better at this magic thing." She opened her bag, and pulled out the *Lagabóc*.

18

CORDELIA'S RULES FOR HER
DAUGHTERS

•

*If You Make a Mess, You Have to Clean Up After
Yourself. Unless You Can Hire Someone to
Do it for You.*

T HAT WENT WELL," Jonathan said as he maneuvered
the Mercedes home from the game. Traffic was light as they
drove on the freeway. "You surprised me with the *Lagabóc*."

"I surprised myself," Reggie said with a laugh. She sank
back in her seat. Satisfaction rippled through her. Troubles
still loomed, but some of her worries had been assuaged.
She would be content with that. For now.

They pulled up to Nate's house. The long driveway led
them away from the street onto the privacy of the property. His closest neighbors lived in front of the house and
on the hillside below him. No one could see into or onto
the property.

Jonathan parked at the far end of the driveway. Nate's

BMW wasn't there. Reggie climbed out as Jonathan came around to get her. He blocked her path.

"Interesting news about Kristin and Tennyson's engagement," he said. "I don't know that I'd be making plans for the future in their situation."

"I think it speaks of hope." She leaned against the car. "I'm glad they're planning for the future. It's optimistic."

"So you don't still think it's a bad time to start a relationship?" He braced his hands on either side of her.

A shy smile slid across her face, and heat flared in her cheeks. She was grateful the dark hid the blush. "I don't think it's an ideal time, but sometimes you can't prevent things."

"Good to hear." He bent forward and kissed her, gently, sweetly, pulling softly at her lips.

She sighed, a tender release from deep in her chest. Could she let herself risk her heart to this man? How could she be enough for a man like him? Even if she was a fairy godmother, she was still just Reggie. Was she special enough? Forget the special. Was she enough at all?

"Let's go inside." He tugged on her hand and led her toward the house.

"We can't." She pulled back a little. "It's Nate's house."

"He's not home."

"Doesn't matter. I'm a guest here."

"He'll never know."

"I'll know."

Jonathan chuckled. "You are a little bit . . . old fashioned, aren't you?" He kissed the top of her head. "I like that. So we don't go inside." He lifted her and placed her on the hood of his car.

Reggie gasped. "Jonathan, we can't . . . you can't—"

"Watch me." He unbuttoned her blouse and flipped the

material from her shoulders to expose her collarbone. He touched his lips to the skin and lightly drew his tongue along the bone.

She squirmed as the sensation unfurled in the pit of her stomach. Beneath her, the heat from the hood of the car buttered her thigh. When Jonathan lifted his head, the cool night air chilled the skin of her throat in sharp contrast to the warmth beneath her legs. Her skin prickled in a sensory explosion.

"Jonathan, the neighbors. They'll see."

"No one can see back here." He pushed her blouse down her arms until it hooked on her wrists.

"Your car—"

"I don't care about the car." He unbuttoned her shorts, then slowly pulled the zipper down. With each click of the teeth, her senses buzzed. In one move, he pushed the shorts and panties over her hips. Her body didn't listen to her protests. She lifted up to ease the removal of her clothes.

"That's right. Let me see you." Perching her on the edge of the hood, he splayed his fingers low over her belly. His thumb slipped between her folds and rubbed the exact spot that throbbed with her need. She nearly jumped off the car, but his touch felt so good. Her own slickness lubricated the tiny circle his thumb made.

With his free hand, he unhooked her bra and released her breasts. The straps caught at her elbows and the lacy cups dangled at her waist. The moon lit his appreciating gaze, and she let her head drop back. Jonathan placed his lips at the base of her throat and traced a trail to one nipple. He laved it with his tongue, then let the air hit it. The acute contrast between the heat of his mouth and the cold of the air tightened her aureole to a not quite painful hardness. He waited until she almost grew uncomfortable, but before she could cover herself, he sucked the tip into his mouth. His tongue rolled over the nipple, shooting electric energy through her. He sucked her in and breathed her out, in and out, in and out, until each pull echoed in her womb. His hand lingered on her belly, his fingers seeking the recesses of her intimate regions. Her entire body trembled at the attention from his mouth and thumb. Her mouth opened as little sounds escaped. She grabbed onto the hood ornament beside her and twisted it in an effort to retain control.

Jonathan stepped back then. Her body and mind contracted in shock and disappointment, until Jonathan undid his pants. Heat coiled within her as she saw his erection spring out. He slid her closer to the edge. Her hands behind her back, she propped herself on her arms, her feet braced on some ridge on the front of the car.

He reached into his pocket and removed a foil envelope. He ripped off the top and rolled the condom down the length of his penis. Stepping between her legs, he slid himself into her waiting depth.

Her throat tensed with the moan of ecstasy that rose from her core. She muffled it, but above her Jonathan grinned.

"No one can hear you but me, and I want to." He ground himself against her so that every inch penetrated her.

She rocked slowly from side to side, feeling him inside of her. When he pulled out, she sucked in air as she emptied of him. She wanted him back inside, deep and hard.

He thrust forward again, this time bending his head to take in a nipple. She writhed at the exuberance of the sensations. The stars twinkled above her, but she couldn't tell if they were real or just a result of the building force within her.

Jonathan's breath came faster, and each inhale and exhale stirred her hearing to a keenness that elevated all her other senses. He pushed into her again and again, slow at first, then faster and harder, and faster still. She was at his mercy, bound to his tempo by her position on the car, and the exquisite agony built higher and higher.

And then above her, he let out a low, drawn-out hum. He slid deep into her and stayed there. With intense little quakes, he tightened his muscles, pushing deeper and grinding his groin against her. She arched so that the sensitive nub, so highly stimulated by his earlier play, met his loins, and she shattered. She cried out into the night, not caring who heard or saw.

As her breathing subsided and the electricity in her blood cooled to a steady glow, she remembered where she was. She would never have considered herself adventurous enough to make love on the hood of a car in a driveway. What had Jonathan done to her? But she felt no shame.

Jonathan pulled out of her and placed his forehead against hers, still breathing heavily. "Mercedes is a great car. I will never buy anything else ever again."

She laughed, astonished at herself and the abandon that had seized her. Now sensibility returned. "We really should pull ourselves together before Nate comes home." She shivered in the cool air.

He nodded. "And before you catch a cold."

She doubted she would ever feel cold again.

"At least our clothes won't be hard to find." He grasped the lacy cups of her bra that still dangled in front of her.

She giggled as he pulled up her bra from her waist. She rehooked it in back and then set to work to reassemble herself. He cleaned himself then returned to help button her blouse.

"I can do it," she said with a chuckle.

"I know, but I prefer doing it myself." He paused. "No,

actually I prefer going the other way." He unbuttoned the button he had just fastened.

She swatted his hand away. "I'll never get inside if you keep this up."

"I can live with that." He unbuttoned another.

She gasped in fake outrage and turned from him to finish fastening her shirt. "There."

He placed his hands on her waist and lifted her from the car. He placed her right in front of him so that their bodies touched. "Hmmm. It's just an easy lift back to the hood."

Her gaze flew to the spot, and then she noticed the hood ornament. It was twisted and askew. "Did I . . . ?" She pointed. "I'm sorry."

Jonathan's eyes crinkled in amusement and he gave her a wry half-smile. "I am never having that fixed."

HE LEFT HER half an hour later, after he saw her inside, after he saw she couldn't repress her yawns any longer. Truth was he heard his bed calling as well.

But he doubted he could sleep.

Something had happened tonight, and it troubled him more than he cared to admit. Oh, he was happy that Reggie and Kristin seemed to hit it off. Kristin appeared to be a great choice for godmother, just as Reggie was. Two different women with different strengths to balance out the job. He also trusted the old godmothers. He was thrilled that Reggie had decided as he would have—that the godmothers were innocent of the murder ascribed to them. The more he heard about the Council and its tactics, the more he believed the godmothers. And if they were right about the Council, then logically their worries about Lucas Reynard would also have a basis in fact. Reggie treaded toward danger, a volatile situation over which she had little control and still too little magic. She wouldn't back down either, and he had pledged his help to her. But even that wasn't what troubled him.

It was his own reaction to Reggie. When he had met Tennyson Ritter, his first thought hadn't concerned a man in trouble, but a possible rival. For Reggie.

Tennyson, to the best of his judgment, was damned good-looking. For a few minutes, Jonathan had thought Reggie might find the taller man attractive and intriguing. Jealousy clawed in him like a beast, a hideous creature. Until he had learned about the engagement. Only then had he relaxed around Tennyson, but he had still felt the need to claim Reggie. And he had.

But now he realized he was wrong. He hadn't claimed her; she had claimed him. He hadn't expected her to acquiesce to sex on the car, but she had. And claimed him as surely as if she had branded him.

The depth of his emotions overwhelmed him. He wanted to see how many other ways she could surprise him. He wanted to hear the stories of her childhood. He wanted to know what books and movies she liked. What music. He didn't know enough about her, and he wanted to learn it all. What made her laugh? What made her cry?

He wanted to plan days, weeks, years with her. He wanted a life with her, children.

He froze.

He was insane. He could have none of these things with her. Especially not a future. Not when he hadn't been honest with her.

His destination required no thought. He drove the Mercedes through the night as if it were on autopilot. Sliding his card into the parking garage kiosk, he waited until the arm lifted, then drove in. When he saw Nate's car, he parked next to it. With a fiery anger, he struck the steering wheel with his hands. Pain flooded him. Good. He hoped he had broken bones. The orange light of the garage showed that the BMW was locked. He stared at the car.

Never had he loathed anyone as much as himself and Nate. They made quite a pair. Deceit, games, anger, secrets, and the knowledge that he was responsible for everything gnawed at him. When this was all over, he'd make it up to her. If she let him. But how? What if his dilemma never ended? What if it never resolved itself? She had her own problems to deal with. She didn't need his. His ordeal concerned only himself; hers concerned the world.

He didn't matter; she did.

He leaned his head against the headrest of the seat. Damn. Would she be better off without him or should he stay to help her? Even now he didn't know which choice was more selfish. One would let him dump her problems, the other would let him use her. He had never thought of anyone beside himself first.

She needed help—the godmothers, old and new, needed help. He could help, but what if the truth got in the way? How was he helping if he didn't know whether he was helping?

Stay or go? Stay or go?

The questions whirled in his head until he was dizzy. His last thought before he fell into the most restless sleep in an eon of restless nights was that Nate probably would still make it home at his usual hour.

19

CORDELIA'S RULES FOR HER
DAUGHTERS

•

Remember Not to Judge a Person by His Appearance,
but it Can Give You Clues About
His Personality.

REGGIE WOKE UP when her cell phone rang. "Woke" was too harsh a word. Her hand flopped around the nightstand as she searched for her phone. Her eyes were still shut, although she tried to open them. What had happened to her? She used to pop out of bed in the morning.

She touched her phone and clenched it in her had. A quick glance at the face told her it was 6:15 A.M. She recognized the number from the bakery.

"Hello?"

"You can't come back here this morning."

She recognized Alfred's distinctive accent. "What's happened, Alfred?"

"They're tearing the place apart."

That shook the cobwebs from her brain. "Who's tearing what apart?"

"The bluidy Council. Are you no' listening to me? They're searching your apartment and the bakery too."

A sense of violation filled her. Why was the Council searching her apartment? "Do you want me to come—?"

"Are you daft? I just told you no' to. They're looking through everything. And sounding giddy about it."

Uneasiness stole across her. What could they find in her apartment? "Thank you, Alfred." Wait. "Alfred, why are you telling me this?"

"They made Tommy and Joy cry, the bluidy bastards. Tommy and Joy love you, and I'll be damned if I'll let the Council make them cry again. If that means I have to warn you, then I'll warn you, by God."

That made sense. She doubted he would go out of his way to help her. "Thank you, Alfred."

"Humph. I'll call when it's safe to come by. Tommy and Joy need to see you."

"I'll try. Please tell them I'll be fine. Tell them I miss them too."

"Yeah, yeah. Damn it, they're coming."

Reggie heard nothing, and then the connection ended. Well, what had she expected from the gnome, a declaration of support?

She stretched in the bed as waves of anxiety rolled over her. Had they discovered that she had seen the godmothers yesterday? But no proof could exist in her apartment. She'd been here at Nate's for two days now.

She froze. Icy tendrils of fear clutched at her. The copy of the *Lagabóc* was in her apartment. If they found it . . .

Before the covers were fully off her, she had jumped from

the bed. She ran into the living room. "Nate? Nate? Are you here?"

Muffled rustling drifted from the hallway.

"Nate?"

A minute later she heard his door open and his lumbering footsteps. He appeared in front her, bedecked in his gear. "You sound frantic."

"I am. The Council is searching my apartment. The copy of the *Lagabóc* is still there."

"Shit." Nate's gaze focused on her. "Get dressed. I'll take you over there."

She shook her head. "The Guards are still there. Alfred said he'd call when they've left."

"They're still searching? Then we might have a chance. I'll leave right now."

"No, Nate, you can't—"

But he had already started to shimmer and then vanished a moment later. Damn it, he couldn't risk himself, not for her. She had to get over there. Well, she could transport. She had proven that the other day.

But it would probably be better if she didn't show up in her nightgown.

Annoyed at the delay, she dashed back to the bedroom and threw on the first things she could find. She didn't know if they matched or not, but none of that mattered. She was dressed and ready to go in under two minutes.

She concentrated on the back entrance to the bakery. With luck the Guards wouldn't be behind the building, but inside. The air squeezed out of her lungs, and dizziness gripped her. Her vision went dark, and she thought she might be sick. A moment later, before she even felt the need of a breath, she stood in the alley behind the bakery.

She leaned against the wall, drawing in deep breaths and

willing the world to stop spinning. Transporting sucked. It sucked worse when she did it herself. She'd rather ride a donkey. There had to be a better way.

Of course, there was a better way. Not for transporting, but for sneaking in. She looked around. There. That napkin would suffice. She picked it up and shook it off. If her mother saw her wearing garbage, she would throw a fit.

With her wand, Reggie poked a hole in the middle of the paper. Hopefully the napkin would have enough strength to hold together. She poked two more holes for her arms to go through, and then tore off a few inches from the length. Now she needed some kind of belt to hold it together. Reggie trolled the ground again and found a broken rubber band. This would do.

She looked for a secluded and hidden spot where she could undress. The spot behind the dumpster would provide her with some privacy. Gross. But she had no choice.

Her mother could never find out about this.

She darted behind the large metal container and found that she really was hidden here. She peeled off the clothes she had just put on at Nate's, laid the altered napkin on top, weighed it down with a tiny pebble—the napkin would serve no purpose if it blew away—and touched the wand to her head.

At once the popping and creaking of her bones commenced. She winced. This time she'd change without ibuprofen, and it would hurt. But then she'd be free to get into the bakery and see what was happening.

The change happened much faster this time, but the pain was almost as intense as the first time. The compression of her bones ached with fiery heat that felt like she burned almost past the point of bearable. She could understand why most Arcani forwent transfiguration.

A few minutes later, she shook the final pops from her body and stretched. Her breath was ragged, and the energy cost had been heavy, but the pain had stopped. She was tiny. Her pile of clothes was beneath her feet, including the napkin; she drew it over her head, only to curse a moment later. Wing holes, damn it. Taking off the paper, she drew her wand and produced a scalpel-thin ribbon of fire. She sliced two long openings into what would be the back of the dress without setting it aflame and tried it on again. The openings were a little tight, but she squeezed her wings through. Her alteration gave an interesting cut to the outfit, but with the rubber band tied around her waist, it shouldn't reveal too much.

Now to fly without being seen. With luck, Groundlings might consider her a small bird or a large insect. Arcani would wonder why a sprite wasn't trying to conceal herself. Either way, she would try to avoid people. Especially since the napkin really wasn't attractive. With a squeak of impatience, she dismissed that thought. She so didn't need her mother's voice echoing in her head.

She flew up to the window that looked in on the upstairs landing. The screen banged with every breeze, and she found the loose corner that caused the noise. Wide enough to climb through. At least when she was tiny.

Inside, she flew to the gap between the floor and her door. There she hesitated. If the Guards were inside, there was no way they wouldn't notice a four-inch fairy wearing a white napkin. Too late for her to realize that white wasn't exactly camouflage. Not that she'd had much wardrobe choice.

She knelt beside the gap and peered under the door. The heel of a boot greeted her vision, but around the heel she could see three other sets of boots on the other side of the room. And a pair of stilettos. Sophronia was here.

"Do not tell me you can't find her." Sophronia's voice was strident. "Get out there, and don't come back until you do."

"Yes ma'am." The heels of all four pairs of boots clicked together. Reggie flinched, the sound striking her like the report of a gun. Then the boots flickered and vanished.

"Stupid, useless . . . ugh." Sophronia's shoes approached the door.

Reggie scrambled out from her position under the door and searched for a place to hide. She only had time to press herself against the wall before the door flew open and Sophronia stepped out. Reggie held her breath, but Sophronia's purpose-filled steps never slowed as they passed her and descended the stairs.

Relief nearly caused her knees to buckle. She clambered beneath the door and entered her apartment. A gasp escaped her. She flew up to survey the damage.

It was a wreck. Books and magazines lay on the floor, leaving the shelves empty. Her bed had been yanked from the wall, and the sheets thrown in a rumpled pile. Her kitchen cabinets didn't close properly because of handles and dishtowels jutting from them, and from one cupboard, a container of spaghetti propped the door open. A long spaghetti noodle dropped to the floor.

She closed her eyes at the mess, hoping if she didn't see it, it might hurt less. It didn't work. But she focused on the reason she was here and ignored the anger and debasement she felt. Had they found the *Lagabóc*?

She zipped to the shelving unit and peered behind it. The copy was gone. Perching on the edge of the bookcase, she dropped her head into her hands and wondered what she should do next. She had no excuse for having a copy of the *Lagabóc,* except to help the godmothers. The Council had to know she wasn't following their edicts, and if they didn't know yet, Sophronia would tell them soon enough. Unless Nate had gotten here first. A miniscule spark of hope lit in her.

The rattle of the front door jolted her into action. She flew down to the ground and hid behind the bookshelf. The irony of her hiding place didn't escape her.

The door to the apartment eased opened and someone slunk in, shutting it behind him. She couldn't make out the face quite, but the cap and muffler gave him away. Flying up, she hovered in front of him. "Nate."

He whirled around and looked at her in surprise. "Reggie? You really shouldn't do that to someone. Especially if you're small. I could have swatted you like a bug." He paused. "Nice wings, though."

"Nate, do you have the copy of the *Lagabóc*?"

He shook his head. "No. This is the first chance I've had to get up here. The Guards and Sophronia have been all over this place. You should see Alfred fuming downstairs. Especially when I hid in the freezer. It's a good thing they haven't opened yet. His language is not suitable for the public."

She flew an inch from his nose. "Nate, it's not here."

All humor fled from his gaze, and his shoulders sank. "That means they found it already. I was hoping to get to it first."

"Me too." She landed on an empty spot on the coffee table, which was littered with papers and, she believed, the entire contents of her junk drawer.

Nate circled slowly and examined the room. "They really did a job on this place."

"It doesn't matter." But her voice held no conviction.

"Yes, it does. They had no right to do this."

"Nate, they found the *Lagabóc*. They have evidence of me being a traitor." Her tiny body trembled. Fear coursed through her veins like shards of glass. "What happens now?"

Nate bent over. "First, I think you should become normal again."

She felt the drain on her energy as he spoke. "You'll have to leave then."

He furrowed his brows. "Why?"

"Because this napkin won't last as I grow, and I'm really too shy to parade naked in front of you. Despite being your housemate."

"You're wearing a napkin?" He peered at her closely. "You're wearing a napkin. I don't think you're going to start any trends.

"God, I hope not." His joking was helping her maintain her equilibrium. "The clothes I came in are in the alley behind the dumpster. I'll just put something on from my closet, but if you could retrieve those while I change . . . ?"

"Sure. I'll wait for you downstairs. We can discuss what to do next . . . after." Nate left the apartment.

With a touch of her wand, her bones began creaking again. The pain was more severe. Probably because she'd expended so much magic energy all morning. She untied the rubber band from her waist and the napkin billowed away from her. She tore it from her body and winced as a major spasm clenched her, then stretched her body.

The change was even faster now. The pain was still there, but the time through it was less. During the transformation's final snaps and creaks, Reggie selected clothes from the strewn contents of her dresser and closet. Pulling on the plain cotton T-shirt and jeans sapped most of her remaining energy. She sat on the couch to recover and hit the button on her answering machine.

Three messages. The first one was from Joy's father congratulating her on becoming fairy godmother. The second one warned her that the warranty on her car was about to expire, but if she dialed— She skipped that one. The third was from her mother.

"Reggie dear, I don't know if it's better to try this number or your cell. I left a message there as well. Luc invited us to dinner again tonight. Just a casual thing. I told him we'd be happy to come. He especially asked for you. I know it's last minute, but you can make it, right? Be here at seven."

Luc? Tonight? How could she possibly . . .

Wait. Maybe she could do some sleuthing. She could find evidence that the godmothers were innocent and that the Council needed to watch out for this guy. Then maybe she could convince them that the theft of the *Lagabóc* wasn't a bad thing, just helping the good guys. After all, the fairy godmothers were supposed to be independent thinkers. And doers.

Right. Because Luc would leave something incriminating lying around. But she had to try.

The doorknob rattled. "Come in, Nate. I'm dressed," she called out.

When the door pushed open, she realized her mistake. The blond hair and spiked heels didn't belong to Nate.

"I knew you'd come back here." Sophronia gloated. Her expression beamed with victory and triumph. She had her wand drawn and pointed at Reggie. "Don't move."

"I wouldn't dream of it." Reggie held up her hands like a cliché in an old western. "But Sophronia, you're wrong about the godmothers."

"Ha! They're out to destroy the Council, and they've brainwashed you as well." Sophronia walked toward her, targeting her wand on Reggie. "What will your mother say?"

"My mother? Is that all you care about? Humiliating my mother?"

"Don't be silly. That's just an added bonus. You copied the *Lagabóc*. There's no excuse for that unless you're trying to use Merlin's magic. When word of your betrayal comes out, I'll be a hero. I captured you. My place on the Council is assured. No one would dare replace me during the Time of Transition after this, and I may even be called to the Prime Council in London."

"Congratulations?" Reggie's heart hammered in her chest.

"Are you mocking me? You're just like your mother. She never understood what was important either." Sophronia sneered.

All that was missing was a mustache for her to twirl. Reggie would have chuckled at the image, but she knew she was in too much trouble. Besides, the truth was more important than trying to best Sophronia. "I didn't betray the Council."

"You stole the *Lagabóc*. Well, you had a cheap copy of it anyway. How did you get it?"

"Tennyson needs to study it. He said there's a—"

"He told you? You've been in touch with Tennyson Ritter?" Sophronia's eyes lit up. "This just gets better."

"Yes, but you don't understand. He's not fighting the Council either. Well, he kind of is, but not really." She was babbling. She clenched her fists in frustration. "If you'd let me explain—"

"You don't have to explain anything. You've been in league with him. Kristin too?"

"I've met her, but—"

"They're going to give me medals for this. Now stand up." Sophronia twitched her wand.

"Where are we going?" Reggie stood without removing her gaze from the tip pointed at her.

"To the Council. I'm sure they'd like to question you about the *Lagabóc* themselves."

"Sophronia, you've got to listen to me. The Council is wrong about the godmothers and Kristin and Tennyson."

"Why should I believe you? You've done nothing to allay our suspicions since you were chosen. Well, now it's too late. The Council will hold you until your trial. I'd start thinking about what you're going to say. You have to convince us all, not just me." Sophronia pointed the wand at her. "Give me your wand."

"What?"

"Give me your wand. I don't want you trying anything." Sophronia touched the tip of her wand against Reggie's neck.

Reggie didn't move. Despair filled her. Opening her hand, she called to her wand, which flew up from the debris on the table into her palm.

"That's better. I'll tell them you cooperated," Sophronia said, but Reggie heard the glee in her voice.

Slowly, Reggie held out the slim rod. Tears gathered in her eyes. She couldn't part with it. Not when she had had magic for such a short time. It felt right in her hand. It belonged to her.

As Sophronia grabbed the end of it, a loud spark flashed. Sophronia yelped and jumped back. "Damn it. You attacked me!"

"No, I didn't," Reggie said, still holding her wand. She tried to approach Sophronia, but the woman backed away.

"I didn't want to resort to this." Sophronia lifted her wand.

The door burst open. Nate crashed into the room, wielding his wand. "*Glaciá.*"

Reggie had covered her head when Sophronia aimed

her wand. When Nate had burst through the door, she had crouched down. Now there was silence. She lifted her gaze.

Sophronia wasn't moving. Except her eyes, which darted in every direction.

"What did you do?" Reggie asked.

"I froze her." Nate shrugged.

"Won't she get frostbite?"

Nate laughed. "I keep forgetting how much you don't know. She's not cold, just frozen. She can't move. It's a simple spell. I can teach it to you."

Reggie approached Sophronia, while the woman's eyes glared at her. Thank goodness clichés weren't real, because she'd have several daggers in her breast by now. "I thought magic was intuitive."

"A lot of it is, but that doesn't mean there aren't spells you can learn." Nate pointed at Sophronia. "Like this one. What was she about to do?"

"She wanted to confiscate my wand and take me to the Council for trial." Reggie turned to Nate. "I can't leave her like this."

"You want me to release her?"

"No. She won't listen to me. Can she hear me?"

"Every word."

Reggie faced Sophronia. "I'm sorry, Sophronia, but I can't let you take me right now. The Council is wrong about the godmothers, and I'm going to try to prove it, but I can't if I'm locked up. I need twenty-four hours. If I find the evidence, I'll turn myself in to the Council."

"You can't do that," Nate said behind her.

"But if I find something—"

"And if you don't?" He stared at her.

Nate was right. She couldn't trust the Council. She turned back to Sophronia. "*If* I have evidence."

"I can make the freeze last twenty-four hours. It won't hurt her. She'll just be a little hungry."

Reggie laughed quietly. "No, I couldn't do that. Not even to her."

Nate tilted his head. "You sure?"

"Yes. I'll tell Alfred to unfreeze her in about an hour. We'll be gone by then." She touched Sophronia's face. "I'm sorry. I really am, but I have to do this."

Sophronia's eyes glittered in fear and pleading.

Reggie whipped her head to Nate. "She isn't in pain?"

"No, except from her own thoughts. I can't help with those." Nate's chuckle rumbled low in his throat.

"Okay. Let me . . ." She gripped her wand. "I can't lose this. Magic feels so right."

"You're frightened." Nate sounded uncertain.

"I am. I've just frozen a Council member—"

"Well, technically I did," Nate said.

"You know what I mean. I think I've chosen my course." She sighed, then turned to Sophronia. "Twenty-four hours. I'll tell Alfred."

She ran from the apartment and heard Nate follow her. She found Alfred behind the counter serving the first morning customers. "Alfred, I need a favor."

Alfred placed an éclair in a pink box, took the customer's money, then looked at her. "Do you think I'm here for your convenience, missy?"

"Never that, Alfred. I just need some help."

The gnome dusted off his hand on his apron, then signaled Brandon to take over at the counter. "What is it?"

Not wishing to be overheard, she bent over and whispered in his ear, "In an hour I need you to go to my apartment and release Sophronia. Nate froze her."

A rare grin split the gnome's face. "Did he now? Good for him. But why would you have me free her?"

232 • GABI STEVENS

"Shhh. Could you please just release her? In an hour?"

Alfred drew his hand down his face. "Yeah. Yeah. I'll do it."

"Thank you." Reggie turned away, then pivoted back to the gnome. "If you hear anything about . . . me, or something, can you please tell Joy and Tommy that I'm all right? That I'm thinking of them and that I'm . . . I'm . . ."

"Yes, I'll tell them." The gnome drew his face to the side. "Now go before you get all maudlin on me."

Trust Alfred to strike the right chord. "Thank you, Alfred."

Nate took her by the elbow. "We'd better go. The Guards might come back."

She nodded, then scrunched up her face. "We'll have to transport, won't we?"

"They'll catch us if we walk." Nate led her to the back of the bakery. "My house is safe."

When they stood in the alley, she realized her legs still felt weak and shivery inside. "I don't know that I have the strength to transport myself."

"Don't worry. I've got strength enough for both of us." He hesitated only a moment, and then placed his arm around her.

She squeezed her eyes shut as the traveling started, and a moment later, they stood in Nate's living room.

Nate released her abruptly. But the transporting had caused vertigo again, and she lost her balance. Without meaning to, she reached out to keep herself from falling and grabbed a fistful of his muffler. She stumbled back, pulling the material with her.

Nate's head jerked back, and the scarf slipped.

20

❧

CORDELIA'S RULES FOR HER
DAUGHTERS

•

Surprises Should Always Be Handled with
Graciousness, Not Hysteria.

WITH A SNARL, he whipped the material from her hand and turned his back to her, but not before she caught a glimpse of ruddy fur and a long curved tusk.

"Nate?"

He said nothing, but wrapped the muffler around his head.

"Nate?" She laid her hand on his forearm.

With an angry movement, he snatched his arm away. Deep in his throat, he growled, but didn't turn around. "Get away from me."

The guttural tone of his voice gave her pause, but she pushed past her trepidation. "Nate, look at me."

He didn't.

"Nate." She grabbed his arm again.

He roared then, a horrible sound filed with pain, wrath,

and strength. Anger thundered in his chest, the vibrations rolling over her, and she steeled herself against crying out in fear. Her ears rang from the noise. She summoned every ounce of her courage to prevent her from bolting. This was Nate. "I'm not going anywhere."

He pivoted and faced her, his blue eyes blazing. She had never seen such a feral glint in anyone's gaze before. For a moment she almost believed he didn't recognize her. She almost couldn't recognize him.

He circled her like a beast would stalk its prey. His voice was low and ominous. "You should. You should run from the monster."

She forced her tone to remain calm. "You are not a monster. You are my friend."

"Friend?" His laugh bellowed from him like a howl. "You call this your friend?"

With a single slash, he rent the silk from his face. She hated that she flinched when she saw the snout and tusks where his nose and mouth should be. Coarse fur covered his face. He whipped the cap from his head. Long tufted ears pointed up from a mass of unruly fur. He yanked the gloves from his hands to expose claws where fingers should be. He ripped his shirt from himself to reveal a barrel chest that swooped into a scooped waist like the torso of a greyhound. "Is this what you wanted to see?"

He released a roar so loud and terrible that the birds in the trees outside flew up in fright.

He towered above her, wider and taller than any man she had ever met. Lifting his hand, he struck an attitude as if to slash her with his claws.

Tears filled her eyes; terror, her soul. Overcoming the urge to flee, she stepped closer to him and placed her hand on his chest. The fur there crinkled under her palm. "Oh, Nate."

His chest rumbled beneath her hand.

She lifted her gaze to his. "You are my friend."

He froze. For a moment she didn't know if he would strike her, but she stood firm. Then he backed away from her. "I don't need your pity."

Before she could respond, he strode from the room. A moment later she heard a door slam somewhere in the house.

Her knees buckled, and she fell to the couch. Tears fell in anger and shame at herself. She had felt fear. She had been horrified. He was still Nate, and she was the monster. After all he had done for her, was doing for her, how could she have reacted to him in such a cowardly manner?

She understood so much now—his attire, his voice, his penchant for privacy, his tendency to withdraw. But it created so many more questions in her head—why had no one ever heard of him, what kind of creature was he, and most importantly why was he this way?

Guilt sat like a hot stone in her stomach. She hadn't meant to reveal his secret, especially if he hadn't wanted it exposed. She admitted her curiosity to herself, but she respected him enough not to have wanted to hurt him in this way.

So in the last twenty-four hours she had met the new godmother, been branded a traitor and thief, frozen a Council member, exposed a beast, and, oh yes, had sex on a Mercedes. No one could say her life hadn't become interesting.

She had tonight to find concrete evidence of Lucas Reynard's activities and find a place to stay. She doubted Nate would let her stay here now.

And with that thought guilt rushed back through her.

Five minutes passed, then ten, but still she heard no sound from Nate's end of the house. She stood and realized she felt woozy. Too much magic this morning and not enough food.

A brief survey of the kitchen showed her enough ingredients for French toast. She whipped the batter together, grilled the bread, prepared two plates, and poured out syrup. Then she sat at the table and ate alone, staring at the other plate. She shoveled a few forkfuls into her mouth, then dropped the fork to the table. She scrounged around for a tray, placed the second plate on it with silverware and a small creamer of syrup and walked it to Nate's door. She knocked.

No answer.

She knocked again. She received no response again.

"Nate?"

"I can't believe you're stupid enough to think I want to talk to you now." His voice growled through the door.

She swallowed hard. "I made you some breakfast."

"What?"

"I'm not asking you to see me, but you need some food. We expended a lot of energy today."

"So you thought you'd fry me up some roadkill?"

"No, it's regular French toast, but if you prefer roadkill, I'll see what I can do." She hoped the humor would work.

Silence greeted the attempt.

"I'll just leave this tray here, then. Let me know if you want me to hunt down that roadkill for you." She put the tray on the carpeting in front of the door and walked away.

Before she reached the end of the hallway, she heard the door open. The dishes rattled, so she knew he must have picked it up, but she resisted looking back at him. He could approach her. Without turning around, she said, "When you've finished, just leave the tray in the hallway. I'll get it later. Unless you want to get it yourself."

She heard no response, but she hadn't expected one. She returned to the kitchen and finished her breakfast with a much better appetite than when she had started.

Only after she finished her French toast did she remember all the fun stuff that had happened this morning at the bakery, like leaving Sophronia frozen in her apartment. She needed to talk to Jonathan.

She dialed his cell, but after ringing five times, his voice mail picked up. Her message was simple: "Call me when you have a chance." She flipped her phone shut and stared at it with dissatisfaction. Maybe she should just go back to bed and start this day over.

With a sigh, she cleaned her dishes and put everything away . . . or where she thought everything went. She checked the hallway, but Nate had not placed the tray back yet.

Her phone rang. Snatching it up from the table, she noticed the number was Jonathan's. "Hello?"

"Hey, babe, what's up?" His voice sounded deeper, gruffer on the phone.

Without expecting it, tears filled her eyes. "I'm in so much trouble."

The words spilled out of her, leaving him no time to respond to anything. Sobs and sniffs punctuated the torrent until she had told him of the search, the *Lagabóc*, and the freezing of Sophronia. She told him of her plan to attend tonight's dinner with Luc and try to find evidence to convict him.

Jonathan broke in at that. "You can't be serious. Reggie, he's dangerous."

"I don't have a choice. Especially now. Alfred has probably freed Sophronia by now, and she has probably informed the Council that they have another rogue fairy godmother on their hands." Her voice broke. "If Nate wasn't there . . ."

He paused. "What did Nate do?"

"He was the one who actually froze Sophronia. And he transported me back." A fresh wave of pain washed through her as she remembered the result of his kindness. "He's been a great help to me, and I don't know how I will ever pay him back."

"He won't want any kind of reward."

"Doesn't matter. He's a friend, and I won't forget what he's done for me."

"He's gotten you into trouble, that's what he's done." He sighed. "He has secrets."

"Don't we all?" She was losing patience with him.

"What if his secrets are terrible?"

"Are you doubting my ability for judge for myself?" She heard the shrillness in her voice. "I thought he was your friend."

"He is. It's just . . . never mind. I don't want to argue with you over Nate. Look, you can't just waltz into Luc's place and expect to find anything. What if someone warns him that you're working with the godmothers? What if Council members are there?"

"That's a chance I'll have to take. Do you have a better idea?" She waited. "I didn't think so."

"I don't like the idea of you going to Luc's alone."

"I won't be alone. My parents will be there as well."

"Humph."

"Your voice sounds off a little. Are you getting sick?"

"I don't think so. Must be the connection." He cleared

his throat. "Promise me you won't do anything rash tonight."

"I'll try not to, but I only have until tomorrow. That's when I promised to turn myself in to the Council. Maybe I can find something to prove that the godmothers are telling the truth."

"I can't talk you out of this?"

"No."

"You're making me age before my time, you know that."

She smiled. "You're too pretty anyway." Had she really said that?

"Right. That's my problem." He laughed, but it didn't sound like the laugh held much humor. Did she hear a tinge of sadness?

"I'll be safe." *I hope.* "I'll call you after I come home." She closed the phone and drew in a deep breath. He was right. She might be making a colossal mistake by going to Luc's. But she had to go.

She dug her fingers into her hair and let her head drop. What if her courage failed her? No, that was a silly question. Her courage was irrelevant. She had no other options. The bigger concern was if she failed.

A noise in the doorway caught her attention. Nate appeared carrying his tray. He was dressed as he always was—scarf to his eyes, hat pulled low over his forehead, gloves, long coat. He nodded at her. "Thanks for the breakfast."

She smiled. His appearance was the best news she'd had today. "You're more than welcome." She hesitated, then took the risk. "So you don't want that roadkill?"

Nate's gaze pinned her, then his shoulders started to shake. His chuckle, rough and rusty sounding, filled her with relief. "You aren't afraid of me."

"Should I be?"

"Yes."

"Oh well. I guess I fail." She took the tray from him and started to wash the dishes.

"I could do that for myself, you know."

"Yes, but it's the only way I can repay you for everything you've done for me. And it's little enough."

Nate shook his head. "You are an amazing woman, Regina Scott."

"I'm just washing dishes." She knew she had to speak about what happened. As she finished up, she said, "I didn't mean to . . . see you."

"I know." Nate's voice held an empty note.

Reggie wiped her hands and faced him. "I'm not going to ask, but if you ever feel like telling me—"

"I won't."

"Okay." She lifted a corner of her mouth. "And if you're more comfortable not wearing all that stuff, I wouldn't mind."

"I would."

She nodded. "Consider the subject closed."

"Thank you." He walked to the coffeemaker and poured himself a mug. "Want some?"

Her eyes widened. "In all the excitement, I forgot to drink some this morning."

"Adrenaline will do that to you." He filled a second mug and handed it to her. "So what are your plans now?"

"I'm going to spend my day trying to figure out how to sneak around Luc's house tonight without getting caught."

The mug hesitated halfway to his mouth as he looked at her. "Good luck with that."

"You aren't going to try to stop me?"

"Would it work?"

"No."

He shrugged. "Then why bother? For the record, I think it's stupid and dangerous."

"You and Jonathan. You're more alike than you know."

He looked at her for a moment. "You may be right about that."

21

CORDELIA'S RULES FOR HER
DAUGHTERS

•

A Guest Has Almost as Many
Responsibilities as a Host.

WHEN THE MEAL was served, Reggie plastered a
smile on her face. She could only hope it didn't look fake
as she took in Luc's charming face and the élan with which
he treated each of his guests. Behind that debonair mask
lay a criminal whom she ached to expose. But how? She
had no idea what she was looking for, or where she should
begin to look for whatever it was she should be looking for.

She had a headache.

The food was as exquisite as the dinner the other night.
At least it looked that way; she couldn't really taste anything; her mind was elsewhere. The others were enjoying
the meal. Ian fawned up at Luc, while Del pouted at the
lack of attention from her fiancé. Her mother maintained
an air of polite interest, but Reggie recognized the calcu-
lating appraisal of the gathering behind Cordelia's expression. Her father simply ate.

There were a few other guests—the enthusiastic wizard from the other night, a wizard who worked as a successful businessman in the Groundling world, and others she didn't recognize—eleven in all. Thank goodness no Council members were present. Sophronia would have reported her by now.

That thought brought her back to the reason for her presence here. She needed to find some evidence of Luc's plans, of his desire to reveal the existence of the Arcani and magic, and to rule the world. How hard could that be?

She wished Jonathan were here to help her.

Darkness had fallen by the time the meal had ended. Reggie still hadn't found a chance to explore on her own. Looked like she had to resort to Plan B. Not that she had a Plan A, but Plan B sounded as if she had organized something better than a "visit" to the ladies' room. But how else could she justify traipsing around someone's house during a party? If the bathroom ploy didn't work, she was going to plead a migraine and ask to lie down.

The party moved into the spacious living room where carafes of coffee sat on the bar, along with the means to fix up the coffee—sugar, cream, crème de menthe, Bailey's, and other add-ins. Once again, a laden pastry cart filled with tempting delights stood ready to serve.

This would be the perfect time to slip away and—

The doorbell rang.

Luc perked up at the interruption. "Ah, he said he would join us for dessert, and his timing is impeccable." Luc crossed to the entry and escorted Jonathan inside.

Reggie snapped her mouth shut when she realized it was hanging open. If she didn't know what granting a wish entailed, she might have accused someone of doing just that for her.

Jonathan greeted the other guests, spending a little extra

time with her mother, as he made his way through the room toward her. Dimitri poured coffee for everyone as a maid passed through the room serving cakes and pastries to those interested. In the congenial chaos, Jonathan reached her and sat beside her on the sofa.

"Why didn't you tell me you were coming?" she whispered.

"I wasn't going to until I talked to you. You didn't really think I could let you do this alone?" he whispered back. "I called Luc and asked if I could join you all for dessert. He sounded thrilled."

"I'll bet. The great Jonathan Bastion, wand maker extraordinaire, added to his collection."

Jonathan's brows arched. "Collection?"

"Look at the people he invites to his dinners. Last time it was Tiberius Herald and other important business and social folk. This time it's more of the same, with some repeats." Reggie indicated the crowd with a wave of her hand.

"Don't forget the newest fairy godmother." Jonathan placed his arm around her.

"I haven't forgotten that." Reggie frowned. "If what Kristin told me was true, and I don't doubt that it is, then Luc would love to have me on his side."

"I know. That's why I had to come. Someone needs to watch over you as you watch out for the rest of us." He squeezed her shoulder.

A trickle of warmth bathed her at his words. She couldn't say no one had ever cared for her—her parents had always loved her in their own way—but she was accustomed to watching out for herself. It was nice to be told that someone else cared about her welfare.

"As much as I appreciate that, I still have to search this

house. I haven't seen anything so far." The dessert cart approached them, and behind it came Luc. "Damn. I guess I can't leave now."

Luc eyed Jonathan's arm draped around her shoulder. "I see you two are getting along. Does my heart good. May I recommend the Linzer torte or the Dobos torta? They are spectacular tonight."

The maid waited with a cake knife in her hand.

"I'd love a slice of either," Jonathan said.

"Or perhaps a sliver of each," Luc said.

With a nod of her head the woman sliced a thin piece of each cake, laid them on a plate, then looked at Reggie. "And for you?"

"Just a scoop of the sorbet, please," Reggie said.

Luc chuckled. "I forgot I am competing with a baker."

She felt as if she wore a mask when she smiled up at him. "I'm not the baker, but the dinner was more than enough for me."

"A pity you couldn't join us for the meal, Bastion," Luc said.

"I had too much business to attend to," Jonathan said.

"Ah, yes, your wands. Anything interesting in development?"

"Always, but I can't share. It would be premature." Jonathan fended off the inquiry with grace. Reggie wondered what exactly wand technology entailed, but now wasn't the time to ask.

"Ever so careful." Luc nodded. "I've heard of the secrecy surrounding your operation."

"Secrets must be kept," Jonathan said with a smile.

A shiver of unease skittered down Reggie's spine. Today had been a day for secrets. Actually, for the revealing of secrets. That she had stolen the *Lagabóc* and was working with Kristin and the aunts. That Nate was hiding his beast-like form beneath his odd attire.

"Is that why you practically disappeared seven years ago?" Luc asked.

"My wand makers live all over the world. Their hours are my hours. I cannot hold regular business hours. It was just easier to withdraw and keep to myself."

His words struck her. There was so much she didn't know about him, so much she had to learn about him and his business. But with Luc preoccupied with Jonathan, here was the opportunity she was looking for. "Will you excuse me please?" She shot a look at Jonathan and hoped he understood what she was about to do.

He gave her an almost imperceptible nod after first giving her a look of exasperation. "And so I couldn't be here for the dinner."

She stood and smoothed her skirt.

Luç said, "I completely understand, but as a good host, I have to ask if you've had a chance to eat."

Jonathan took a bite of his cake. "I stopped somewhere for some roadkill." Jonathan's voice was a little gruff from the bite he had just taken.

Her head whipped around. Impossible. It couldn't be. He gazed up at her. With those blue eyes.

She froze. Her heart screamed a denial of what her mind knew.

The room faded from her consciousness. Luc's laugh at Jonathan's joke added an eerie soundtrack for the turbulence of her thoughts. Roadkill. Nate had said that exact word to her earlier today in the same voice, gruff and gritty, just as Jonathan had said it now with his mouth full of cake.

Those blue eyes looking at her belonged to Nate.

She hadn't seen it before because the rest of Jonathan

was so beautiful. His thick blond hair, his straight nose, the strong chin, the white teeth, his lean build, his style, they all created a picture where that one trait, those blue eyes, didn't dominate. All Nate had were the eyes.

Jonathan. Nate. Oh God. Her stupidity drowned her senses, flooded her consciousness until even breathing hurt. Their names were the same. Jonathan Bastion, Nate Citadel. Clever joke that.

Cold seeped into her bones, into her gut, as ideas, evidence, slipped into place. She had never seen Nate by night; she had never seen Jonathan by daylight. Nate had been so willing to help her, Jonathan had been so sure she could count on Nate's help. Nate having all the information Jonathan had found; Jonathan so free with Nate's hospitality.

Well, sure, they were the same person.

But how? Why?

Nate was wider, taller, and looked like a monster. Jonathan looked like an angel, but a monster was on the inside.

Why didn't he tell her?

He had been lying to her, hiding from her this whole time. Why hadn't he told her? What did he want from her?

Her cheeks felt icy beneath her fingertips. She didn't even know that she had lifted them to her face. They trembled as she lowered them to her side again.

Jonathan jumped to his feet. "Reggie?"

"I feel sick." She rushed from the room into the hallway.

He followed. She knew he followed, but she couldn't look at him. As soon as she was out of the living room she searched for a way to escape, but she was too slow. He caught her on the arm.

"Reggie." He turned her around.

She stared up into those blue eyes and cringed. How had she not seen?

Luc came into the hallway a moment later. "Reggie, my dear, you don't look well. Can I get you something?"

"No, no, I . . ." She stopped as she caught sight of Jonathan's eyes again. "I need to get out of here."

"Of course. This way." Luc led them up the stairs to a bedroom. Jonathan held her upper arm the whole way. She didn't have the strength to pull away.

"Please feel free to use this room. Shall I send for something?" Luc asked.

"No, I . . ." She yanked her arm out of Jonathan's grasp and whirled away from him. "I'm not ill."

Jonathan stepped toward her.

"Don't!" Her voice was as sharp as a dagger. Jonathan drew back.

A look of understanding dawned on Luc's visage. "I'll leave you two alone." He backed out of the room and closed the door.

Jonathan crossed toward her. "Reggie—"

She twirled out of his reach. "I hope the joke was worth it. I hope you got what you needed."

"What are you talking about?"

"Did you have a good laugh? Good times, right? Lots of fun. Let's see how easily you can fool her. How stupid you could make her feel. She's new. She doesn't know anything about magic yet. I couldn't have been much of a challenge. You should have set your target much higher. Certainly someone prettier, someone more at your level."

He put his hands in front of him. "Reggie, I don't know—"

"I trusted you." Her voice rose. "Did you think I would never find out . . . Nate?" She spit the name out as if it were poison.

He stilled. "Oh, God."

"You sold me. I knew I wasn't good enough for you, but

you made me believe. You persisted. I didn't believe you would ever be so cruel. I was so stupid." She shoved her fingers into her hair and clenched her scalp. "You could never be interested in me. I'm not your type. I don't have anything you could want. What reason could you have to see me? You must have enjoyed yourself."

"I did, but not how you think." He reached out his hand to her.

She swatted it to the side. "Don't touch me."

"You have to listen to me."

"Why? What makes you think I want to hear anything you have to say, Jonathan or Nate or whatever your name is?"

"It's both, okay?" he shouted. "I'm Nate and Jonathan, but it's not what you think."

"Oh, so you didn't lie to me? You didn't deceive me?"

"I did. I did lie to you." He sank onto the bed. "But I didn't mean to."

"You want me to believe that?"

"Yes. I wanted your help."

"Help? You could have asked."

He laughed, but it was an angry, disbelieving laugh. "Because you would have listened to a monster."

"You didn't give me that chance. Instead you seduced me and acted like you cared about me."

"I did. I do."

"You've certainly proven that."

He bounded up and grabbed her wrist. She tried to wrench free, but his grip was too strong. "You will listen to me now."

She glared at his hand. "It doesn't seem I have the choice."

Yes, she did. She had magic. Why couldn't she remember that? She concentrated and visualized the hallway.

"No, Reggie, don't . . ."

Her breath squeezed out of her, darkness enveloped her, and she dematerialized. A moment later she stood in the hallway.

Magic was awesome.

Except for the nausea. Despite the dizziness that engulfed her, she stumbled farther down the hallway and fumbled with a doorknob. This was a smaller room. Inside she crouched against a wall and waited for her equilibrium to return.

Please don't let him find me here, please don't let him find me here.

She clutched her wand close, hoping the words would be enough of a shield to keep him from following. A minute passed. She listened for a door opening, for footsteps, anything that would indicate Jonathan had moved or left or something.

Her breath hitched as she tried to keep from crying. She wouldn't give him the satisfaction. She had more important things to do, like catch a bad guy.

An unnatural calmness overtook her, but she accepted it willingly. She had a job to do. She could concentrate on stopping Luc.

And here was her chance.

22

CORDELIA'S RULES FOR HER DAUGHTERS

•

Snooping Is Rude, Especially if You Get Caught.

SHE HAD VANISHED from his grasp.

Damn. Damn, damn, damn, damn, damn. Shit.

She shouldn't have been able to do that. He had been holding her, damn it. She should have taken him with her. Somehow she had separated herself from his grip. That took finesse, more finesse than she should have. Amazing. Even through the haze of disbelief, he had to admire her.

He had totally screwed up.

How was he going to tell her that he hadn't meant to lie? That he had strong feelings for her? That he was sorry for his actions? She'd never believe him now.

And she certainly wouldn't help him lift the curse either.

He dropped his head into his hands. He had never screwed up this badly before.

His growl reminded him of his other self. They were alike, he and Nate, in more ways than one.

He had to stop thinking of Nate as someone else. He was Nate. All parts of him. And he was a monster. Only by day he could use a mirror to recognize it.

Who else but a monster would have tried to manipulate a novice fairy godmother? In the seven years since the onset of his daily transformation, he had never done anything as deserving of his curse as what he had done to Reggie. Not even his original transgression had been as bad as this mess. He was worse than a monster. He should have told Reggie the truth. He should have trusted her to see past his outer hideous form and help the man inside. Instead he had used the man outside to hide the monster within.

God, what was he doing? Wasting his time feeling sorry for himself? He didn't matter any longer. He never had. Reggie needed his help.

Ineffectiveness swamped him. He couldn't stay in this bedroom. He couldn't help her from here. Urgency dogged him as he left the room and returned to the party downstairs. He surveyed the room. She wasn't there.

Luc appeared at his elbow. "Did you two work things out? Is she *well*?" A knowing tone colored his words.

Jonathan wanted to slash that look of sympathy from Luc's face. Luc was a different sort of monster, but Jonathan recognized him. It took one to know one. "Not yet, but I'm working on it."

Luc nodded. "The path of love is seldom smooth." He clapped him on the back, then moved on to his other guests.

Jonathan searched the room. Where was Reggie? If she wasn't here, she must have transported somewhere . . . Oh hell, she wouldn't leave. She had a mission. She was searching Luc's house. Alone.

That sense of urgency grew stronger.

Reggie was placing herself in danger. His heartbeat accelerated, and he tried to calm himself enough to come up with some sort of plan to cover her activities. Should he try to find her and protect her? Should he stay here and keep Luc under observation?

She wouldn't be happy to see him. Okay, so he could help from here. Monitoring Luc would be his priority. Then if he needed to, he could rescue Reggie. Ready to pretend interest in the party, he moved closer to the conversation.

THE LAST WAVE of nausea passed as she pushed herself upright. A quick sweep of her surroundings told her that this room was little more than another bedroom. She didn't believe she'd find anything in such a small bedroom, but she gave it a quick search anyway. The neatness, lack of clothes in the closet, and empty drawers told her it was unoccupied. Reggie peered into the hallway. It was empty. She slunk out of the room and hurried away to another room to see if she could find anything.

Another bedroom and a bathroom later, she opened the door to the master suite. Her pulse sped up. This was Luc's room. Surely she'd find something here.

She slipped inside and closed the door behind her. Where to start? She didn't think the bed held any secrets. The crisp corners of the comforter and the plush pile of pillows showed the work of a meticulous housekeeper (somehow she couldn't picture Luc making his own bed), but not a place to hide something. But there was still the closet, drawers, and desk to examine.

She started with the closet.

While she didn't approve of snooping, pushing herself past her level of discomfort proved easy. Her task was important. The huge walk-in proved worthless, except to show that Luc had a fondness for expensive and well-tailored clothes and fine shoes. And she had thought her mother was bad. Her hand brushed along the top shelf. Stacks of empty shoeboxes shifted at her touch, but she found nothing of substance.

The desk was next. She opened the middle drawer. Quills, pens, paper clips, and other miscellaneous supplies, but nothing incriminating. Of course it would help if she knew what she should be looking for.

Another drawer held notebooks, newspaper clippings from the *Quid Novi*. She flipped through the notebooks. They were filled with French poetry, if she could guess from the appearance of the writing. She couldn't tell if he had copied it or if it was original, but apparently Luc had a hobby.

A piece of paper listed names, including her family's, but that wasn't evidence of anything. Nevertheless, she pocketed it, just in case. Nothing pointed to Luc's plans.

In the bottom drawer, she found several files. These looked promising, but they were labeled in French. Like most Americans, she spoke one language. Still she riffled through the contents in case she recognized anything.

One file, labeled MAISONS, held articles about local houses. In English. Why would Luc have such a file? Then she found a picture of the house she was in now. A Groundling couple—he with a friendly smile and a double chin, she with short graying hair—stared back at her. They were an older couple, slightly plump and happy-looking. The accompanying words told of their beautiful home in Rancho Santa Fe and the decorator they had used. Handwritten notes appeared in the margin and red ink circled the picture with the name Dimitri written beside it.

A second article was clipped to the first. This one was

from the *San Diego Union*. It was the story of the death of the same couple in a freak sailing accident. Their bodies had been recovered near their overturned sailboat, but the cause of the accident was unknown. The article also mentioned how they had just sold their home in an unusual and quick sale and the heirs were having difficulty finding what the couple had done with the money. The date was less than three weeks ago. Luc had told her a friend had loaned him this house. She shivered. Somehow she knew that he was behind the death of this couple.

This was evidence. She could show these clippings to the Council and they could investigate.

If they believed her.

So it wasn't great evidence. She needed something else. Nevertheless, she would send the file home and show it to the Council.

She stopped. Where was home? Not Nate's . . . uh, Jonathan's. She couldn't send it to the bakery. The Council might find it. For lack of a better idea, she folded the articles and stuffed them into her back pocket. Thank goodness this had been a casual evening and she had worn jeans.

Half an hour later, after finally succumbing and checking the bed too, she accepted that Luc had hidden nothing further in his bedroom. She needed to find his office or a study, someplace where he might keep . . .

She stopped. She was so stupid. Luc had Merlin's Gifts. If she could get one of them, that would be evidence indeed.

She peeked out into the hallway. Good. No one had missed her yet. Or at least they weren't looking for her. Luc probably thought she was still pouting over Jonathan. Her heart clenched at that thought. She felt bruised by the entire episode. How was she going to recover from the hollow pain that mortification and embarrassment left in her gut?

She drew a deep breath and steeled herself. Right now the bigger dilemma was how to get to the art-filled room without being seen. There was only one set of stairs, and if she took those, she'd be noticed and have to rejoin the party. A balcony opened off of Luc's room. Maybe she could get down from there. Easing the door open, she sneaked outside.

The balcony overlooked a patio and yard. By day the view would be lovely. Now shadows hid the hills and contours of the land. But the shadows also hid her.

If she remembered the layout of the house correctly, Luc's room was over the kitchen area. Surely she'd find a door there. But if someone was in the kitchen . . . She wouldn't think about that now.

At the corner of the balcony, she leaned over to plan her descent. Enough light poured out from the windows to give her a view of her self-imposed obstacle course. If she hung from the bottom rail, the drop wouldn't be too far. She hoped. Too bad she had never taken up rock climbing.

Thank goodness she hadn't worn a dress. She hoisted her leg over the railing and balanced on the outside. The drop seemed higher from this side of the balustrade. Clutching the bottom bar, she lowered herself over the edge. The rim bit into her stomach. She maneuvered her hands to the lowest point, wincing as stucco grabbed at her shirt and scraped her side. She wouldn't escape this move without a few scratches and bruises.

One, two, three. She gulped in a breath, swung out, and let go. The slowest second ever followed as she hung in the air until her feet crashed into the ground. She rolled before her knees jarred any further. Taking inventory of her parts, she stood. All here, still working. So far, so good.

To her right were sliding glass doors to the living room, but on the left was a door to the kitchen and another one farther down. She chose door number two.

A quick twist of the doorknob told her the door was locked. She tapped her wand on the hardware, but the door still wouldn't open. Luc probably had some protections on his house beyond the simple Groundling technology. She looked at the tip of her wand and followed her instincts. Picturing a key on the tip of her wand, she felt the power surge down her arm into the wood. She placed the wand at the keyhole and turned.

Click. The door opened. Hmmm. Unlocking doors seemed to be her thing.

She poked her head in first. The door led into a small bedroom. Although tidy, it was being used by someone. The abundance of black clothes led her to believe that she had found Dimitri's room.

When she had visited the other night, Luc had led them past the main stairs to another hallway. She slipped from the room and oriented herself. To her satisfaction, the hallway appeared right where she thought it should.

She slunk into the hall and its enveloping darkness. The artifact room was at the end. She hurried to the door. It opened without a squeak. She was in.

Looking for a light switch, she patted the wall. When her fingers brushed against a plastic knob, a soft glow lit the room. She didn't want to risk more light, so she left the dimmer switch where it was. No sense in making it brighter than was necessary.

The artwork once again took her breath away, but disturbed her at an even deeper level. Every painting took on new meaning now that she knew what Luc—really she should be calling him Lucas—had planned.

The staff stood in the corner. Now that she looked at it, it looked aged, powerful, much more than the prop she had thought it was before. She reached out for it.

A hand clamped down on her arm. "Looking for something?" Harsh Russian consonants grated against her ears. Dimitri's grip was like a bracelet of rock.

She had already done this once this evening. She concentrated and tried to transport from the room.

"That won't work. This room is magically protected. You can't do magic in here. It reads only the footprints of myself and Mr. LeRoy."

"You mean Mr. Reynard."

Dimitri's eyes widened, and she enjoyed his surprise. For a moment. Then his expression changed and became harder than before. "You know. I'm sure Mr. Reynard will want to talk to you about this."

He pulled her to a door she had not noticed at the other end of the room. Despite her attempts to pull free, he had no difficulty in dragging her with him. A simple tap of his wand opened the door. He pushed her in and passed his wand over the space. "You will stay here until I have spoken to Mr. Reynard. Your magic won't work in here, but you're welcome to try." He slammed the door shut, and darkness engulfed her.

She lifted her wand. "Light."

Nothing, not even a fizzle. Maybe she could transport. She focused on the outer room, felt power surge through her, but she stayed within the darkness. A second try left her slightly drained, but no farther from her prison. She stepped to the door, nearly smashing her nose against the wall when it was closer than she thought. The back of her hand hit the knob. She bit back a curse word. That would leave a bruise.

She grabbed the handle and tried to turn it. It wouldn't budge, not even after she shook it and kicked it, which wouldn't leave a bruise, but rattled her bones. So much for unlocking doors.

She searched for a light switch and finally found one, but when she flicked it, nothing happened. Great. She pressed her back against the wall and sank to the floor. Hugging her knees to her, she waited in the dark to see how the rest of this evening would play out.

"THE GROUNDLINGS HAVE no idea who we are or how much power we have," Ian, Reggie's soon-to-be brother-in-law, said.

Jonathan regarded him. Ian really was kind of a prat. He wondered if Reggie felt the same. And then he cringed at the thought because he knew he couldn't ask her.

"Perhaps it is time they found out," Luc said.

Ian seemed too eager at this response. He seemed to be eating up Luc's ideas.

"What of their numbers?" asked Reggie's father.

"We have magic." Ian shot his future father-in-law a patronizing look. "How can they even think to be our equals?"

Jonathan hid his distaste for the conversation. But better Luc talked here than looking for Reggie.

Luc's creepy butler appeared in the doorway and nodded to Luc. Luc rose from his chair. "Excuse me for a moment." He walked to Dimitri.

This couldn't be good. Dmitri leaned forward to speak with Luc. For an instant, a sharp frown appeared on Luc's face, then it disappeared. He looked over his guests and met Jonathan's gaze. Jonathan crossed to the pair.

"Is there a problem?" he asked, hiding his disquiet with a smile.

Luc's face transformed into a mask of congeniality. "I'm afraid one of my cooks has cut himself. He'll be fine, but I would like to check on him. Please don't disturb yourself. Have another drink. I shall return in a moment."

Right. Because he believed the guy. "Sounds good."

Jonathan took a few steps toward the living room, but watched where Luc and Dimitri went. He waited until the two men had turned their backs to him, then he pivoted and followed them.

They had turned down the hallway that led to Luc's art collection. A feeling of dread grew in Jonathan's stomach. Luc had no reason to abandon his guests unless Dimitri had discovered something. And if Dimitri had discovered something, that something was probably Reggie.

The two men strode down the hallway. If he judged from the quickness and length of their steps, they were confident no one would notice their absence. He'd also say they wanted to get to their destination as fast as possible.

He stayed a safe distance behind them, waited until they stepped through to the art room, then stole up to the door to listen. He couldn't hear anything.

He peered through the opening and realized that the room was empty. He crept inside and saw a second door at the other end of the room. It was ajar. From inside he heard voices.

"What were you looking for?" Luc said.

"Nothing." Reggie did not sound convincing.

"Please. I am not an idiot." Luc's voice had lost its polish. "Dimitri told me you know my name. He found you reaching for the staff."

"I don't know anything about a staff."

"Reggie, Reggie." Disappointment colored Luc's tone. "I thought you were smarter than this. Dimitri, fetch Mr. Bastion."

Jonathan pushed through the door. "There's no need to fetch me. I'm right here."

23

❧

CORDELIA'S RULES FOR HER
DAUGHTERS

•

Etiquette Is Knowing How to Act in All Situations.

LUC'S EYES NARROWED. "How convenient. You've saved me the trouble of hunting you down."

"That sounds so uncivilized." Jonathan stood beside Reggie and tried not to notice how she leaned away from him. "I'll come peacefully."

Luc turned to Dimitri. "Keep them here until my guests leave. We shall deal with them after the party."

"Won't your guests realize we're missing?" Jonathan said with a calm he didn't feel.

"Nonsense. The two of you have already created a stir. Your earlier 'fight' generated gossip in the room. Thank you for that performance by the way. You've made my job so much easier. My guests all understand how young love needs time alone to discuss things. Together. I just have to tell the others you've left." Luc examined him with a disdainful gaze. "And to think you are considered one of the most powerful creatures in the Arcani world." Luc left the room.

Dimitri smiled at them. "You have no magic in here." He started to close the door.

Reggie started forward. "Wait. Could we at least have a—"

The door shut.

"—light."

The darkness was complete.

He took out his wand and said, "Illuminate." Nothing happened.

"You really think I haven't tried that?"

He pulled out his cell phone. No reception in here, but at least it provided some light.

"Well, that's going to do a lot." Reggie sighed. "Why are you here?"

Although he couldn't see her face clearly, he heard the exasperation in her voice. "I came to help."

"Really? You're doing a great job. Now Lucas has an excuse for our absence." Reggie sounded annoyed and scared. "Have you considered I don't want your help?"

"Absolutely, but I came anyway." He put his wand back in his pocket. "Did you find anything?"

"No." Then she stirred again and pulled out a sheet of paper from a pocket. "Maybe. I found a list of names." She reached it toward him.

He took it and read it by the light of the phone. He recognized most of the names. "What do you think this is?"

"A list of possible important recruits to his cause. Every Council member is on there, as well as the richest families in the area."

"Sounds reasonable. Anything else?"

She hesitated. "No. Nothing definitive."

"So you did find something else."

"Just an article about the Groundling couple that owned this house before Lucas. They're dead now."

"And you think Luc killed them?"

"Yes. I was hoping the Council could investigate."

Her voice sounded disheartened now. She was right. He wasn't helping her. Time to do something productive. He tried to examine the space. "So where are we anyway?"

"A room off the art room."

"Have you explored it?" He reached his hand out and brushed against her.

She sucked in a breath. "Don't touch me."

He felt the hurt in her voice like a physical pain in his gut. "Reggie, I know you're not happy to be here with me now, but we should work together."

Her hesitation said more than words could. "You're right. What do you want to do?"

"First, what do you remember about this room? It was light in here when Luc was here." He held up his phone. Its tiny screen did little more than draw the eye to it. It certainly didn't illuminate anything. Oh yeah, the phone was a brilliant idea.

"There's no furniture except an empty bookcase against the back wall."

"That's all?"

"That's all I remember. I was focused on Lucas and Dimitri, not taking in the decorating." Her voice was snappish.

"So really this is more of a large closet or storeroom than a real room."

"I suppose."

"Okay, we'll start against the door and go in opposite directions until we meet in the back. Feel around for anything—a vent, an opening, a crack."

"Fine."

Holding his hand in front of him until he touched the wall, he gingerly moved into position. They lined up shoulder to shoulder. The scent of her hair wafted up to him, and he nearly leaned into her to smell it more thoroughly until he remembered she wouldn't welcome his attention.

She moved away first. Right. They were searching for a way out. He patted the wall in front of him and found a light switch. He flicked it.

"I already tried that. It doesn't work." Her voice was smug and brittle at the same time.

He cringed to hear it. She was hurting, and he hated himself for being the cause of her pain. "Look, Reggie, I never meant to hurt you."

"I don't want to talk about it."

"But I do."

"What makes you think I want to hear any more of your lies?"

"I was Nate the first time I met you, the first time I showed up at the bakery. Do you think I could have introduced myself as a monster then?"

She hesitated, and he hoped it was a thought-filled pause. "I suppose I can understand that. But that doesn't excuse your secrecy later."

"I know. But I was under a curse. I was hoping you'd be the answer to my problem. You're a fairy godmother. I thought you might have a way to lift the curse from me."

"You could have asked."

"Right. Jonathan Bastion, the man who used to fill the papers with his exploits, his affairs, who later became a recluse. You couldn't have looked at me without revulsion or judgment. No one else did."

"I didn't know who you were. I wasn't an Arcani. I was

busy taking classes at a Groundling school, trying to start a bakery with my friends. Of all people, I would have understood."

"But I didn't know that. I couldn't tell anyone. I didn't want pity."

"Because deceit is so much more admirable than pity."

"I was cursed. Until you know how that feels, don't pretend to understand me."

"Then don't pretend to predict my reactions."

Their voices had become successively louder until Reggie shouted the last words.

After a moment of silence, she said, "Let's just keep looking."

The room wasn't big, so they reached the shelves in little time. The shelves were fixed and wouldn't budge even under his persistent pressure.

"Well, that was a waste of time," he said.

"Why? Do you have somewhere else you need to be?"

"Snarky doesn't suit you." He found the wall and sat down on the floor.

"I find snarky quite comfortable."

Silence followed. He flipped the phone shut to save the battery. No light spilled in from under the door. This room was sealed, and they were stuck. He could hear her breathing, moving, getting comfortable, the occasional sigh, but she didn't say anything else.

"So why were you cursed?" Her voice broke through the darkness.

"Seven years ago, I was seeing a woman."

He heard her sniff of disdain. He ignored it. "I was young, arrogant, and not nearly as smart as I thought I was. If you remember the papers—"

"I don't."

He hadn't wanted to relive his history. He hadn't acted honorably with the women he dated, but he had been young. And stupid. "I dated a lot of women. Then I met Diana Verlund. Her parents were wealthy Arcani. She was a couple of years older than me and well known for her humanitarian and environmental causes. We met and dated for a while. When she found out that I wasn't as serious as she, she wasn't happy. But then she found out that I had been dating other women while dating her. Worse, one of them had asked me to invest in the development of an exclusive, luxury Arcani resort in an unspoiled area of the South Pacific. I said yes.

"Frankly, the plan was irresponsible environmentally and fiscally, but Diana accused me of thinking with my . . . uh, nether parts rather than my brain."

Reggie snorted at that.

"Really, when it comes to business matters, I don't. The business venture wasn't sound, and I did come to my senses, but only after Diana cursed me. She told me that since I act like an animal, I might as well experience how it feels to be one."

He paused. He hated to admit it, but Diana had been right. "The next day at sunrise I transformed into a beast."

"And that's when you withdrew from society."

"Except at night. As soon as the sun goes down, I'm Jonathan again. Doesn't matter where I go in the world. In daylight I'm a monster. I can only be Jonathan when the world sleeps. Not much of a life." He let out a mirthless laugh. "It was easier to avoid everybody."

"Where is Diana now?"

"Last I heard she's in Africa doing everything she can for the Groundlings and the animals there."

"Have you ever tried an apology?"

He slammed his fist against the floor. "Damn it, Reggie,

don't you think I did that? Diana laughed at me. She said I'll change back when I change."

"Clearly you haven't done that yet."

"Clearly. I've done research, I've tried spells and potions, but nothing has ever worked."

"Is that the research the librarian was talking about?"

"Yes. I've been going to the Academy regularly for the past seven years hoping to find some counter curse. I said I was writing a book as my cover."

"I told you you're a good liar." The humor in her voice sounded caustic.

He paused. He didn't want to tell her the next part, but he owed her the entire truth. "You might as well know that I made a copy of the *Lagabóc*."

"I know. I went with you, remember?"

"No, I mean I duplicated the copy we made. So I could study it on my own." The words gave weight to the darkness. He felt as if it was crushing his chest.

Silence fell again.

"So as your backup, you thought you'd seduce me in the hope I could change you back." Her voice was small in the dark.

"No."

"Oh, please. We both know you wouldn't be interested in someone like me except for what I could do for you."

"Yes. At first, sure. But you surprised me."

"I'll bet. Especially when you discovered that I'm so new at this that I couldn't help you."

"No. I mean I hoped you could, but then I got to know you."

"You expect me to believe that? That you weren't using me to get access to the godmothers, the ones who still have power? Or Kristin? She's a Rare One, you know. I bet she has the power to uncurse you."

He felt his frustration grow. "What can I say to make you believe me?"

"Why should I believe you? You had so many chances to tell me the truth, and you never did. When Nate . . . uh, you were teaching me magic. When I was at the university with Na—you. When we talked about ourselves." Her voice hitched. "After we made love."

"How could I? I thought you would run."

"I didn't run this morning when I discovered Nate . . . you. Didn't you think maybe then would have been a good time?"

"You were frightened of me."

"Yes, because you tried to frighten me. But Nate was a friend. I trusted him and hated myself for my reaction to him. Did you know that? I hated myself."

He couldn't reply. She was right. He had no argument.

The silence returned and stretched into the darkness.

SHE DIDN'T KNOW how much time had passed. She did know that she had fallen asleep, and when the door opened again and she tried to move, her legs wouldn't obey. They had fallen asleep, and her neck hurt.

But nothing hurt as much as her heart.

Lucas walked into the room followed by Dimitri. "Now, where to begin?"

She was still shaking the grogginess from her mind. Jonathan blinked at the light, but he seemed more alert than she. "What time is it?"

"Late. My guests were enjoying themselves. And then I decided to rest a while." Lucas crouched down to their level and looked her in the eyes. "Don't worry. Your parents think you went home with Jonathan. They won't be looking for you for a long time."

She jerked her gaze away.

Lucas grabbed her arm. "Shall we start?" He pulled her to her feet, then grabbed her around the waist when her legs threatened to collapse beneath her. She had no feeling in them yet.

Jonathan jumped up. "Don't touch her." He lunged at Lucas.

With a quickness that showed training in the martial arts, Dimitri swept Jonathan's legs from beneath him, and Jonathan fell to the floor. The Russian drew his wand.

"I thought you couldn't do magic in here," Jonathan said as he righted himself.

"*You* can't," Dimitri said.

Her legs were buzzing with needles and pins as circulation returned. Lucas's arms encircled her waist. As she pushed him, his hand pressed against her pocket. The paper crinkled.

"What's this?" Lucas reached into her pocket and pulled out the list and the articles. He chuckled. "A guest list and newspaper clippings. What did you hope to prove with these?"

"That you killed those Groundlings."

"Tsk, tsk, tsk. Foolish girl. This isn't evidence. A list of people I should know in my new home. And the tragic story of the former owners of my house. Do you really think my morbid fascination with this couple proves I murdered these Groundlings?" He touched his wand to the papers, and flames consumed them. The acrid smell of smoke remained long after the flash disappeared.

"And now you have nothing." He brushed his fingers together as if ridding them of dust, and then gripped her jaw. His fingers dug into her skin, and Reggie forced herself not to flinch. He forced her gaze to his. "How much do you know?"

Resolved to say nothing, Reggie clamped her lips together, but a fresh sense of betrayal struck her when she saw Jonathan beckon Lucas closer. How could she have been so wrong about him?

When Lucas leaned in, Jonathan smiled. "Bite me."

Shock and a bit of reluctant admiration stole into her.

Lucas drew back and backhanded him across the mouth. Jonathan sprung forward ready to throttle him, but Dimitri trapped his arms behind him. A trickle of blood appeared in the corner of Jonathan's mouth. In the doorway, two other men appeared. Dimitri shoved Jonathan toward them, and they grabbed him by the arms.

"Usually it's ladies first, but we had a volunteer." Lucas jerked his head toward the other room, and the two men lifted Jonathan into the light.

"Sit tight, Reggie. Your turn will come." Lucas winked at her.

She shivered as the door closed again, leaving her in the darkness. The darkness no longer disturbed her. She knew it held no monsters. She had seen the monster. It was Lucas.

From beyond the door she heard an indistinct voice, and then a thump, followed by a cry. What were they doing out there? Every now and again, she heard laughter, and more rarely she heard a groan.

Her imagination provided pictures she didn't want to view. Each minute grated on her nerves, but she couldn't be sure when a minute had passed.

Wait, she could tell the time. Feeling along the floor, she searched for Jonathan's cell. There. She flipped it open. Four forty-eight A.M. Almost seven hours had passed since she had begun her search.

Another half an hour passed. Knowing the time didn't help. The sounds and voices had varied in tone, all indistinct, but she knew they weren't having a conversation out there. All too soon, or was it much too long, the door opened again. She jumped to her feet and swayed a little as the blood rushed from her head.

"I see you were expecting me." Lucas strolled in.

"Where is Jonathan?" She crossed her arms over her chest.

"Come see. Perhaps then you'll be more willing to talk." He motioned her into the outer room.

Jonathan sat slumped in a chair, his hands tied behind his back. One eye was swollen shut, blood oozed from the corner of his mouth, and a red bruise covered one cheek. Several gashes appeared where his sleeves had been. As if in silent mockery, the Caravaggio hung on the wall behind his left shoulder.

Her hand flew to her mouth. "Jonathan."

All her anger with him was forgotten when she saw him. He looked up and gave her a crooked smile. "Hi, babe."

His words were slurred. Tears welled in her eyes at his attempt at levity. "Don't talk . . ."

Lucas stepped between them. "Do you want to save him, *chère*? Tell me what you have discovered and whom you have told."

"And then what? You aren't going to let us go."

"You are right, but there is no need for this unnecessary pain." Lucas waved his hand in Jonathan's direction.

"Don't say anything, Reggie," Jonathan said from the chair. He tilted his head and focused his uninjured eye on her. "The new day always brings new possibilities."

She looked at him and understood.

24

CORDELIA'S RULES FOR HER DAUGHTERS

•

No Situation Warrants the Loss of One's Dignity.

SHE HADN'T ANSWERED Lucas's questions. Half an hour of silence had earned her several slaps across the face, one particularly nasty blow to her cheek, and a return to the storage room. The darkness permeated through her. Dismay grew in the pit of her stomach, and her cheek throbbed. She cradled it in her palm.

From the other side of the door, she heard a scream. Jonathan. She felt so ineffectual. Why was she a fairy godmother if she couldn't rally her powers?

Why couldn't she?

Just because Lucas said she couldn't didn't mean she wasn't able to. She was a fairy godmother, damn it, and therefore she had greater powers than expected. She sat on the floor and closed her eyes, letting the darkness flow over her, become a part of her.

There. She found the footprint of Lucas's magic.

It wasn't a wall exactly, but she felt it push back, contain her. With patience she examined the sensations, and in a few seconds she found a chink in the wall.

Picking her way through the spell, she reached beyond the barriers he had set up and felt herself expand into the openness. She didn't know how she had done it; she just did it. Lucas's magic would prevent her from physically breaking his constraints, but she could break them metaphysically.

Into that openness she released her power. She concentrated on the space beyond the barrier. "Help me."

The words glowed red in her consciousness. She felt the power surge through her, and then it drained her, leaving her on all fours and trying to breathe.

Something thunked in the corner of the room. What had she done? Tapping the ground, she found Jonathan's phone. She grabbed it and shone its light on that area. At first she didn't see anything, but then she saw a knot of wood. Attached to that knot was a staff.

The staff.

She grabbed it and nearly yelped when the wood burned in her hand. A strong blast of air blew her back and stole her breath before subsiding. A hazy glow emanated from the staff. Leaning against it, she stood.

A new sound came from outside the room. She took the staff, still warm in her hand, and struck the door with it. The knock resounded throughout the room, but the door remained shut. Then she remembered something.

She breathed in and focused on the anger and fear she felt. The frustration and desperation. Power surged within her. This time when she rammed the door, she also said, "Behave."

The door exploded outward. Wood chips scattered through

the room. The boom's echo disappeared as she took her place in the doorway, clinging with both hands to the staff. The men whirled in surprise.

Except Jonathan.

Jonathan sat rigid in the chair, his eyes shut. The muscles in his neck corded. New streaks of blood colored his face, and more trickled down his arm. His shirt was ripped, and his hair matted with sweat.

But that's not what caught her attention.

Although his expression held the vestiges of pain, triumph curved his lips in a sly smile. And then she heard the telltale popping and cracks.

Dawn had arrived.

As she watched, his nose elongated and his canine teeth grew longer and thicker, curling up at the end. Coarse oranged-red hair sprouted from his arms and face. His ears took on a distinct pointed shape. As the seconds passed, his chest grew wider, rounder, broader. The shirt ripped more as his torso became bigger, stronger. His fingers lengthened, and the nails sharpened into claws. His pants hung more loosely at his waist as his stomach hollowed out even as the side seams separated as his thighs grew massive. His feet broke out of his shoes.

His eyes opened. He had hidden so much when he was Nate. So much of him wasn't human. So much was pure animal. He was completely transformed. Only his eyes remained the same. His gaze fell directly on her. Despite the frightening exterior, she found a strange beauty in him now.

Clasping the staff to help support her, she stepped toward him, but he shook his head. Then she remembered their audience.

He slid his gaze from her and looked at the ropes that bound his hands. His mouth curled into a semblance of a smile. He turned his head slowly until he had the four men in his gaze. By simply tensing his arms, he snapped the ropes that had bound him. The pieces fell to the floor.

The two henchmen stepped back. Even Dimitri looked paler.

Jonathan stood. In the deep gruff voice of Nate, he said, "Bet you're regretting that last hour now."

"Impossible. You can't do magic in here." Lucas's eyes had a wild glint in them.

"I didn't do magic. This is who I am." With the lithe, graceful movement of a predator lunging after his prey, Jonathan pounced. Claw raised, he landed in front of Lucas. With a single slash, blood gushed from Lucas's face.

The blood seemed to goad Dimitri into motion. "Stop him!" Dimitri shouted.

The three men jumped into action as Lucas fell to the floor clutching his face.

The mêlée was a blur. Jonathan moved so quickly she wasn't sure where he stood from one moment to the next. Dimitri picked up a club and swung it at Jonathan's head, but Jonathan twisted, and the wood shattered over his shoulders. The other two men tried to attack from different sides at once, but Jonathan was too fast, and they were only able to deliver glancing blows. He roared as he fought, the sound adding to the horror of the fray. More than once she saw the henchmen recoil and scream as Jonathan's claws sliced at them and met flesh. The artwork rattled on the wall, and the Caravaggio crashed to the ground.

It was horrible to watch. "Jonathan, no! You are not an animal!" she cried.

He looked up for a moment, just as Dimitri stabbed a knife into his shoulder. Jonathan swept his arm out, knocking Dimitri and the knife from him.

A second later, Reggie felt a sharpness pressing into her neck. She let out a yelp.

Jonathan looked at her and froze.

Lucas drove the tip of his wand into the side of her neck. Lucas grabbed her arm and forced it behind her. "Yes, Mr. Bastion. I suggest you cease your travails."

The men panted as Jonathan stilled. Dimitri picked himself up from the ground.

Lucas stood behind her, but she could smell the coppery, tangy scent of his blood. A few warm drops fell on her neck and she shuddered.

"While you may have the physical advantage, I have the intellectual one." He shoved his wand harder against her neck, causing her head to bend to the side. "Hold him."

Jonathan growled, but didn't move as the two men picked themselves up from the floor. Bleeding and limping, they appeared a little hesitant, but they grabbed his arms.

"You just have to know a man's—" Lucas chuckled "—or beast's weakness. And she is his."

Dimitri hurried to his boss. "Sir, your eye."

She hadn't looked at Lucas yet, but at those words she turned. A deep gash marred Lucas's face on the left side. His eye hung against his cheek and blood flowed from the wound.

"Sir, we must take care of that."

"I must take care of this first." Lucas pressed the wand into her neck again. "Tell me who knows about me."

"No one," Jonathan growled.

"I don't believe you think I'm serious." The wand twitched in Lucas's hand.

"No one," Jonathan bellowed. "Just us. The godmothers."

"So then, with you gone, I can continue my work."

He removed the wand from her neck and pointed it at

Jonathan. A blast of power shot from the end, and Jonathan jerked back.

"No!" she screamed.

The staff blazed in her hand. Energy flowed from the staff into her, renewing her, giving her strength. She cast off Lucas's grasp and ran to Jonathan. A hot wind blew through the room. The two henchmen dropped their grips on Jonathan and backed away as if in fear of her. She propped herself under Jonathan's shoulder and tried to support him. She lifted the staff and rammed it into the floor. "Home."

A great flash filled the room. The heat grew almost unbearable, and then it died away.

They were no longer at Lucas's. They were in the bakery.

Alfred stared at them, and Joy and Tommy came running out of the kitchen.

Reggie swayed on her feet. She let the staff fall to the ground. "Hi, guys." Then the room grew black and everything disappeared.

Jonathan caught her as she pitched forward. He ignored the pain that shot through his arm as his action tugged on his shoulder wounds. He scooped her up and held her against him, although he hated to do it. His fur was so coarse, so rough, and so matted with blood.

Alfred ran in front of Tommy and Joy, brandishing his wand. "I dinnae know who you are—"

"It's me. Nate," Jonathan said.

"Nate?" Incredulity filled Alfred's voice.

"Nate? You're not wearing your costume," Tommy said. "You must be more comfortable like this."

The simple acceptance in Tommy's face surprised Jonathan. Tommy showed no fear. Until he saw Reggie. "Is Reggie sick?"

"No, Tommy, but she's hurt. I need to take care of her."

Too much magic. Damn it. She had used too much magic. He was fine. He had just been waiting for an opportunity to strike. It took more than one blast to stop the beast. "Where can I take her?"

Alfred had been gaping, until the question snapped him into action. He whirled to Joy, who had been backing slowly away. "Dinnae worry, Joy. Reggie'll be fine. She just needs to rest. Why dinnae you go back to the kitchen?"

Joy nodded and dashed into the other room.

Tommy's eyes shimmered with tears. "Why isn't she waking up?"

Alfred turned to Tommy. "Tommy, I need you to help Joy. Make sure she is no' scared, okay?"

"Okay, Alf. Nate, you promise to take care of Reggie?"

"I promise, Tommy."

Tommy ran into the kitchen.

Alfred's eyes narrowed. "You're really Nate?"

"Yes, and I'm sorry. I didn't want to upset Tommy and Joy. Reggie would hate that." Jonathan looked around. "I can't stay here."

"You're probably right, but the lass does no' look like she's in any shape to travel." Alfred frowned.

"She won't have to. I will."

"You dinnae look so good yourself."

"I'm fine."

"Sure you are."

"Don't worry about me. I'll take care of her."

"You have no' done the best job so far." Alfred reached out and wiped Reggie's bloody cheek with a rag.

"I know that," Jonathan growled.

"Dinnae bark at me, you daft beast. I'm here to help." Alfred picked up the staff and stared at it. "This is a powerful thing."

"Don't let the Council get it."

"I won't. Now you'd better go. They've been watching us. You need to take her—"

"Home." He knew where to take her. Without waiting for Alfred's response, Jonathan transported. In seconds he was standing outside Cordelia's house. Reggie's mother would help.

Reggie hadn't stirred since she collapsed at the bakery. Her breathing was shallow. Her pallor was off. Her eyelids appeared blue and her lips were almost white. Too much magic. She didn't have the skills yet.

He kicked at the door. And then he kicked again. And again.

The door opened revealing Cordelia in her robe. "Honestly, there is no need—" Cordelia stared up at him and screamed. Then she saw Reggie in his arms and screamed louder.

"Move over, woman. She needs a bed." He pushed past Cordelia and strode into the house.

The screams had summoned Vincent and Del. And Ian, although he lagged behind the other two as if he wanted to assess the situation before getting involved. They all stopped short when he appeared. None of them moved or spoke.

"Her room. Where is her room?"

Del blinked and pointed to the stairs.

Jonathan took them two at a time. His strides were huge, but he cradled Reggie to him so that he didn't jar her at all. At the top of the stairs, he bellowed, "Which room?"

Del was first up the stairs. She ran in front of him and opened the second door on the right.

He carried Reggie in and laid her on the bed he found. Although he hated to leave her even for a second, he ran into the bathroom and grabbed a washcloth. When it was wet, he returned to Reggie's side. With infinite care, he started to wipe the grime and blood from her skin.

"I can do that." Cordelia walked in, back erect, carrying a bowl filled with water. She took the washcloth from him and started to clean her daughter.

Jonathan stood back. He didn't want to hand the job over, but he was afraid his clumsy paws might hurt her.

The rest of the family came into the room. Her father turned to him, then looked away. "What happened?"

"Too much magic." Jonathan felt the guilt. She had pushed herself beyond the limits for him.

"The blood?" Vincent asked.

"Mine. And others. Not hers. The story can wait. We need to help her."

Reggie looked so fragile there on the bed. Her dark hair rioted on the pillow, a stark contrast to her skin, which still lacked color. He couldn't detect the rise and fall of her chest. His own heart cramped in his.

Cordelia wiped Reggie's neck, then lifted one limp arm to cleanse it. Jonathan winced at the fear and determination in Cordelia's face.

It was his fault. He stared down at Reggie, willing her to stir, to wake, to yell at him again and be angry.

Ian stepped forward. "Yes. Well, thank you. We'll take it from here. You can . . . uh, leave."

Jonathan loosed a deep growl, and enjoyed seeing the color drain from Ian's face. "I'm not going anywhere."

"Jonathan, stop being a bully."

His gaze flew to Reggie's face. Her eyes were still closed, but she *was* breathing, and she leaned into Cordelia's hand as it stroked her face. Reggie's voice had been weak and whispery, but he had never heard anything more beautiful in his life.

"Jonathan isn't here, dear," said Cordelia, wiping Reggie's

neck with the cloth. A bright red mark left by Lucas's wand remained after the cleansing.

"Yes, he is." Reggie rolled her head to the side. She opened her eyes and caught his gaze.

He moved forward around Ian and Vincent and completely ignored Del, who had pressed herself against the wall. Cordelia's eyes widened, but he ignored her as well. He knelt beside the bed and gazed at Reggie. "How are you doing?"

With trembling fingers, she reached up and cupped his face. "My Nate."

He grabbed her hand and lifted it from him. "Don't touch me."

She sighed. "You stupid man. You got shot."

"Just in the shoulder. He couldn't aim well with just one eye." He placed her hand beside her. "It takes more than one puny sorcerer to bring me down."

"He blasted you. How was I supposed to know you're too stubborn to die? You frightened me."

"*You* frightened *me*. How could you have used so much magic?"

"I needed to save you."

A hint of warmth filled him at her statement. "Does this mean I'm forgiven?"

"Maybe." She drew in a deep breath and laid her head back.

"Enough. Don't tire yourself." He wanted to reach out and stroke her hair, but he felt dirty. He stood and faced her family. "She needs food and water."

"Call a doctor first." Reggie said, but her eyes drifted shut. "Jonathan was shot."

"I'm fine."

Cordelia looked at him. "Jonathan?"

"Yes." He faced Cordelia, bracing himself for the horror he knew would appear in her face.

She stared at him, but her expression never changed. "Maybe you should clean up."

That wasn't what he expected. "She needs food. Something to give her strength."

Del straightened up. "I'll do it." She left the room.

"You'll probably need something else to wear too. I'll bring you some sweats," said Vincent, and he disappeared after his daughter.

Cordelia bent over Reggie again and brushed her hair from her forehead. "My poor baby."

Ian stepped closer to him. "Are you really Jonathan Bastion?" A look of revulsion distorted his face.

Jonathan glared at him, and Ian stepped back.

"Don't be a putz, Ian," said Reggie from the bed.

"I don't know what you mean, Reggie," said Ian, drawing himself upright. He still fell short of Jonathan's chin by a good six inches. "I have the right to know if this mon— m-m-man means us harm."

"But that's not what you asked, putz," Jonathan said.

Ian opened his mouth to speak again, but Vincent walked in. He carried sweats and towels. "I thought perhaps you'd enjoy a shower."

"I'd like that," Jonathan said.

"I think you'll just fit into ours." Vincent gestured to the hallway.

As Jonathan left the room, he heard Cordelia ask Reggie what happened. In a halting, weak voice, Reggie started explaining, starting with the *Lagabóc*.

When Jonathan returned, his fur damp from a quick shower and the sweats dangling from his waist, he felt better. He had used one towel to staunch the blood from the wound and had torn a second towel into strips to hold the pad in place. A sloppy bandage at best, but it would serve. He would replace the towels as soon as he was able. He had also ripped the sweats at the knees so they would fit better. His old clothes were a loss. He left them with the ruined towels. Shirtless wasn't his choice, but he doubted Vincent had anything that would cover him in this form.

As he walked into the room, Del jumped. He didn't blame her. He still did that when he saw himself in the mirror. Reggie sat up in the bed with a tray of food in front of her. She smiled at him, then finished her tale.

"And then I transported us to the bakery, and I don't remember anything else."

"This is incredible." Cordelia sat back on the bed.

Jonathan looked at the shocked faces of Reggie's parents and sister. And then he noticed an empty spot against the wall. "Where's Ian?"

"Right there . . ." Del pointed at the other side of the room, but Ian was gone. "Where did he go?"

Uneasiness stole into Jonathan. Ian was too much of a stooge to accept their story without arguing. His absence didn't bode well.

Del said, "I'm going to look for Ian." She dashed from the room.

Cordelia looked up at Jonathan. "I do believe there is more to her story than just what Luc has done."

Reggie shook her head. "Mother, don't bother him now."

"She has the right to know, Reggie. I plan to be a part of your life for a long time." Jonathan crossed his arms over his chest. He hated that he wasn't covered. The coarse hair on his arms rubbed against those on his torso. He had never felt so exposed in his life. But Reggie's reaction, a mixture of surprise and delight gave him strength. "I'm cursed."

"I think we already knew that," Vincent said with a hint of impatience in his voice.

"I've been hiding for seven years because of this." He held his arms wide. "I came to your party because of Reggie. I was hoping a fairy godmother could find a counter curse."

"You were using Reggie?" Cordelia's gaze grew frosty.

"We've already discussed this, Mother." Reggie placed her hand on Cordelia's arm.

"I'm willing to make it up to her, but now is not the time." Unease prickled along his spine. "We have to decide what to do."

"I know what to do." Reggie turned her face toward him. Her dark brown eyes captured his gaze. "I'm going to turn myself in to the Council."

25

❧

CORDELIA'S RULES FOR HER DAUGHTERS

•

Know Your Priorities.

A RE YOU INSANE?" Jonathan glared at her.

"You know, I haven't decided if I've forgiven you yet. Don't push it." She pushed herself up, only to be pushed back onto the bed.

"You can't get up." Jonathan scowled at her. "You almost died earlier."

"Watch me." She swung her feet off the bed and tried to stand, but her legs wouldn't hold her and she fell back onto the mattress. She glanced up at Jonathan. His head cocked to the side as if to say, "I told you so."

A deafening boom reverberated through the house. The windows shook, and the doors rattled. "What was that?" she asked.

Vincent ran to the window. "Sophronia is outside with about two dozen Guards."

Sophronia was here? She glanced at Jonathan, who had rushed to the window.

"They're setting up for another attack." He turned to them. "We need to set up more protections."

"I'm on it." Vincent ran from the room, brandishing his wand.

Cordelia jumped to her feet. "Ha. You aren't doing this without me." She turned to her daughter. "Don't you dare move." And she left the room.

A second loud boom crashed through the house. Reggie fisted her hands into the bed covering as the sound dissipated, but she noticed a tiny crack in the plaster. Good thing her parents lived in an exclusive neighborhood. Groundlings would have noticed the explosions.

Her father had better hurry with those shields, but even that was stopgap. The extra protections could buy them time, but no individual protections could withstand an assault from the Guards forever. Reggie struggled to get off the bed.

Jonathan held her down. "No, you don't. We've told you to stay in bed."

"I have to see her. She's after me. I'll turn myself in, and she'll leave everybody else alone."

He shook his head. "Sophronia won't be satisfied until she inflicts some damage on your mother. They've already put something on the house. I felt their footprint. They can't come in, but my guess is they've put a spell over the house so we can't leave either."

How much more could she muck everything up? Not only did the Council know that she was a traitor to them, Lucas now knew that she was onto him. Sophronia was attacking her parents' house in an effort to find her, and so she had involved her family. And she had exposed Jonathan. How many more lives could she ruin?

"I think Ian was the one who told Sophronia we were here." Jonathan looked out the window.

"Ian?"

"Don't tell me that surprises you?"

"It doesn't." And now Del was going to be affected by this. Chalk up another wrecked life to her total. "I'm getting up." She placed her feet on the ground.

"We'll go somewhere else. I'll take you." Jonathan swept her into his arms.

"We can't get through. You said they placed a shield."

"I can. I don't need magic to break through." He straightened to his full height.

"Put me down." She shoved against his chest. "I'm not fighting. If I can talk to the Council, maybe they will believe me. Lucas's threat is bigger than me. I don't matter, but we have to stop Lucas."

"They won't listen." He carried her toward the door.

"It doesn't matter. I can't keep placing everyone in danger. Put me down." Reggie punched his arm. He winced, and she remembered his shoulder wound. She patted the makeshift bandage gently. "Sorry."

Jonathan looked down at her. "Reggie, they're here to arrest you, to shut you away."

"I know. Now will you put me down?"

He blew out a puff of air. "You are so stubborn."

"I know. That's how I got through childhood and started a bakery. You're sweet to care, but I have to do this." She placed a kiss on his cheek.

He placed her on the ground and stepped back. "How can you do that?"

"Do what?"

"Kiss me?"

"Because I . . ." She stopped and drew a deep breath. "Because I think I love you."

He froze, and she felt her cheeks blaze. "I just thought you should know before I . . . uh, become a prisoner."

He struck his chest. "How can you love this?" His voice rumbled with an animalistic timbre. "I lied to you, deceived you, and, hello, I'm a monster."

"I'm not perfect either, you know." She waited.

"Damn it, Reggie, you have no business loving me." He paced to the other end of the room and whirled to face her. "I won't let you."

"Excuse me?"

"You know what I mean." He glared at her.

"Why are you so upset?"

"Because I care about you. Because I may just love you too."

She stared at him, then she threw her arms around him.

"Stop that." He peeled her arms from his neck. "Don't touch me."

"You are so cute when you're cranky." She stroked his cheek again, and almost laughed when he pulled away. "But I don't have time now. I have to turn myself in."

"Reggie, you can't."

"What do you want me to do?"

"Stay with me," Jonathan said. And she watched that big, strong monster wilt before her.

She stared into his eyes, those beautiful blue eyes, and her heart broke a little. "I can't."

She started out of the room, only to be knocked back by a third crash of magic against the walls.

As the final ripples of the magic died down, Sophronia's voice sounded through the house. "Good morning, Reggie. I know you can hear me."

Reggie shivered. The magically enhanced voice reached every corner of the room and vibrated under her feet.

"Don't do this to your family. Come out now, and we'll make sure they are safe."

Even though Reggie couldn't see her, she could picture Sophronia with a wide, triumphant grin on her face.

Jonathan stepped beside her. "You can't listen to her."

"Perhaps you need a little incentive," Sophronia's voice continued. "We can work out a little trade."

What was she talking about? Reggie crossed to the window and peered out. Two Guards held Del by the upper arm. What had Del done?

Behind her, Jonathan growled. "She can't be serious. The Council can't condone kidnapping."

Cordelia rushed back into the room. "Sophronia has Adelaide."

"I know, Mother." Defeat dragged Reggie's shoulders down. "Don't worry. I'll make the trade. Sophronia will call off the attacks as soon as I go outside."

"Are you crazy?" Cordelia grabbed Reggie's hands. "I'm not letting you go out there. This isn't some sort of bargain, one daughter for the other. You're staying here where you're safe."

Shock didn't describe how she felt. Her mother was defending her? "But—"

"Actually, I'm thinking she should." Jonathan leaned back against the wall.

Reggie gaped at him.

"I have a plan."

SHE DIDN'T LIKE it. She didn't like it at all. Someone was going to get hurt.

"Don't you think—"

"It'll work, honey," her father said.

"It will work, Reggie," Jonathan said.

Cordelia just nodded.

"Fine." Reggie crossed to the front door and flung it

open. Five minutes had elapsed since she had told Sophronia she was coming out. She stood in the doorway and blinked into the sunshine, then stepped over the threshold. She reached the edge of the flagstones in front of the door and felt her father's shield roll over her shoulders and allow her to pass. It worked. Daddy's magic was meant to keep out anyone not in the family, not keep anyone in. She took another two steps and hit the barricade of the Guards' magic preventing her from leaving.

"I'm here, Sophronia."

"Yes, you are. Where is your wand?" Sophronia called.

"Right here." Reggie removed her wand and laid it on the ground. "Stay," she whispered as if it were a trained pup. She would need it in a moment.

Reggie lifted her hands in front of her. "I'm ready."

Sophronia lifted her wand, and the two Guards who held Del stepped forward bringing Del between them. Del's expression looked miserable. Reggie longed to shout out some words of encouragement, but knew she couldn't. Not yet.

Four more Guards broke rank, brandishing their wands. They would have to remove the shield before Reggie could step through. Sophronia joined them. Clearly she had wanted to add her signature to the magic that would bring down the house of her rival. The triumphant gloat on her face made Reggie almost eager for the next part of the plan.

With a sudden flick, Sophronia removed the first part of the barrier, and the Guards followed with their own like movements. A moment later Reggie felt the magical curtain lift and knew she was free to walk through. She hesitated.

"What are you waiting for? You haven't changed your mind?" Sophronia shouted, her triumphant look taking on the aspects of anger.

"Not at all." Reggie took another step, waited until she

saw Sophronia's shoulders relax a little, and then she pivoted back toward the house. "Now!"

With a roar to silence all other roars, Jonathan bounded through the front door on all fours. She hadn't realized he could run on all fours, but understood the reason at once when she saw his speed. The Guards, stunned by the unexpected attack, dropped their grip on Del.

Reggie opened her palm, and her wand flew up into it. She turned again in time to see Jonathan rise up and grab Sophronia under one arm, then swing around and tuck Del under the other.

By now the Guards had shaken themselves from their shock and raised their wands.

Reggie raised her wand. "Don't. You'll hit Sophronia."

By now Jonathan had returned to the protection of the house's shield, which her father had altered to recognize him, and Reggie ducked under the shimmering protection as well. The whole event had taken less than a minute.

She ran into the house and shut the door behind her. Jonathan had released both women and gave his attention to Del.

"I hope I didn't hurt you," he said.

Del smiled and rubbed her ribs. "Well, I've never had quite such a hard hug before, but I'm sure I'll survive."

Sophronia stared up at Jonathan. Fear glittered in her eyes. "What the hell are you?"

Jonathan turned on her, and Sophronia jerked back. "I'm hurt you don't recognize me. I'm Jonathan Bastion."

Sophronia's eyes grew wide. "Impossible."

Jonathan's lips curled around the tusks that protruded from his snout. "You should know by now that little is impossible."

Affecting a disinterested air, Sophronia faced Reggie and scowled. "You'll regret this."

Reggie placed a fist on her hip. "I don't think so. You've been stubborn and obtuse and have refused to listen to anything I've had to say. Well, this is your last chance."

"Oh, I'm all atremble with anticipation," Sophronia said.

"Shut up, or I'll make you my lunch," Jonathan said.

"Stop it, Jonathan." Reggie stepped between them. "Sophronia, I'll release you as soon as I've had my say. Sit down."

Jonathan gave Sophronia a slight shove, and she plopped into a chair. Her eyes widened as she stared up at Jonathan.

Reggie shot him an exasperated look, then turned to Sophronia. "Right now, I have no proof but my word that Lucas Reynard, also known as Luc LeRoy, is making an attempt to seize control of the Arcani world. Kristin and Tennyson discovered his plans and their reward was derision from the Council. They aren't your enemies. Neither are the godmothers."

"I've heard this story before," Sophronia said, affecting a bored tone.

"No you haven't. You've never listened. It's the truth. I'm making one last attempt to make you hear. If nothing else, you will know what we do."

Sophronia sniffed.

"You may not believe me now, but my guess is soon you'll realize that I was telling the truth. Then you'll have no excuse for your actions. You can do the right thing and be unselfish for the first time in your life and help us."

Reggie leaned on the arms of the chair so that Sophronia had to look up at her. "What reason do I have to lie?"

For a moment Sophronia looked at her, then her eyes narrowed. "I have no idea what motivates you."

Reggie straightened up. "I pity you. I just hope when you realize you're wrong, it's not too late."

Jonathan grabbed Sophronia by the arm and hauled her

from the chair. "Get out. Your stench bothers me." He opened the door, tossed her out, and slammed the door.

The three of them looked at each other.

"Can she leave?" Del asked.

"You father's spell keeps people out. It doesn't keep people from leaving. If the Guards reset their barricade, then it might take a few minutes for them to figure it out."

Del sat on the chair recently vacated by Sophronia. "I guess I'm with you guys now."

Reggie took her sister's hands. "I'm sorry, Del. We didn't give you much of a choice."

Del shook her head. "No, no, you don't understand. It was my choice. I saw the bastard outside with Sophronia. Ian. He was at her side. He betrayed you." A fat tear plopped against her cheek.

"Oh God, Del. I'm so sorry," Reggie said.

Del gave her a fierce smile. "Look, I won't pretend that I'm not hurting now, but no one messes with my family. Better now than later. I'm glad I found out before we were married."

Reggie looked at her sister with undisguised surprise.

"I know. I didn't know I was strong either." Del shrugged her shoulders.

Jonathan chuckled.

Cordelia and Vincent ran into the room. Cordelia's face broke into a relieved smile, and she kissed Del on the cheek. "Adelaide." Then her expression changed. "What were you thinking?"

"I had to find the godmothers. Reggie needed help."

"Did you find them?"

"Not exactly, but I did reach Aunt Lily. Well, I left a message on her cell, but apparently she was near it, because she called me right back—"

"Get to the point, Del," Cordelia said.

"Sorry. I told her what was happening and she told me to bring Reggie to—"

"Don't tell us," Vincent said.

"Why?" Del asked.

"The less we know the more convincing we can be. Your mother had a brilliant idea."

Cordelia blushed. "I did."

A wave of magic blasted the house again. Reggie rushed to the window. A new phalanx of Guards stood outside, wands at the ready.

"We can't stay here," Jonathan said.

"You won't, but we will," Cordelia said.

"You can't, Mother. They'll bring the house down around you," Reggie said.

"That's the plan. And when they do, they'll find your father and me bound and gagged. By our own daughter. For shame, Reggie." A bright laugh tinkled from Cordelia's lips.

"I don't—"

"Don't you see? You need someone who can feed you information about the search for you and the godmothers. I know my reputation. No one would ever believe I would become some revolutionary. And I am a good enough actress that they will believe my heart has been broken by my two renegade daughters."

Reggie's eyes filled with tears. "You'd do that for me? For us?"

Cordelia stroked Reggie's cheek. "Darling, I may be shallow, but I'm not stupid. I know what's important, and this is."

Another blast hit the house. Cracks appeared in the stucco.

"Sophronia never saw us. We've been 'tied up' for hours now," Cordelia said. "Ever since you came home."

"But now we have to get to a safer room." Vincent took Cordelia's hand. "Good thing California has earthquakes. Our houses are built with safe zones."

Within five minutes, her parents were tied to straight-back chairs in one of the rear bedrooms. Most of the attacks landed on the front of the house.

"Be ready to transport as soon as the barriers are breached," Vincent said. "They'll have to remove their spell in order to come in. That's when you can leave too."

Her mother said, "Try to call on occasion. I will be worried."

"We will, Mother," Reggie said. She could scarcely believe what was happening. Her parents were sacrificing their house for her.

"Now the gags, and then don't forget to put some magical bonds on us as well," Cordelia said.

"Got it," Jonathan said.

"Be careful," Cordelia said.

"You too." Reggie felt her throat tighten.

"Take care of my girls," Cordelia said.

"I will," Jonathan said.

Reggie slipped a gag into her mother's mouth then kissed the top of her head. Del took care of their father.

Jonathan summoned his wand and placed a simple binding spell on them. "Thank you."

Vincent winked and nodded at him.

A loud crack from the front of the house told them that the walls had broken.

"Come on." Jonathan grabbed Reggie's hand. Del followed behind them. "Where are we transporting?"

"Your house," Del said.

"Got it." Jonathan hugged Reggie to him. "Can you transport yourself?"

"You bet." Del's eyes gleamed with excitement.

"Ready then?" Jonathan focused on the gap in the wall.

Another blast widened the jagged slit in the Sheetrock. Daylight poured in through the opening. The Guards gathered just outside. Sophronia waved her wand, as did some of the Guards who stood a little aside from the bunch waiting to storm the house.

Reggie felt the tingle from the use of magic, and a moment later, another blast shattered the wall. Her father's spell faded as the Guards ran into the room.

"Now!" Jonathan held her tight.

She saw Del shimmer, then felt the tightening around her chest as the air rushed out and blackness engulfed her.

26

❧

CORDELIA'S RULES FOR HER
DAUGHTERS

•

You Can Always Rise from Adversity.

WHEN THE BLACKNESS receded a moment later, Reggie gritted her teeth against the wave of nausea that struck her. But it was smaller this time. Maybe she was getting used to this mode of travel.

She opened her eyes to find several people staring at her. The aunts, Kristin, and Tennyson were here. She searched quickly for Del and saw with relief that her sister had arrived safely.

"Our little army keeps growing," Rose said.

"Where are we?" Reggie asked.

"One of my houses," Jonathan said. "They've been using it as a base since our first date. Although I'm afraid it won't be safe for very much longer now that my loyalties are in question."

"We're on it. We'll have a new place in a few days," said

Tennyson. He stood in front of Jonathan. Unlike the last time the two men met, Jonathan towered over Tennyson.

Hyacinth scrutinized Jonathan. "Hmm. Del warned us, but you're even more . . . impressive than I imagined."

"Hyacinth," Rose said, scolding her friend.

"What? It's not as if he doesn't know what he looks like." Hyacinth faced him again without a hint of shame or fear. She nodded. "I'm glad you're on our side. I think we can use you."

"Thank you, I think," Jonathan said. Reggie recognized the amusement in his voice despite its gruffness.

"But he's only like this by day. At night he's human again." Reggie took his hand.

Lily looked at him. "What will it take to break the curse?"

"She said I'd change back when I had changed." Jonathan's voice held no emotion.

"Do you think you have?" Lily asked.

Jonathan shrugged. "I'm not a very good judge of my own character."

"I am," Reggie said. "Sophronia won't keep your secret. Everybody will know what you've been going through these past seven years. You've been exposed not only as a traitor, but also as a beast. You sacrificed everything for me."

"You're more important than my stupid secret."

She smiled. "See? You've changed."

"Then why haven't I changed back?"

"Have you tried?" Kristin asked.

"Of course, I've tried. I've tried for seven years." Jonathan's voice held a low rumble.

"Don't growl at her," Tennyson said.

Kristin sent him an impatience-filled look, then focused on Jonathan again. "Have you tried today?"

"No."

Reggie felt a stirring of hope in her heart.

"Go ahead, Jonathan, dear. Try now," Rose said.

He looked at all the expectant faces and slowly retrieved his wand. He touched the top of his head with the tip.

For a moment nothing happened. Reggie felt her stomach drop in bitter disappointment. And then she heard the first pop. In a few seconds, his body was twisting, writhing, cracking into its other form. His eyes had scrunched shut. Sympathy, anticipation, and yes, even a little revulsion appeared on their faces. For Reggie, the only thing going through her mind was seeing Jonathan suffer and knowing she could nothing to ease his pain.

His body continued to contract. It grew smoother, leaner, paler. The tusks drew back into his skull, his mouth grew smaller, lips formed. His claws retracted, his spine straightened, his ears grew round . . .

The popping stopped. Jonathan drew in a deep, ragged breath and straightened up. Nobody spoke. Tears formed in Reggie's eyes.

Still clutching his wand in one hand, Jonathan lifted his other hand in front of him. He stared at his fingers, then flipped his hand over to see his palm. He ran his fingers through his blond hair, and felt the top of his ear.

She stepped forward and touched his smooth cheek. His face was bruised from the beating he had received. A cut ran from his mouth, but it wasn't bleeding. He would have two black eyes in a day, and his brow was swollen, but his eyes, those incredible blue eyes looked down at her.

Rose gasped. "Who did this to you?"

"Lucas." Jonathan shrugged.

"I don't know. I think you might look better as a beast," Hyacinth said. "I'll get the first-aid kit." Hyacinth bustled from the room.

Reggie stared up at him. "I can't believe it took me so long to figure out you and Nate were the same person."

A slow grin split his face. Then he let out a whoop, grabbed her, and swung her around. Her laughter joined his as they spun around. Then he placed her on the ground, tilted her face up, and kissed her.

Tears of happiness spilled down her cheeks as they shared their joy. His tongue gamboled in her mouth, and her hands delved into his hair, sliding through the smooth length.

"If you can do that, you can't hurt too badly," Tennyson said.

They broke apart, and Jonathan laughed again and clasped his shoulder. The towel had slipped when his size had changed, and the blast wound looked raw and ragged. "It hurt less when I was Nate."

Concern wrinkled her brow, but he kissed her forehead. "I'm fine. I've never felt better."

She glared at him, and he laughed. "Okay, I've felt better, but I'm not going to let some flesh wound spoil this day for me."

Lily beamed at them, and Rose nodded in approval. Tennyson's arms were around Kristin, who watched with a huge smile, and a few tears trickled down Del's face as she watched her sister.

Jonathan turned back to Reggie. "I can kiss you. It's daylight, and I can kiss you." He did it again just to prove his words, then he grabbed her hand and pulled her to the door. He threw it open and ran outside. The sun hit his chest. He threw his arms wide. "Seven years. I haven't felt the sun in seven years."

He ran back to her and pulled her into the sun. Holding her face between his hands, he kissed her.

"I'm kissing you in the sun," he said with wonder in his voice.

"That's all well and good," said Lily from the doorway, "but unfortunately, we don't have time to let you enjoy it."

"And we have to patch you up first." Hyacinth beckoned them inside with the first-aid kit.

Irritation streaked through Reggie. She knew they were right, but she wanted Jonathan to enjoy this moment. Jonathan however just nodded and returned to the house, never releasing her hand.

Tennyson shook his head. "Man, we have to find you some clothes."

Jonathan looked down and laughed. Her father's sweats hung from his hips in a shapeless mess. At least they covered the personal parts. And the beating he had taken wasn't pleasant to look at either.

"I don't know. He has a nice chest," Kristin said. "I wouldn't mind looking at it some more."

Tennyson scowled at her, but Kristin just laughed and kissed him. "I'm just teasing you. And besides, after that kiss we witnessed, I'd say Reggie has her own designs on that chest."

Reggie smiled despite the heat that crept into her cheeks.

Jonathan concentrated, and with a flick of his wand, a shirt and some decent shorts appeared on the coffee table. He grabbed them. "If you will excuse me . . ."

Del stepped forward and touched his arm. "Your transformation . . . it . . . it looked like it hurt."

He nodded.

"And you went through it twice a day?" Del asked.

He nodded again.

Reggie considered that aspect of his curse. She knew how much pain was involved with transformation. He had had to endure it twice daily for seven years. She glanced at the other faces in the group. They were somber as they all ruminated over his response.

Jonathan shrugged. "I got used to it."

Tennyson stepped forward. "I hate to ask this now, but do you think you'd be willing to change back if we ever need it?"

The celebration was over. A crisis awaited them. The future was uncertain at best, and theirs was precarious. They were fugitives, each of them. The Council was looking for them, and so, most likely, would Lucas. Her parents were risking themselves to provide a link to the Arcani world and give them information as they needed it. People had already died.

Jonathan eyed Tennyson. "Yeah. I would."

Tennyson almost clapped him on the back, then seemed to remember the injuries. "You're a good man."

"Wait. What happened to the staff?" Reggie asked.

Jonathan gave her a crooked smile. "I told Alfred to hide it."

"He's helping us?" Reggie's eyes grew wide.

"Yeah. I think he likes you more than he lets on."

"Well, he would have to, wouldn't he? He acts like he can barely tolerate me." Reggie closed her eyes and concentrated on the staff. There. She'd found it and felt its answering call. A moment later it materialized in her hand. She held the staff as if she were a monarch.

"The Living Staff." Tennyson's voice held a tone of reverence. "I have got to get back to the *Lagabóc*." He ran off to a room in the back.

Kristin laughed. "That's my academic. He has to look it up in his books."

"Where are we going to keep it?" Reggie asked.

"Send it to the Sanctum. That's what I do with the Ruby Sphere," Kristin said.

Reggie looked at the staff and said, "Sanctum."

The staff disappeared from her hand, but she could still

feel its presence on another plane, safe and secure. She smiled. "Cool."

"I think we need some lunch," said Rose.

"I'll come help," Del said.

Reggie shot her a surprised look.

Del shrugged. "I want to help, but I doubt I'll ever be a fighter. The least I can do is learn how to cook for us."

Reggie shook her head in amazement as her sister disappeared after Rose.

Kristin pulled out a notebook and a pen. "Right. What's next? We need a plan." She wrote "New Headquarters" on the paper, followed by a list of requirements. Lily joined her on the sofa.

Hyacinth approached Jonathan with the first-aid kit. He took it from her. "I think I can handle this by myself while I change." Jonathan walked into a bathroom off the living room.

Reggie looked around. Eight people. "We're not a very big army, are we?"

Hyacinth looked up at her. "Size doesn't matter." She winked.

Lily clicked her tongue. "Really Hyacinth, sometimes your sense of humor . . ."

Kristin chuckled. "The numbers aren't great, but we've got more than those against us have."

"What's that?"

"A reason to fight. The right."

"So eight of us here, ten if you count my parents . . ."

"Twelve with Zack and Callie. You haven't met them yet, but they're helping us on the outside." Kristin went back to her list.

"And don't forget Stormy," said Lily.

"Who's Stormy?" asked Reggie.

"The last godmother. But she won't turn twenty-seven until next month," Lily said.

"She won't have powers until then, so we can't contact her yet. We don't want to leave her unprotected, and as long as no one knows, they won't bother her," Hyacinth said.

Reggie felt a surge of protection toward Stormy. She looked at Kristin. "It's like I already know her, and I'm already angry at the threat against her."

"I know. It's like instant best friends," Kristin said. "At least we have a month to get to know each other. And when it's time, we'll welcome Stormy."

Jonathan came out from the bathroom fully clothed. Reggie hid a pang of disappointment. Too bad. He did have a nice chest to look at. His face looked terrible, but at the same time beautiful.

"A month will give us time to heal too," Reggie said.

"Hey, I'm good to go right now." He cocked his head to the side, and she followed him into the backyard. He sat on a bench and pulled her into his lap.

She tried to climb out. "Your shoulder. I don't want to hurt you."

He tightened his hold around her. "You can't hurt me, Reggie. Not this way." He leaned back and closed his eyes as the light hit his face. "I don't think I'll ever take the sun for granted again."

"As long as you don't get sunburned," she said.

He laughed. "I don't think I could complain even about that." He kissed her then, slowly and leisurely.

When he broke away, she said, "I suppose you think this means I've forgiven you."

He searched her face, then nodded. "Yeah, but I expect I'll still have some groveling to do. Is this a bad time to plan for the future?"

Her heart rate increased. "Yes."

"Okay, just checking. You'll let me know when we can, all right?"

"I will." Her smiled melted inside her and warmed her every corner.

"So now?"

She drew in a deep breath. "We wait. And we plan. And we hope that Sophronia listened to me at least a little."

"We'll get through this, Reggie."

"I know." Because the alternative was too horrible to contemplate.

"In the meantime I think we should enjoy every second we can."

"I'm all for that."

"I do love you, you know. You, not the fairy godmother, not the bakery owner, you."

She sighed and snuggled against him, hearing his heart beating through his shirt. "Good, because if you think Diana knew how to place a curse, you have no idea what I'm capable of."

He jerked back for a moment, stared at her, and then he laughed in the bright sunshine.

AUTHOR'S NOTE

Did you know that 54 percent of individuals with Intellectual and Developmental Disabilities (IDD) never receive a phone call from a friend in their lifetimes?

Tommy and Joy are two special characters in my novel. I created them from the heart and from experience. You see, my own daughter has IDD. She doesn't have Down syndrome, and genetic testing has proven inconclusive, but, really, the diagnosis is irrelevant to our family. She is funny, and happy, independent, goal-oriented, responsible, and just a joy to be around (thus the reason I named my character Joy). Of course that doesn't mean she isn't a typical teenager as well—she can be surly and obnoxious, just like any other kid. In fact she is normal in more ways than not.

But the isolation my daughter faces at school and in public because of her disabilities is sometimes (okay, always) hard to take. She wants nothing more than to have friends, to be included, and to participate and contribute to society. Luckily, we found a wonderful program two years ago at her school.

Best Buddies is a non-profit organization that matches individuals with IDD to a peer buddy whose job is simply to be a friend. Anthony Kennedy Shriver founded the group in 1989, and today Best Buddies has over fifteen hundred chapters in middle schools, high schools, and colleges around the world. They have programs in communities and an employment program (most of the difficulty people with IDD have holding a job is because of missing social skills, not the ability to do the work). You can find more information about them at their website (www.BestBuddies.org).

Tommy and Joy could conceivably work as bakers (especially with magic) and do a wonderful job at it. I tried to express Joy's difficulty with communication accurately, using my daughter as a model. But like Joy, if you teach my daughter a process, she will never make a mistake. My daughter often does cook and bake for herself, and we implicitly trust her.

So I'm putting my money where my mouth is. For the five years following publication, I pledge 10 percent of my royalties from this book to Best Buddies in support of their programs. I hope you will help me support this worthy organization, not only because you like my book, but because everybody needs a friend.

—Gabi Stevens

TOR
ROMANCE

Believe that love is magic

P lease join us at the Web site below
for more information about this
author and other great romance
selections, and to sign up for our
monthly newsletter!